This Lighter Realm

To marcin,

From one artist to Anotha
— Enjoy the adventure!

Love,
A.J. Fogden

AJFogden x

**Grosvenor House
Publishing Limited**

This book is published by
Grosvenor House Publishing Ltd
Link House
140 The Broadway, Tolworth, Surrey, KT6 7HT.
www.grosvenorhousepublishing.co.uk

This book is a work of fiction. Any resemblance to
people or events, past or present, is purely coincidental.

A CIP record for this book
is available from the British Library

ISBN 978-1-78623-637-1

To both of my grandfathers.
I hope you are proud of me.

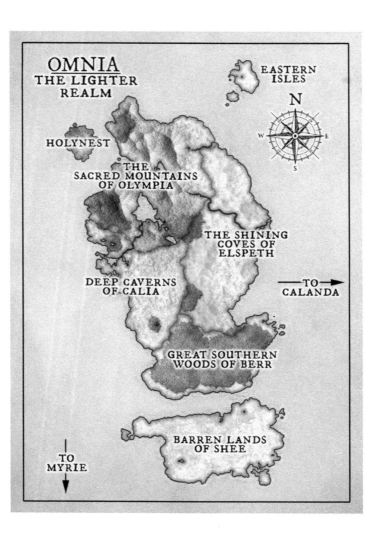

Character List for
This Lighter Realm:

DARKER REALM CHARACTERS:

Evanie Harley – Noble Lady, war nurse, resident of
  Abbeville, member of the House of Light *(Eh-va-nee)*

Sebastian Harley – Noble Lord, soldier, twin brother to
  Evanie, member of the House of Light

Penelope Harley – Noble Lady, war nurse, elder sister
  to Sebastian and Evanie *(Pen-el-uh-pe)*

Henry Harley – Noble Lord, soldier, elder brother to
  Penelope, Sebastian and Evanie

HOUSE OF LIGHT:

Seraphyna Lux – Youngest of the Omnia siblings,
  Highest Lady of the House of Light *(Se-ra-fee-na)*

Ethelde – Professor of Light *(Eth-el-duh)*

Clancy – Student of Light's History

Lorna – Student of Light's Scrutiny, adoptive sister to
  Isoletta of Water

Conaire – Student of Light's Wielding

Leora – Member of Light

Ulric – Member of Light

Old Davisham – Count of Scylla, Warden of Royal Isle, father to Lindera

Lindera Ilene – Wife of Florean Ilene, Countess of Ilene, heir to County of Scylla

Florean Ilene – Husband of Lindera, Count of Ilene

Earl Luz – Noble Lord

HOUSE OF AIR:

Aella Caeli – Third youngest of the Omnia siblings, Highest Lady of the House of Air *(I-el-uh)*

Corentin Caeli – Husband to Aella, General of Air, Lord of Air

Horus – Professor of Air

Aviana – Student of Air's History, sister to Clancy

HOUSE OF EARTH:

Herminia Arbour – Third eldest of the Omnia siblings, Highest Lady of the House of Earth

Dagan Arbour – Husband to Herminia, General of Earth, Lord of Earth

Rosaleen – Professor of Earth

HOUSE OF FIRE:

Aidan Omnia – Second youngest of the Omnia siblings, Highest Lord of the House of Earth *(I-dan)*

Eithne Omnia – Wife to Aidan, daughter of Ethelde, General of Fire, Lady of Fire *(En-ya)*

Lord Ambustian – Noble Lord, Court Physician

HOUSE OF WATER:

Daileass Omnia – Second eldest of the Omnia siblings, Highest Lord of the House of Water *(Di-le-ass)*

Isoletta Omnia – Wife to Daileass, General of Water, Lady of Water

HOUSE OF DARKNESS:

Domhnall Omnia – Eldest of the Omnia siblings, Highest Lord of the House of Darkness *(Dom-null)*

Melaina Omnia – Wife to Domhnall, Lady of Darkness *(Mel-i-na)*

Darsey – General of Darkness

MENTIONED DECEASED CHARACTERS:

Domhnall XXXIV – Father to Omnia siblings, King

Arista – Mother to Seraphyna, Domhnall XXXIV's last wife

Adrienne – Mother to Domhnall, Domhnall XXXIV's first wife

Oralee – Highest Lady of the House of Light, 700 years before Seraphyna's time, Mistress of the Eastern Sun

Luke – Highest Lord of the House of Light after Oralee, Master of the Western Skies, brother to Oralee

Hestia – Highest Lady of the House of Fire, sister to Oralee and Luke

Donovan – King and Highest Lord of Darkness, brother to Luke, Oralee and Hestia

BEFORE ALL

Before all there was darkness. And still darkness remains.

Only ever to be overcome by light.

Within all of us is darkness. No matter how much someone insists that they are enlightened, the sun always sets in them. If there was no darkness, there would be no purpose for light, no reason for it to exist. Darkness is overwhelming and eats away at our happiness, our love for others, because, whilst darkness may be the absence of light, darkness is also the absence of love, too.

"Evanie? Evanie? Evanie!"

"Hmm..." I reply distractedly.

"Evanie, you're daydreaming again," my sister, Penelope, scolds.

"Sorry, Penny, do carry on," I reply, resting my heavy head on my hand.

"I was saying that I received a letter from Henry yesterday," she carries on. "It didn't have much of a tone of hope in it."

"So, nothing from Sebastian, then," I sigh, focusing my thoughts again on the mysterious figures lining the Abbeville street that is home to the war hospital we work at.

"No, Evanie, nothing from Seb. But at least we know Henry's alive, does that mean nothing to you?"

"It does, Penny, it does, but I feel as though I barely know Henry. When we were living in London and in Hertford, he was always away at Eton or Cambridge, hardly ever at home. And when he was, Penn, he paid no attention to me, just to the games of cricket he played with you and Seb. Seb has always been there for me, he's my twin brother. We were chosen to be together throughout all of our miserable little lives, now this goddamn war has separated us."

"Just keep an eye out in the newspapers to check if he's alright, Evanie, I'm sure he's alive. You'd know if he wasn't."

"You're right, Penn, I would," I agree, nodding my head lightly. The hospital is hot and the atmosphere tense, French orders being flung from one side of the ward to the other.

"Miss Evanie, please, you are needed," the matron sighs, handing me a roll of bandages and a clipboard. A plump, happy French woman, the matron hops from bed to bed, asking quick and stern questions to the men. Most of them have practically recovered but are still shell-shocked. Men who have been sent home for severe injuries are becoming more frequent by the day, and some are so desperate to come home they shoot their trigger finger off so they are sent back. I suspect that the patient I am sent to see has a similar injury, so I tut and saunter off to the entrance hall. The man is my final patient of the day, a young boy who must be but two years older than me. He says nothing during the time that I tend to his wounds, he just stares aimlessly at the walls of the hospital, yellow with age and neglect. I greet Penny at the gates and we set off to our house. The walk is not too long and certainly not unpleasant, but it's not to home, it's just to a house.

The light merges with the horizon as the sun sets, creating an ominously dark glow over Abbeville. I watch the skies closely after the sun sets, counting the amount of fighter planes that fly overhead. I lose count eventually. Penny calls me in after the clock chimes 11 and I go to sleep with the thoughts of painful death plaguing my mind.

The morning of the summer solstice of 1916 is bright and the people of Abbeville almost forget that the country is at war. The restaurants open early and ladies sit on sunny terraces and discuss the letters they have received from their husbands, fathers and brothers. I wait all day by the post box of the house Penn and I are renting, just hoping that something from Sebastian comes for me. I long to see his untidy cursive scrawled across the page, my name slanted at an angle and my address, which I hate, under it. I wish I could see his face again, a sight which has been out of my reach for six months. My father does send constant letters to Penelope and myself, and they do cause us much amusement since he sends us articles from *The Spectator* and *The Times*. He's incredibly witty and fun, our father, a stark difference from my mother, who is quiet and diffident. Henry sends the odd letter, too, but they are nowhere near as anticipated as the fortnightly ones from Father.

I finally give up waiting by the post box, nothing will come.

"Good morning," a light voice lilts as it floats past.

"Yes, quite," I reply as the owner of the voice turns towards me.

"Waiting for a letter?" she asks. The girl, woman, looks at me in a cautious way. She wears her hair down, long red locks flowing down her back. She sports a floor-length gown, bright yellow in colour, causing her to look quite out of place in the busy Abbeville streets.

"Yes," I reply. "From my brother."

She bows her head solemnly and smiles. Her pearly white teeth show, and she almost radiates light as she shines upon the street.

"My brothers are fighting in a war, too," she explains. I nod, though not in surprise: everyone's brothers are fighting in the war.

"On our side?" I ask, noting her British accent.

"No, against me," she explains, surprisingly.

"Against you?" I furrow my brow. "Is he fighting on the German side?"

"No, against Light," she mumbles, looking around distractedly.

"Against Light," I state. "Right, good day, miss, I must be off." I start to walk away, very much concerned that I have met one who is quite insane.

"Wait." Her hand is on my shoulder.

"I'm sorry, Miss, I must be off." I shake my head and take another step.

"Are you Evanie Harley?" she asks nervously and quickly.

"No," I state, alarmed at her knowledge of my identity. "Please, do let me go."

"I know you are her, Lady Harley, if I may call you that." The girl says. I look straight into her eyes. She must be my age as she has no wrinkles or blemishes; her skin seems as pale and radiant as her teeth.

"How do you know me?" I ask, widening my eyes. "I don't even know who you are!"

"Seraphyna Lux, Lady, if you please," she tells me, sticking out her hand in greeting. I do not take it.

4

"What do you want from me?" I scowl at Seraphyna.

"I don't want anything from you, I have something you want," she smiles warmly, almost stopping the breeze.

"I don't think so, Lady," I snarl, again taking another step back towards where Penn is sitting in the café waiting for me.

"Please, Evanie, if you want to see Sebastian again then you should listen to me," Seraphyna urges, putting a hand on my shoulder.

"Sebastian..." The word passes across my lips like a breath, one which has not been taken in weeks.

"He is in danger, I can feel it, Evanie, come with me and you can save him."

"Impossible, he is in Flanders, I doubt you've been there and seen him," I disagree, however much I wish that this isn't true.

She doesn't even look at me or say anything, but the streets of Abbeville mould into red splatters and white sheets.

Suddenly, ever so unexpectedly, I'm not in Abbeville anymore, I'm in Belgium, mud and debris littering the rough boarded paths that are below my feet.

"How... what?" is all I can let out. Seraphyna looks at me knowingly.

"Take me back!" I demand, not looking around.

After standing dumbfounded and staring at a wall for thirty seconds, I finally have the strength to hold out my hands and see that I have, in fact, not died and gone to hell. 40 soldiers or so line the walls of the trench, either reloading guns or casually fingering through decrepit books. I gaze along the line; no one notices me. My brother stands not in the line nor lies in a bed dying in the makeshift infirmary. I sigh in anger but with relief.

"He's not here, please take me home, I don't even know you!" I plead, pulling at the scratchy nurse's uniform that somehow, I am in, despite the fact I had changed out of mine hours and a city ago. "Seraphyna."

Pointing at the door, Seraphyna goes white and I watch in horror as my brother is escorted out of the cabin by an armed soldier. A gun is pressed to his back, but my brother says and does nothing about it. I wonder if we are in a German trench, but when I hear the soldier, an old wrinkled man, bark gruff orders at Sebastian I don't think more about it. My brother, white and withered, stands with his face to the muddy wall of the trench.

"What are they doing?" I demand desperately. "He's on their side, he's not a German!"

"Shooting him for desertion. Shell-shocked. Ran away three days ago because of the gunfire. It was too loud. He's lost friends... brothers," she whispers.

I shake my head, trying to run forward to stop him. My arm is yanked back but then I'm pulled towards the wall. As I blink, the scene changes, and I too am facing the same wall Seb is. He doesn't notice Seraphyna or I, he just continues to stand there. He breathes heavily, small tears forming in the corners of his eyes,. Seb never cries. He begins to murmur and I hear faint words of prayers, which I find strange as we both find religion an odd thing, so Seb never prays. Seb always said the day he died he would sing as he did. He does not sing. He is a changed man, a changed man indeed. The soldier holding the rifle yells into the air, counting down from three. When the count gets to one, Seb draws a sharp breath and even lets a tear fall into his dusty face. Zero does not come, and neither does the shot. Alarmed, he turns, his sandy hair that is littered with sand and dust shaking as he does so. There is no pause before the gun goes off.

The sound is a horrible one, as I would expect, but it makes me jump even more than anticipated so I leap out of the way. I follow that the intention was for Seb to be shot in the back, but a round, Crimson rose wound has formed along his abdomen.

"Sebastian!" I call, yet it comes out as a whisper amongst the shouts from soldiers rushing to aid my brother. The man who shot Seb looks pale but smug and doesn't go to help Seb but also doesn't push his aides away. However, despite the help, I can see that Sebastian is slipping away, struggling to hold on. The light behind my brother's eyes does not fade, it stays alive, almost as if he is using all of the little light and hope he has left to cling to all he has been given.

"Can you not do anything?" I gasp at Seraphyna. "You brought us here on a whim in a split second, can you save his life? Please, I'll do anything..." I stare desperately into her eyes, watching me closely and contently.

"How cruel do you believe this world is, Evanie?" she asks me calmly, holding my clenched fists gently.

"Too cruel," I state. Shaking my head in despair because I know I speak the absolute truth. This world is too cruel, too absent of a light. "I can't go another day without knowing that Sebastian lives somewhere on this earth. Please, do something, anything." My breathing becomes ragged and slower as I glance back over to where my brother, my dear brother, is dying.

"The only way I can save him is by taking you to a world where there is a war far worse than this, where brother is fighting brother who is fighting sister who is fighting sister. Greater numbers will be lost than you could imagine, the hope drained out of you forcefully. But I know, Evanie, that in this world that I call my home, you were once worshipped as Mistress of the Eastern Sun, a miracle for mankind. Come with me, and you will leave everything but your brother that you love, but you will see the rebirth of a brighter place, a Lighter Realm," Seraphyna explains, still holding my trembling fists.

"And will he live in this world?" I question fiercely and determined, not confused or questioningly as I should have, given I had been told that in a past life in a brighter place, I was a goddess. I do not think twice about the mistakes I may be making; all I care about is saving Sebastian. Lonelier I shall be if he is gone than if I leave everyone else I know.

"You have my word," she nods. I brace myself, bow my head and glance back over to Seb. No chance except this one, so I nod fervently and say:

"Take me there then, and I will do all I can to help you."

A thin, loose smile spreads across her face as she takes my hand and nods. Light blinds my eyes and I find myself screaming, not in pain like I expected, but in shock. The moulding of my surroundings looks as easy as clay, I feel like a hundred years has passed and I have been pulled in all directions, turned inside and out, but a light sits in my heart, rising me above the clouds, to forever keep me above what is below me.

MISTRESS

"Welcome to the Lighter Realm, Evanie." I hear a soft voice whisper. I am not shaken awake, but I feel a quake under me. I am lying upon a field of cotton, where I seem to have fallen from the sky. I am no longer wearing a scratchy nurse's outfit, just absolutely nothing. Sub-consciously, I cover my chest.

"Stand up, it'll be fine." Seraphyna smiles, offering me her hand. I take it and as I rise, the cotton seems to weave itself in the air as if an invisible loom was suspended there. The fabric is woven and dyed before my eyes and sticks lightly to my skin, hanging loosely in a floor-length yellow gown.

"This is where you live?" I ask in horror, gazing at the ruined buildings that line the field.

"No," she states. "This is Elspeth. We must be going, Evanie, we're not supposed to be here."

I look out to the horizon where a turquoise sea shines in the sunset.

"Evanie!" I hear a yell from the other side of the cotton field.

"Seb." The word is like a song, a beautiful high note from a lyre. He comes running towards me, arms extended. Still barefoot, I run in his direction, too, and we meet in the middle. The embrace is wonderful, a feeling I had not felt in half a year.

"I missed you so much, Evanie," he whispers.

"Seb…" I breathe. "It's been too long, way too long."

"Am I dreaming?" he asks. "Or am I in heaven, I remember dying, so that seems logical, but that must mean you are dead too. Oh, Evanie, I'm not dead, am I?"

"You're not dead," Seraphyna steps in and confirms. "You are in a Lighter Realm, welcome, Sebastian."

Seb stares straight at Seraphyna. I know that look better than the back of my hand, but as well as that, it's mixed with confusion. Seraphyna only reads the confusion behind his eyes.

"I promise that I will explain everything when we reach the Eastern Isles, but please, I urge both of you, we must head towards the sea. We are not safe here, this is my brother Daileass's territory."

A small fishing boat-sized vessel waits for the three of us in the harbour. No rowing is required as it moves at Seraphyna's command. Sitting in the boat, I take some time to embrace what a crazy and unbelievable situation this is. I can barely fathom it and the thoughts make my head go cloudy. The dizziness makes me feel seasick so I rest my heavy head on Seb's shoulder.

"I'm so glad you're alive, even if we'll never see Henry or Penn again. As long as I have you." I sigh into his arm, which is covered in a cape and a cotton shirt, which matches the dress I am currently sporting.

"Evanie, Sebastian, I welcome you to the Eastern Isles of Light. This is my home," Seraphyna beams as the boat pulls into a harbour marked with a wooden post. The island that we land at is tiny, barely fitting a palace-sized building and a few wooden huts. A larger island sits to the rear of our landing ground; however, it looks almost empty.

"Phyna!" I hear someone yell. A young girl runs down the steps to the harbour and offers Seraphyna her hand to get out of the boat. Behind her, four other figures step down to the docked boat. The vessel rocks slightly as Sebastian and I clamber out, managing to stay afloat on willpower.

"What took you so long?" one of the people asks. An elderly-looking woman stands over Seraphyna, a dominating figure. She looks upon her with such stern love that I wonder if this is her mother, then erase that thought, as she looks too old. Grandmother, perhaps?

"I'm sorry, Professor, but it took me a while to track her down," Seraphyna sighs. The woman, whom Seraphyna called professor, takes my hand and smiles that same stern but caring smile at me.

"What is your name, dear child?" she questions with authority and purpose, which causes no hesitation from my part.

"Evanie Harley, Madam," I reply confidently, paired with a confident grin, showing I am no longer intimidated by this new land.

"Mistress Oralee of the Eastern Sun, I never thought I would have the honour to meet you, Lady." The professor drops a curtsey. "My name is Ethelde, Professor of Light. Mistress, what an honour it is."

"Thank you?" I say questioningly. Ethelde drops my hand gently and moves on to greeting Sebastian.

"Master Luke of the Western Skies, what an honour!" Ethelde smiles, again bobbing a well-choreographed curtsey for him. Sebastian murmurs his thanks and starts up a polite conversation with her, asking to be called Sebastian. I don't think he is particularly fond of the title by which he was addressed.

I meet three other members of what Seraphyna calls 'the Faithful House of Light'. The three students are all around the age of myself and Seraphyna and study what they call the branches of learning (Scrutiny, History and Wielding, I hear). They are all as bright and enlightened as their Highest Lady, the title which Seraphyna holds.

"What is the Darker Realm like?" one of the students, a tall young man named Clancy, asks me as we ascend to the palace.

"Excuse me, what's that?" I ask, very confused with the terminology used.

"Where you come from," he continues. "And I wouldn't answer a question with a question, even if you are unsure of yourself, it shows weakness."

"Right, sorry," I apologise and carry on. "Well, our world is different," I conclude.

"Any more?" he asks earnestly. "As a student of History I must find out all I can about the structure of the realms. Myself and Lorna have been working on an experiment about returning ourselves to the Lightest Realm. It's harder to return up the scale than down, what you did is almost a miracle, it must have hurt very much…"

"It was not pain," I confirm. "It was an odd sensation I suppose, a light inside of me I have never experienced before. I felt invincible, like even the sun was on my side."

"She's definitely a bright one, Lorna," he tells the girl to his left, a woman who holds herself well and with purpose. I am on his right. "Phyna was right, it's definitely the Highest Lady of the Eastern Sun, I'd know her the best after reading about her so many times in the scriptures."

"I think you might find, young Clancy, that I would know her best if I saw her. I have read every book in the library of Light there is, and I out of all people know that she is the right woman." Ethelde steps in.

"The right woman." The words seem so familiar to me, a phrase repeated over and over in this same spot, the repetition in my head almost makes me go mad, insane, as the spiral of light in front of me transforms into a night, a day, then a thousand years all at once.

"She is the right woman," the figure standing in front of me mutters to the men holding my chains. I pull harder but they would not come off, they are tangled with strands of fire and streams of water and are weighed down with boulders of Darkness.

"I never thought I would see you again, brother," I snarl. "What do you want from me? My place at the top of the House of Light? Well, I'm afraid I can only award that title to those worthy of it. When I die, the Sun Crown will pass to Luke, not to you. I cannot give you want you want, Donovan, no matter how hard you try."

"Cut her down," is the only command that Donovan, Highest Lord of Darkness, gives to the men beside me.

"In peacetime? In my own territory?" I cackle, shaking my chains and producing a breath-stopping and ominously terrifying sound.

"No one shall hear of it, they do not care about your heart or flesh, you are no queen."

"I am no queen but I wield more ancient and horrifying magic than you, Donovan. I curse your house and those who have conspired against me, they shall crumble when a traitor within the Palace of Darkness lifts light from the ashes that it will become. The tide will go in, the flames shall burn out, and

forevermore shall light overcome darkness. Heed my warning, brother, this is a misfortune of your house."

The darkness cuts through me but I feel no agony, no pain. All I feel is the light fighting back. I laugh manically as I fall to the ground in surrender. The whirlwind is not unhappy, as I know that this curse shall topple darkness, fire and water.

"Oralee, no!" *Luke cries in agony from across the meadow. His hand is under my neck as I stare up at the stars. I watch as I fade, a new star forms and becomes brighter.*

"Star Oralee, the Eastern Sun," *I smile at Luke.* "A beautiful creation." *I laugh as my eyes droop.*

Darkness. Nothing but.

"Damn you, Donovan," I whisper, feeling like I have just hit the ground again after living a thousand lives.

"What was that, dear?" Ethelde asks, hearing my whisper.

"I had a brother called Donovan, didn't I, he killed me, and I had another brother, Luke, I believe, who succeeded me as Highest Ruler of Light?" I recall to Seraphyna, who has her hand on my shoulder in concern.

"Perfect." she nods faintly, her yellow-flecked eyes bright and wide. "How do you know?"

"I just saw it all, the formation of the Eastern Sun," I explain, shaking my head in disbelief. "I saw everything as though I was her, I was a woman called Oralee and she was killed by her brother and as she faded a star formed to the east of her eye."

"You are her, Evanie, in a past life here. Before you passed through the realms, you were Oralee, you were one of the only ones of the last royal family to be of the

House of Light. Oralee was succeeded briefly by her brother but her family was banished from the throne by my ancestors. I have brought you here, Evanie, because you still possess the memories and powers of Lady Oralee, Mistress of the Eastern Sun. Light is under immense pressure. We have been the weakest house for years, ever since you died, and now I fear the last of our territory is in danger of being taken over by Darkness. Our house could be got rid of instantly. I am young, Evanie, I know little in the ways of a warrior, but you, Lady Oralee, are the one way in which all of the houses may live in harmony."

"I said I would do all I could to help you in exchange for saving my brother," I nod at Seraphyna. "First, I shall need some explanation of the basis upon which your realm is founded."

"It will take a long time, I tell you," she warns me. "Please come into my home and I can tell you over a meal." The path towards the palace is not how I saw it in the recent memory, which was a straight and simple path; now it is twisting and lined with dead bushes.

The inside of the Palace of Light is warm and every corner has a hanging lantern housing a single firefly.

"This place is beautiful," Seb gasps, tracing his fingers over the wallpaper, which is scattered with fireworks and spots of colour that almost emit light themselves.

"It's home," Seraphyna laughs. "I've done some renovations of some parts, but sacred places like these I just couldn't bring myself to change. They are the pictures I saw in the books about the House of Light, and I wanted it to stay that way. Please, do come in." She leads the way to a large oak door. Lorna, the sprightly girl who smiled at me warmly, opens the door and leads us both in.

"Phyna, can I get you anything?" Lorna asks once we have sat down in a small parlour, with windows that stretch from floor to ceiling.

"No, it's fine, thank you Lorna," Seraphyna replies.

"Evanie? Sebastian?" she asks.

"I think we're fine," Seb replies and I nod in agreement. With a snap of Seraphyna's fingers a meal appears. Apples as golden as rings, meat that tastes similar to pork and falls off pristine white bones are presented to us.

"Are you ready?" Seraphyna asks me and Seb. We both nod in agreement with full mouths.

She takes a deep breath and beams a beautiful smile. "Then I shall begin, we may be here for some time."

"We have a saying here," Seraphyna tells us. "Which is the one thing all of the houses agree on. If you must know one thing, it is this:

Before all, there was darkness, and still darkness remains. Through it ran a cool river of water, dividing the darkness in two. From that water sprang life, plants, animals and earth. From the mouths of the living, air was breathed, weaving its way around everything. From the air sparked fire, warming the universe from corner to corner, but woe betide those who should meddle with it. Finally, from the fire, a light grew, overcoming darkness, its only foe."

I nod, shocked at how well I seem to know the passage, my lips tracing the words at the end, the formation of light.

"Is that what actually happened?" Seb asks her, looking just as, if not more, bewildered than I.

"Not exactly. It is generally just a saying to tell us what is right, the order in which the houses were created, and what is wrong."

"What is right and what is wrong?" I question.

"Well, it tells us the purpose for all of the houses: darkness the head, water the pace, earth the life, air the breath, fire the temper and light the heart. The origin of the houses is debated. It is agreed among the faithful houses, Light, Air and Earth, that the founders were simply the first wielders of our ancient magic and their legacy lives on through the hearts and souls of the members of the house." She pauses slightly, wetting her lips as she looks into Seb's eyes. "The noble houses, Darkness, Water and Fire, believe that the founders were the elements themselves and the legacy is within the magic spun by their hands. That is one of the ways the houses are split, but still this is a six-sided war, and we are the weakest side." Seraphyna bows her head in reminiscence, her expression solemn.

"Right," I exhale.

"The royal family came into existence over 7000 years ago, 3000 years after the original civilisations were set up. There have been three main dynasties, two smaller ones. My family has been ruling over Omnia, our land, for over a thousand years, but Omnia is now lacking a king or queen."

"Why?"

"Our country has been in a dire state of war for years," she explains. "A terrible, horrifying war. A fight for the throne like no other. My father died thirteen years ago, and ever since then each house has been competing for their place on the throne. What you must know is that this generation of royalty is exceptionally rare. My father, King Domhnall XXXIV, had six children, each of a different house. The eldest is Domhnall, named for our father, who is Highest Lord of Darkness; he is married to Melaina, Lady of Darkness. Once my father passed away, when I was three, Domhnall, who is seventeen years older than I, took me into his court and his wife raised me. I still, to this day, believe that if it were not for her kindness towards me, I would have been of Darkness. Light is love; it controls the heart. Domhnall is the eldest so it was assumed that he would take the throne. However, when he stormed the Royal Palace, Daileass, the next eldest and my brother of Water, had arrived. When the time came that the next eldest of my siblings, Aella and Herminia, were chosen for their houses, they decided that, although they were still young, they wanted the throne, too. Aidan was chosen for Fire four years later and he joined the fight, as well."

"And you?" I ask.

"I was twelve, the youngest you can be, when I was chosen for Light. A choice day comes every four years and is the one day per quaternary of sacred peacetime. To break that peacetime curses your house. Domhnall and Daileass chose together, Aella and Herminia together also, and Aidan and I chose alone, Aidan eight years ago and myself four, along with Clancy, Conaire and Lorna, the students. When I was chosen, I was young, but not stupid. I was almost thirteen and knew much in the ways of my duty. I sought not to claim the throne, but to end the fighting and abolish the monarchy, for the houses to rule together. That's all I wanted, that's all I want."

"Peace." Seb nods, but then contradicts himself and shakes his head. "Peace doesn't seem achievable here."

"Oh, no!" she yelps. "No, now that you two are here, peace is almost certain, possible. That peace is achievable, have faith, Sebastian, I beg of you, and you will see the light within you. I promise."

"I'll try," Sebastian promises, reaching out to touch Seraphyna's hand. I do not see it at first, but a small orb of light erupts from the end of Seraphyna's index finger. She looks very embarrassed and retracts her hand to her lap.

"What can I do?" I say, changing the subject and setting aside the gold plate that is on my yellow-clad lap.

"Fight," Seraphyna states. "Domhnall will never give in to me, no matter how much he kicks and screams. You, however, have power concealed within your hand like no other, Evanie. I ask you to find that power."

"How?" I ask desperately, as I most definitely want to know.

"It will come to you in time, Evanie, you have no idea how much Domhnall fears what the curse that you set on his house will do to him. Light's magic is more ancient, despite the house being newest, so therefore it is the strongest. It is wielded by so few that those who do are more powerful than half of the House of Darkness put together. You both must discover your potential, for you cannot turn that potential into triumph without knowing you have it." Seraphyna encourages.

"How long will it take for this magic to appear?" Seb asks, eyes as wide as the jars on the wall, soaking up the knowledge and the light.

"Less time than you expect," she smiles. "Watch this..."

Light erupts from the corner of every room, enveloping everything, not in a dominating way, but more similar to the effects of a welcoming embrace. The path the light etches into the air resembles a lifetime story with all its twists and turns, ups and downs. Finally, the light travels alongside another path, never separated until the light hits the ground.

Darkness blinds me. The light fading back again is slower and more agonised than I would have thought. Eventually, the room is light enough to see Seraphyna and Seb sitting across from me but dimmer than before.

"What was that?" I question quickly, shaking a little too much from such an invigorating experience.

"Oralee of the Eastern Sun's life in light," Seraphyna explains. "Woven within the magic in my heart, from that ancient legacy."

"This legacy..." I gasp, stunned by the experience I am yet to get over. "It's..."

"Amazing," Seb finishes my unfinished sentence for me. "What about me?" I can tell he's now very much invested in who he once was.

"Master Luke of the Western Skies was a faithful brother, leader and follower of Light," Seraphyna explains, pointing to a portrait on the wall of a young man shrouded in white and yellow. Four portraits line the wall of the parlour, three women and a man. I stand without realising that I have and walk over to the wall. The colours on each of the portraits is similar, each in gold with a plaque underneath citing a single name and title etched into the metal. I trace my fingers curiously over the words. The portrait furthest away from me is very clearly Seraphyna, her long red hair flowing over her shoulders like an ignited waterfall that runs like liquid sugar down the side of her face, framing it perfectly.

"That's you, then," I point at Seraphyna's portrait and she nods happily.

"I was so nervous the day that was painted," she reminisces. "The painter was kind though, a wonderful woman, the wife of the Earl Luz. I sat there for hours, but I'm pleased with the result, I think."

"You look beautiful," Seb tells her, and I nod in absolute agreement.

"Thank you," she replies meekly, bowing her head. Her hair still maintains the same shine shown in her portrait, reflecting the dim but welcoming light of the room perfectly. As she moves gracefully to take her place next to me, her hair shifts, falling back into place. It's an odd colour I cannot even begin to describe. It's like copper and caramel and gingerbread stirred around in elegant, flowing strands like a river, catching the candlelight and firelight when it moves.

I turn my attention back to the other portraits on the wall, the two in front of me ancient, with peeling sections of faded paint flecking off the frayed canvases. The gold frames, each seeming to tell a well-worn story, have been polished and cleaned so much that the etching is starting to wear away. The plaques bearing the single names of Luke and Oralee are nearly illegible; the thin script is also at risk of being lost amongst the gold forever. The first portrait, the only one of a man, Seraphyna has already told me is Sebastian, Luke, Oralee's brother and the third Leader of Light. As well as being the only male leader, he seems to be the only one of the leaders not wearing a golden coronet in amongst his dark hair.

"That crown missing from Master Luke's head is the Sun Crown. During his rule, the Sun Crown had been captured by Donovan XX, his brother, and he could not wear it." Seraphyna reads my mind so easily, although I do not know if she actually has or it's just a coincidence.

"What's the Sun Crown?" I ask, moving my bewildered gaze to the next portrait along and tracing the shape of the crown on the woman's head, a truly magnificent accessory.

"Each house had a relic, and the leader of the house, the Highest Lady or Lord, is the holder of the relic. The Sun Crown is the most ancient, created for the founder, over ten thousand years ago. It's much more regal than some relics, like an 'eternal fire'-" She scoffs and waves her hand dismissively. "- or a gauntlet made of leather from a sacred cow."

"Is this," I pause, gazing-skinned woman. "Is this who I was?"

"Yes, Evanie. This is the ancient portrait of Oralee the Great, Mistress of the Eastern Sun," Seraphyna replies.

"She's stunning."

"And powerful," Seraphyna reminds me.

"Of course," I smile, wringing my hands subconsciously. "Who's this last one?"

"The founder," Seraphyna tells me. The painting is so faded I can't make out the face of the portrait, but jet black hair weaves its way into braids around the side of her face. The colour of her dress is also indistinguishable, but the sleeves are long and float upwards with her hair. "Only Light, Darkness and Earth have surviving portraits of their founders, the others have nothing. We do not know any of their names, if they were related, where they came from, nothing about them expect perhaps their gender for some and that they founded an entire land. "

"There are only three others though, shouldn't there be more?" Seb asks.

"There should be more, Seraphyna agrees, "but only three royals, excluding the founder, have ever been chosen for Light. We are the smallest house. The Dukes and Duchesses are on a huge wall in the great hall, as they rule the house in absence of a royal to lead it. It is a funny thing, our system, I know, but I suppose it is just the done thing. It has been the same way for over 6000 years, when the houses became a mainland system, not just six schools on Holynest. The royal family keeps it all together, and now that there barely is one... Well, it has been hard."

"Things will work out," I assure her. She smiles as I say it; she has such a beautiful wide grin.

"If you believe they will, then I suppose they will."

The weeks that pass are hard to get used to. The days are long, with an early rise and late settle. The palace sits high on a cliff overlooking the sea on one side and a meadow on the other. Around the west keep and east wall are dense evergreen woodlands that carry high, shrill birdsong to wake us at dawn. The sounds of the forest are paired with the casual ebb and flow of the sea and the occasional crash of the clear water breaking over the top of the cliff and splashing the milk white walls of the palace, tarnished only slightly by the salt and spray that hit them softly.

Seraphyna's presence is warming, even when the nights are cold and long. Even if she sticks her head into my room, or into Seb's, which she does more often, she brightens the spirit of the area instantly. She carries a youthful glow but a wisdom that even the eldest wise woman could not hold, and Seraphyna is not ignorant of the fact. She spends her days in the library with the Professor, or with Clancy, and many afternoons I find myself joining them. In fact, I spend much of my time with Seraphyna, even if I just watch in awe at all she does.

"Saints, is there anything you can't do?" I ask, one day when I am watching Seraphyna sweep the entrance hall simply by walking next to it. Her long robe graces the cold floors behind her as she glides up and down the passage effortlessly.

"Much," she replies simply. "I only manipulate things. Only objects that the light falls on."

"Even humans? Light falls upon humans," I ask inquisitively. Seraphyna laughs lightly, a tense smile behind her eyes.

"Light doesn't fall upon humans, humans fall upon light." She tells me matter-of-factly. I can tell she's said the words many times, and I almost understand what she means so I don't question her further. "I probably couldn't explain it to you if I tried, Evanie, I've grown up with the fact that there's six houses, six magics, six territories and a family that oversees the peace, although that's the opposite of what we're doing. Our world is too complicated to be explained to you at once, even though I'd like to, but even I don't know everything about this realm." She sighs, picks up the broom and puts it away in a cupboard off the entrance hall.

"Ah, Seraphyna, I was looking for you." My brother, dressed in regal gold and silver, opens the door from the library to the entrance hall. "I found this, I was wondering what it was?"

She takes one look at it and laughs fluently, lightly.

"Why, it's my diary!" she chuckles, taking it with both hands from Seb's. Opening it, she fingers the ink-blotted pages as small ribbons of dust float into the air from the pages. The handwriting is blotchy and childish, the cover a rich red colour and the binding frayed but still holding the parchment together. On the cover a name is written on a haphazardly stuck piece of parchment. I squint to see what it says, looking for some similarity to Seraphyna's name, but all I see is P.B.L Omnia in an untidy scrawl.

"Is it yours?" I ask in disbelief.

"Yes, I was never known as Seraphyna at my brother's court. He despised the name, probably for it was my mother who chose it. My great-grandmother's name was Phinella, so he hoped by calling me Phyna as my common name, his courtiers would come to think that Phinella was actually my name. I love Phyna, it's easier to say than my full name but Phinella?" She pauses to make a vile expression on her pretty face. "No. I prefer Seraphyna much more than that."

She pauses, thumbing through the pages and smiling at certain points, before saying, "I should probably change it now, I haven't dared declare myself of my brother's family for years. It should be S.B.L Lux now, I suppose.

"Oh," she giggles, shaking her head when she's turned the page once more. "Hear this, I was such a dear, funny girl. 'I surely cannot wait for Holy day, I have been practising in my rooms for weeks, perhaps months, waiting to be called up to emerge Baroness of Darkness'." She tilts her head to the side, grimacing. "I wrote Baroness of Light instead of Darkness accidentally, I remember. I bled through the page with ink covering that up, I was afraid that Domhnall would read it and find out that secretly I hated his house and himself. Still, I was too afraid to admit I had a choice, but I let my feet take me to where I needed to go. If I'd let my heart do it, or my head for that matter, I would be in a dark room in the Palace of Darkness somewhere, barking gruff orders at some handmaid, sold as a slave to my household. I would be extremely unhappy, I know that."

"But you made the right choice, now you're here, happy and here, most importantly, you have the power to make a difference," Lorna says, descending the staircase to stand next to Seraphyna. "Excited for choice day?"

"Oh, yes of course!" she exclaims, "most certainly I am!"

"What?" I question, looking at Seb to see if he is confused too. He is.

"Oh, of course, I forgot to tell the both of you. In five days' time comes the most important event in the quaternary, choice day, when young Omnians choose their houses. Very exciting of course, and I would like you both to join me."

"Why?" I question, acknowledging our unimportant roles at this court now.

"Prove your loyalty, so I can show you off, even if no one knows who you really are."

CHOICE

Seraphyna adjusts my circlet, a magnificent golden thing that sits on my head comfortably. She smiles warmly at the completed outfit.

"You just need to follow my instructions, Evanie," she reminds me sternly, throwing her hands back from my dress, which was a subtle cream and white colour much more to my taste, and nodding her approval at the small parade of Ethelde, Lorna and I in front of her. Lorna twists the skirt of her dress uncomfortably, a bitter expression clouding her face.

"I hate this," Lorna exclaims, sighing melodramatically. "This skirt will get caught on the buckles of my riding boots!"

"Oh, Lorna, you are not wearing riding boots..." Ethelde scolds, scuffing the hem of Lorna's dress with her shoes, a neat pair of leather pumps.

"Ethelde, it's fine, we need to go," Seraphyna says. "Clancy, Conaire, where in the sainted suns are you?"

"But, your lightest..." Ethelde protests.

"Now," Seraphyna says surprisingly forcefully, before ordering the door open with her finger. She sends both Ethelde and Lorna toxic and unnaturally fierce stares before ushering us all out of the door angrily.

Conaire and Clancy stumble hastily down the stairs and try their best to avoid the second round of death stares from Seraphyna. Making our way to the cliff side, we watch the bright sky shift over the sea.

Four fillies stand in a row along the cliff looking towards the early sunrise; another is bridled and standing purposely to lead a beautiful gold and ice-white carriage. The fillies that stand alone sport no bridles and I'm surprised when I see Conaire, Clancy and Lorna scramble on to their backs.

"You ride bareback?" I question in wonder.

"How else would we ride?" Conaire replies. "Only the very scum of the realm, men of darkness and water saddle their mares, stallions do not mind as much but they are not as compliant..." He grips the horse tightly with his knees and the mare trots contently and neatly along the cliff's edge.

"Woah girl, slow," he coaxes as he sees Ethelde struggling to get on the back of her horse.

"Let me help you, professor," he offers, grabbing the professor's hand so that she could climb on to the back of her horse.

"Maybe I should have worn riding boots. Saints, I hate riding horses," Ethelde tuts, scrambling on.

"Sorry, professor, it won't be for long, that is, if Daileass keeps his oaths..." Seraphyna sighs, gazing longingly over the ocean before her.

"He will, Phye, he has to," Lorna points out to her. The comment seems to brighten Seraphyna's spirits for she nods, albeit hesitantly, and turns back towards the carriage. It was a beautiful spectacle; I'm still, after five or so minutes, able to find new secrets within its patterns.

"Evanie, Sebastian, you'll ride with me in the carriage, I trust you don't mind as such," Seraphyna says, taking her first step into the carriage before dragging her other foot up with her.

"Of course not, it would be my utmost honour," Seb wheedles, following close on Phyna's heels into the carriage. "Come on Evanie, we'll be late if you carry on with this dallying."

We wait for what feels like an uncomfortably long time for ones who are unfamiliar with each other to sit and wait. About every ten minutes or so, five times in the period we sit there aimlessly, Phyna looks out of the window and tuts loudly. After fifty minutes spent carelessly, Seraphyna finally seems to crack. In a whirlwind rage, she storms to the edge of the cliff, dangerously close to the 50ft drop into the ocean.

Mouth wide open, she yells at the empty horizon. I never thought a human being could shout so loudly and purposefully.

"Daileass, the one that they call Highest Lord of Water," Seraphyna rages. Very suddenly, the sea sits still, as though it's listening. "Adhere to what you owe the House of Light or I swear, brother, you shall pay greatly. Remember that the throne forged by our father, Domhnall XXXIV, still has the crown's eyes and ears, which can spy and hear your treachery. Part these waters now, you're already late, but compare this to what it costs you, not what it costs me. You know these duties must be adhered to, brother, you swore your oaths just as I did." The ocean stirs, rising and falling eerily like the breath of a man under pressure. First come ripples, as small and dainty as flower petals, then the waters become rougher, focusing their anger down one, sharp, endless line. The roar and power of the ocean astounds me, helping me realise finally to never mess with the ocean, and certainly not with Seraphyna.

Blowing a wisp of copper-gold hair from her sea-kissed face, Seraphyna saunters back towards the carriage and signals for the four riders to start their journey. The door is opened fiercely as she cools off slowly, but nowhere near as much as when it was opened the last time.

"Well, that's that sorted..." Phyna concludes simply.

"That was bloody amazing!" Seb exclaims as she takes her rightful place next to him in the carriage.

"Why, thank you." She smiles, opening the window next to her, even able to perform such a task as that so regally. "Wind's good today, though I suppose if one person would keep her oaths it would be Aella," she mumbles to herself whilst she looks out of the window, staring contently into the clouds.

"Hm?" I question as she looks back towards me and Seb. "You talk a lot about oaths, what do they all mean?"

"Well," Seraphyna starts, folding her hands in amongst the chiffon of her dress. "When one becomes a leader of one of the houses, oaths are sworn so that the houses have no excuse not to acknowledge their duties to the realm and to the other houses. On Holy Day, well, Choice Day we call it now-" she clears her throat awkwardly and loses the window again, glancing sideways at the scenery. "-Each house has a role, I suppose. Earth's is to rebuild destroyed temples, fire to provide sacrifices for the houses that believe in all that nonsense, water, as you just saw, must part the oceans for access to Holynest, air is to provide the winds so that the horses' hooves fast enough to match the speed of a hawk, and Light must provide sacred scrolls and holds the power to place the trance over wishers."

"Right," I nod in understanding, Seb does so as well.

"Wait, but what about Darkness?" Seb asks, posing a valuable question.

"What do they have to do?" I continue.

"Grace the island with their '*O Mighty presence...*'" Seraphyna explains, so sarcastically I may never believe her words again. "You see, it was a King of Darkness, Blake IX, who laid the rules for his subjects on Choice Day. I think that you might just be able to tell which house he was of just by worthy assumption."

"Darkness?" I guess, knowing my answer is correct.

"Almost half of the kings are. We've had 210 kings in 7000 years of the monarchy and 101 of those have been male members of the House of Darkness," she explains bitterly.

"Hang on a minute," Seb says, breaking the conversation. He looks nervously behind him and then out of the window. "How are we getting down from the cliff?"

"How *are* we getting down?" I think out loud, repeating Seb's question. It's a 50ft drop onto the beach. I pause, noticing as Seb must have that we are now moving and are dangerously close to toppling off the edge of the cliff.

And we do. But, somehow, the fall doesn't maim, injure or even scratch a single one of us. The glass of the windows does not shatter vigorously, does not crack nor is my breath forced from my lungs violently as it, assumingly, should be. In fact, the experience is one step away from soaring up in the sky with the swifts and the eagles.

So very suddenly, in an explosion of water and sand, we've landed on the beach and are in the belittling shadows of the palace on its cliff.

"What just happened?" I screech, in a state near to complete shock. I look, panicked, at the windows and glass panels of the carriage, still wondering how the drop of dozens of feet hasn't shattered their glass entirely.

"How else do you think we'd get down?" Seraphyna laughs calmly, throwing her head back lightly against the cream velvet behind her.

"Oh goodness, thank God that's all over," Seb gasps, struggling to find proper breath and I know I most certainly agree. Despite the euphoria I felt in the moment, the aftershock of our flight lingers heavily.

Barely any time is given for Seb or I to get over the shock of hurtling at full speed over a 50 or so foot cliff onto a parted ocean path than we start speeding along the seabed.

"Ah, look, if you squint you can see Olympia, those blue-capped mountains over there." Phyna points out a magnificent range peeking over the horizon about half an hour into our journey.

"The two candidates from light today, will they be at the Island already?" I ask shortly afterwards. Lorna, Clancy, Conaire and Ethelde are still cantering along up ahead with a constant beat, the generous and accepted gale blowing us all along.

"Oliv and Adrielle? Yes, I suppose they'll be at Holynest already." Seraphyna nods certainly, gazing out at the scenery of the clear blue seas.

"What happens if there isn't at least three members inducted into the House of Light?" Seb asks, uncertainly, exploring new and unstable ground.

"It hasn't happened before," Seraphyna assures us. "But if it did, then I suppose the Sixth of Suns in the Imperial Academy on Holynest would fall and-" The pause she takes to gather herself is like a scream but Phyna continues as though nothing fazes her. "Well, it would be a grim omen for the House of Light."

Nothing is said until the time reaches 11 o'clock and we've been travelling in the carriage for about an hour.

"Oralee, welcome home..." I hear Seraphyna murmur. Despite my confusion, I gaze up at the incredible sight before me. The island rises from the ocean like a lone traveller, a beacon lighting its way for boats and ships.

Boats and ships.

"I'm sorry, what?" I reply.

Don't be confused.

"Welcome home, Oralee," Hestia puts her arm around my shoulder and points to the central mountain. "That is where you were born."

"Really?" I reply excitedly. "What about you?"

"Yes, me, Donovan and Luke too, of course," she replies.

The ship glides along the water, docking at the natural harbour that glistens along the shoreline of Holynest.

Harbour? There's no harbour.

Hikes up mountains are usually no big deal for me as I live at the top of one but Holy Mountain certainly challenges me, although I suppose I am wearing dancing shoes which makes climbing mountains much harder than I previously anticipated.

Before all has passed and I'm completely aware of what I'm doing I'm at the mountain's summit and at the temples, ready to define the rest of my entire life.

"Good, luck, Oralee," Hestia smiles, crossing her fingers over her heart. She pushes me forward to the circle of professors in front of the crowd, huddled around the wishing stone.

"Are you ready?" one of the professors, I think of Water, asks me as I take my place.

"Yes, sir," I nod meekly and kneel on the wishing stone. The roughness is harsh and cold which I can feel through the fabric of my white dress.

"And what do you wish?" he asks me.

"I..." I stutter "I... I..."

What do I wish?

The thought lingers in my mind as cool ripples of water flow through me, to be followed by overwhelming heat of a fire, burning a hole through my heart.. The wind rushes through my ears like a shrill warning whistle, and I can feel the thick vines pulling down on my fingers, pulling me towards the earth.

"Oralee..." I turn my head quickly but cannot see a thing. The blindness, however, is not because of darkness. My vision is hindered by a thick fog, weaving a deadly, opaque blanket around everything it touches.

"Oralee!" The whispers from the South are quickly drowned out by shouts, determined yet gentle, flowing through me from the East.

"No, Oralee, here!" The South starts to yell, desperately and eerily.

"Oralee." The East continues to call me, not fazed by the South's yelling. It still calls calmly, it's welcoming. I'm apprehensive, but I turn towards the East.

"Wait." I stop dead in my tracks.

Donovan.

"Oralee, you're making a mistake." He says. It's so clearly Donovan. I can't see him, but I can hear him, the proudness and smirk in his voice is all too familiar to my ears. I can just tell it's him, standing right behind me, a cruel hand on my crueller shoulder, breathing down my back, waiting for me to make my decision. Catching my breath, I'm still unable to decide between my brother, my family, my king, the embodiment of Darkness itself it seems, and between kindness, warmth and calm. The sharp, menacing grip I can feel digging into my shoulder tells me I should turn towards my brother, to the South.

"That's it..." He coaxes, the mist echoing the movement of beckoning. All of a sudden, I can see it, a future of Darkness and of cold. I can hear the screams of the East, how they know I'm wrong. I'm wrong.

Oralee, you're making a mistake!

"I don't need someone to make my mistakes for me." I spit, slamming my hand through the mist. To my surprise, my hand does not cut through the fog, but violently hits a stone table, leaving a long, clean crack like a battle scar.

The whole room, finally in my view, is a gorgeous glowing temple, erupting with laughter, not from people anywhere near me, but almost as if the sun herself was laughing with me.

My vision clears enough to see that in front of me is a door, waiting to be opened as though it's awaiting my command, as though no one in hundreds of years has opened it. I don't even have to put my hand near the splintering planks and rusty lock for it to open. I emerge from the temple with my vision finally restored from my encounter with indecision. I turn to see where my future *lies, which table I have emerged confidently from the door of. I could only guess fire as the voice I turned away from was of Darkness. I keep drumming it into myself that I'm part of the House of Fire now, but I just doesn't seem right, not as wrong as being of Darkness, but still wrong.*

Opening my eyes that I closed in anticipation, I read the words that form an arc over the doorway of the temple. I have to read them and reread them over and over again to make sure it's not all in my head. I can see the dark thoughts clouding in Donovan's mind as I face my family as they read the words no other royal has before.

Welcome, fair one, as a member of the faithful and ancient House of Light.

Where am I?

"This is the Temple of Light, Evanie," Seraphyna tells me, drawing an arc in the air in the shape of the dome, more cracked than I remember it to be. When I last saw it.

But you haven't seen it before.

Yes, you have.

"I've been here before," I quiver hesitantly, reaching out slowly to touch the carvings etched into the ancient stone wall. "This path... I've walked it before, Hestia, I know I have."

"Hestia?" Seb questions, confusion building a hazy wall between us.

"Sorry, I meant Luke," I correct myself incorrectly as Sebastian sends a worried look Seraphyna's way. She meets his concern with a knowing smile.

"What did you see, Evanie?" she asks me, placing a much-needed calming hand on my shoulder and ushering me away from the temple.

"I saw, I was fifteen, I think, and my sister was as angry as the fire inside her and my brother as apprehensive as his soul's darkness. Luke was scared, as was I, but the Light showed us the path, and I have walked this path before, I swear it Phyna, I have." I tell her, not completely sure of what I am saying or entirely in the place I stand. My feet are most certainly touching the rocky ground but my mind soars miles above us, in a state of euphoric confusion.

"Of course," Seraphyna nods. "Ah." She stops right in her tracks as a dark parade ascends the hill.

"How did I get here?" I ask Phyna, but she raises a finger and stops ushering me away.

"Stand next to me, don't say anything and resist whatever dark whispers you hear, my brother's a weak man but a crafty one," she whispers, her eyes following the leader of the parade intently. "I'll give him that." The man continues up the hill on a black mare. He's a tall, gaunt man with oily coppery hair and a dim expression. His eyes are unexpectedly bright, a similar green-grey colour as Seraphyna's, yet they're lacking her whimsical, wise wonder and golden gaze.

Next to him is a woman on a white horse with flowing blonde tresses that stir whimsically in the spring breeze. She looks quite frightened as though something gruesome or dangerous is right under her nose and she can do nothing to make it go away. I have a bad feeling the gruesome and dangerous thing is the man next to her.

Each man, they are all men except the scared blonde, dismounts and leads his horse up the hill towards where Phyna has chosen her protective, advantageous ground.

"Little sister." Domhnall sneers, sniggering at the sight of our meek parade. Seraphyna's eyes flit momentarily to where the woman is still saddled on her mare and both of their stern, concerned expressions soften.

"Big brother." Phyna scowls, taking her hand off my shoulder and pacing strongly towards the men and woman, addressing her as she steps regally from her saddle to the dusty turf of the mountainside. "Melaina."

"Seraphyna!" The woman, Melaina, I remember her as Domhnall's wife, exclaims excitedly and twitches nervously. Angrily, Domhnall flicks his hand.

"Silence, woman!" he growls. "No speaking today, understand?" Melaina looks petrified and as though she is tethered like an animal to the end of a thick invisible rope. Nodding fervently, she frowns and bites her lip in defeat.

"I see you made it here alright," Domhnall continues, slurring. "Some of my centaurs intercepted your message to Daileass. Such a shame he forgot about you up there in the Eastern Isles, then again your house is so small that-"

"I'll have none of your games, Domhnall," Seraphyna warns quietly yet fiercely. "That message should never have reached your ears."

"Ah, but you see, dearest sister, it did. I can do what I want, I could knock you and your house from your tiny pedestal in the east with one clean blow and no blood on my hands. Mine or others."

"But that blood's in your veins, and it's yours; that's enough to make you a monster," she threatens.

"The same blood as yours, sister."

"Half. I've learned to ignore the vile fact that we share the same blood. It's one thing I hate about myself."

"Blood is thicker than water," Domhnall reminds her.

"Not as thick as you, though, it seems," Seraphyna quips wittily. I cannot stifle my laughter and the noise means that, regrettably, Domhnall finally notices me.

"And who's this, dear sister?" he grins, yellow teeth showing as he takes my chin in his hand fondly. I try not to be sick at his touch.

"I'm no one, my Lord," I whisper. "Please unhand me."

"She's my handmaid," Seraphyna lies quickly.

"I thought you didn't believe in slaves," Domhnall points out.

"Does it ever occur to you that I pay her?"

"And what about the boy?" Domhnall asks, gesturing to Sebastian, not answering Seraphyna's quick reply.

"My Lord," she says.

"Yes?" Domhnall replies, narcissistically assuming she's addressing him. "What?"

"No, he's my Lord," she tells him. "My husband." *What?*

"Yes, I'm Lord of Light, pleased to meet you," Seb smiles, playing along happily and taking Domhnall's hand to shake it. "Uh… Domhnall, right?"

"Yes, that's correct," he replies curtly. "So, my sister has got herself a husband, never thought that would happen, tell me-"

"Sebastian," Seb confirms.

"Sebastian-" Domhnall pauses and clears his throat, just like Phyna does frequently. "Why in the realm did you want to marry my little sister? She's not honourable, she's not even pretty, she's barely royal having rejected her brother the king, myself, she's practically disowned herself from me, styling herself 'Lux' instead of 'Omnia'. Why, sir, why? You seem honourable."

"Your sister is the smartest, most beautiful, honourable and wonderful woman I have ever met and I encourage you to think the same, sir, if you want your opinions to be correct. I think your wife raised a wonderful woman and she did it well. I assure you, there is nothing about power or money in our union," Seb tells Domhnall. Behind him and out of Domhnall's view I can see Melaina nodding in Seraphyna's direction, slightly teared up, hand over her heart and beaming. I nod back at her and glance over at Phyna, who looks like she was just shot with an arrow of happiness.

"He's silly like that, charming and all," I tell her aside.

"No one's ever talked about me like that," she replies hopelessly, shaking her head, almost in disbelief.

"No broken-hearted young men sailing their boats off the Eastern Isles?" I ask.

"Never." Seraphyna confirms. "I've never really thought about my own romances until now, I suppose."

"And what are you thinking?"

"I'm not entirely sure, but I shouldn't be thinking as such, he's your brother, I'm sorry." She shakes her head, contradicting herself.

"Who's that?" I question, changing the subject and pointing to another parade advancing towards us.

"Oh, that's Aidan, my brother of Fire and his wife, Eithne, Ethelde's daughter," she replies casually.

"Ethelde's daughter?" I ask.

"Eithne was born and raised in the Eastern Isles, and now she's Lady of Fire and my sister-in-law. So yes, that's Aidan and Eithne and behind them is..." She stands on her tiptoes to get a better look. "Oh, Aella!"

As the processions of Air and Fire march up to where Domhnall and Seraphyna are, I see mixed emotions from the crowd I am in. As Seb steps back I can see the confused mix of colours passing across his eyes. He smiles briefly at Seraphyna, who returns his expression, but then looks back at the increasing amount of horses and carriages.

"Daileass of Water and Isoletta, his wife," Seraphyna mumbles to me, answering my unasked question.

"And-" I start, pointing to a couple on the backs of mules, unusually regal, contradicting the entire reputation of their steeds.

"Herminia and Dagan, of Earth," Seraphyna finishes, again reading my mind.

"So that's everyone?" Seb asks her.

"Yes, once all the candidates arrive, ceremoniously of course, we shall begin," she answers.

"How many this year?" Clancy quizzes.

"About 150," Seraphyna replies.

"Hm, about average," he informs us, writing something down on the scroll he's holding in his right hand. I tilt my head, noticing he's left-handed. It makes me think of my father, who also writes with his left. Conaire pops his head out to smile at me, I grin back. His hair blows in the wind and he pats it down irritably.

"Phyna!" I hear a woman shout, followed by another woman, Herminia on the mule, jumping down excitedly and following the other woman, Aella I remember her as, up to where Seraphyna is standing, open-armed and calling their names.

"Aella, Herminia!" she exclaims, embracing both of her sisters.

"Oh, Phye, I've missed you too much. You should come to Berr more often or I could come to *Les Insulae*," Herminia laughs, letting go of Phyna gently.

"Oh, you know Daileass would never let me," Seraphyna replies, glancing in Daileass's direction with a bitter expression. "We could all meet on the Isles, though."

"What about Olympia?" Aella suggests, speaking of her own home. "We have enough room in the stables for all of your horses, Hermie."

"I don't have that many horses!" Hermina exclaims.

"And who's this?" Aella questions, embracing me warmly as though she's known me her whole life.

"I'm Evanie," I smile. "And this is my brother, Sebastian."

"Oh, he's a handsome one, Phye," Herminia chuckles, embracing Seb. Like Aella, she holds onto him as though he's family. Although as far as Domhnall is aware, he is.

"They're my friends," Phyna tells them, comfortable enough to tell them our true identities.

"And where are you from?" Herminia asks me.

"Uh... well..." I hesitate, looking to Seraphyna helplessly.

"They're not from around here," Phyna answers for us.

"Ah, so from across the sea?" Aella suggests.

"You could say that, I suppose," I reply.

"Aella, my dearest," I hear a man call after Aella for her attention and we all look over.

Charging up the hill is a parade of children, some young and so innocent-looking, others older, more aware of the world, storming up the mountain in a sea of purple and white.

"Your lightest, I'd best go and take my place," the professor murmurs sadly, head bowed. Phyna nods and waves to Aella and Herminia as they go to find their respective Lords and places.

"Ethelde... I know it's hard... I'm sorry," Seraphyna says under her breath, holding the professor back. Ethelde looks apprehensively towards where Aidan and Eithne, her daughter, are standing.

"I'm fine," she insists. Ethelde leaves to stand with the other professors in front of the wishing stone. Each Lord and Lady, or in Seraphyna's case, just Lady, stands in front of their house's temple. Domhnall looks confused when Seb doesn't stand with Phyna, but, surprisingly, doesn't say anything.

The process is just as I saw Oralee's years ago. The candidate kneels on the wishing stone and before anyone knows it, it's over.

Each of the candidates are dressed simply, boys in deep wine-purple robes fastened at the collar and girls in a white shift dress, tied at the waist with a length of rough rope. However, each candidate, whether female or male, wears a single pearl on a string around their neck. I notice the pearl changes colour once they've emerged from a temple. Black for Darkness, blue for Water, green for Earth, grey for Air and red for Fire. It stays white though when the first sweet girl emerges from the temple of Light.

"Lady Leora of the House of Light!" Ethelde declares triumphantly.

"Saints be damned, she almost knocked the temple down," Conaire gasps. "I hope Phyna chooses her for wielding."

"Mm, she'd make a good warrior, you can see it behind her eyes," I confirm. I've seen plenty of soldiers pass in and out of Abbeville's hospital, and I know how to tell the weak ones from the natural born fighters.

Darkness. Water. Air. Fire. Fire. Darkness. Darkness. Earth. Water. The list goes on as candidates emerge from the temples of their new house and names are droned out. Isabelle, Elisabeth, Jan, Michael, Fina, Hans, Maryssa, James, Agatha. All types I see, but all have either a frightened or triumphant expression written all over their faces.

Leora, the new, sweet-looking girl looks as though she is in deep conversation with Seraphyna until their concentration breaks when the temple of light does. Stones fly everywhere, the roof is completely blown off. As quick as lightning itself, the stones pause in the air, even the tiny bits of sand, and it feels as though even time does. With force unimaginable to me before now, vines pull up from the ground and push the rubble back into shape almost perfectly, but not pattern-perfect, so that the temple bears one more battle scar. A boy, must be only twelve, emerges from the temple looking fazed and innocent, completely unaware of the fact he had just destroyed a 10000-year-old holy structure.

"Lord Ulric of the House of Light!"

"Only three people have ever destroyed the temple of light like that before," Clancy whispers, almost entranced.

"Who?" I ask.

"Oralee the Great, of course," he replies with a wise smile. "Then of course, Seraphyna and Lorna."

"The temple didn't seem destroyed though," I mutter under my breath.

"It isn't seen by the member of the house as they're still in their trance," Clancy answers, obviously having heard me. "I don't suppose you, Oralee, would've seen what happened."

"You know about my flashbacks?" I question.

"I've studied them before, you murmur things you wouldn't know to murmur, you look frightened when you're not the kind of person to be frightened," Clancy points out, drawing his attention back to the boy, Ulric. "Amazing," he mumbles.

At one point during the choosing of every single one of the young and fresh candidates, Clancy nudges me in the rib excitedly, murmuring that the girl that's kneeling on the wishing stone is his sister, Aviana. Aviana takes little time to make her decision, emerging from the temple of air with a breathtakingly strong gust of wind. Clancy shows no disdain of his sister's choice, only murmuring something partly inaudible about wanting her to become a student of history.

Finally, Oliv and Adrielle, the two candidates that were born into the House of Light, step up. Oliv goes first, obvious fear shrouding him. His decision does dictate his entire life from now, after all. It takes him a good two minutes, flitting between what seems like all six of the houses before the fog drops and he's emerged from the Temple of Fire.

Adrielle's decision is certainly different. It's an eerie process, she stops right between the temples of Light and Darkness, dead still. Slowly, slowly but surely, she treads defiantly towards the temple of Light. Seraphyna nods, as to encourage her on.

But then Adrielle stops again.

She doesn't even walk towards the Temple of Darkness, she disappears from the doorway of Light to the home of Darkness and I can see Seraphyna's head hang in shame and worry.

Adrielle was the last candidate.

Only two new members of Light.

A grim omen for the House of Light.

NOT ALONE

Seraphyna doesn't say anything. She looks Ethelde straight in the eye and frowns. Instantaneously, she takes mine and Seb's hands and glances at us worriedly.

"What's going on?" I ask, but she grips tighter onto my hand. Lorna takes Conaire's hand and Ethelde and Clancy walk towards us. "What's going on?" I repeat, but I can't finish my question properly. The mountainside and the temples, the crowds and the carriages mould into one huge dark void as I am twisted and turned in a hundred directions. I scream, but nothing comes out from my mouth but freezing breath, suspended in air. I can't feel Seraphyna's hand clutching mine any more but when I try to move it the void pulls against it, pulling me through the dark curtain.

It's still light on Greater Isle, although the sun is setting. The sunlight reflects on the ocean as Phyna stands on the cliff overlooking the tumbling waves that crash up against the white cliffs. Tenderly and slowly she reaches down to pick up a stone, a smooth round one. She tosses it in her hand for a while, watching it turn about in her palm. She raises her arm in the air and I expect her to throw it into the ocean angrily, but the action she takes is with something deeper than anger. The stone smashes into tiny pieces, some as small as dust, in the air. The fragments of the stone fly away from her at all angles, some fall into the ocean, others land on the emerald grass. Seb reaches his hand into the air also and with no effort at all catches one of the larger shards of stone and makes a fist around it. Seraphyna collapses onto the ground and then proceeds to sit over the edge of the cliff with her feet dangling over the ocean. Cautiously, Seb sits by her side and turns her body towards him.

"I think you dropped something," he says quietly, opening his fist and laying the stone fragment in her lap. I don't leave the shade of the tree I am stationed under to join them as I feel that only Seb can help the situation now. I'll only end up making it worse. Seb tenderly places one of his large hands on Seraphyna's shoulder as she sobs her heart out, sinking into him. She places her hands over her eyes in despair as her breathing slows, wiping her tears away with her sleeves.

"Seraphyna," Seb says, moving her hands away from her eyes and wiping one of her tears away for herself. She looks over at him sadly, with her head bowed. "Look, we'll get through this together. You're not alone. You have me. You have Evanie, you have your people to help you and your house. It's their house as well, after all. Listen, we'll always be here for you. *You are not alone.*"

Seraphyna opens her mouth to say something but then closes it and places her head on Seb's shoulder once again. Maybe silence is the thing she needs now. The pause isn't too long, however, as eventually she sits up.

"Thank you," she mumbles quietly, as she raises her head and looks Seb straight into his oaky eyes. She tilts her head so as to look upon him closer. He smirks at her, flirtatiously but caringly. Tenderly, he sweeps a lock of her honey hair from her eyes to behind her ear. They both smile together, a beautiful and clear sign they are at peace with each other and with their situation.

The scene is serene, a perfect picture of light and peace. Seraphyna and Seb sit with their legs dangling over the edge of the cliff, overlooking the calm, rolling waves of the ocean's expanse. The sun gravitates towards the horizon as, slowly, they join hands. The two keep looking at each other for reassurance that the scene is real, as the atmosphere feels dreamy and made up. Time passes quickly as we watch the world go by, and very slowly, Seb and Phyna gravitate closer to each other. Finally, Seb is the one to make a much-anticipated move, holding Seraphyna closely as their lips meet. They cling on to each other helplessly, for so much that they need to hold on to.

Suddenly, the situation feels awkward, as though I'm intruding on a classic oil painting and shouldn't be here. I look around to see if someone is near to help me get back to Royal Isle, I'm not going to swim in this dress and these shoes, after all. The rough path down to the dock for the fishing boats is clearly marked with lanterns mounted on wooden stakes in the ground.

The path is quite short, although it twists and turns, and when I reach the dock a boat is about to leave. One of the figures, tall and masculine, is merry and swaying with drunkenness, leaning into his obviously sober friend, whereas the others, stouter and more feminine, are quiet and sombre. I squint in the dim firelight to see who they are as the boat is leaving for Royal Isle and I know most people who live there now.

"Alas, a Lady approaches!" one of the passengers yells, brandishing a bottle of what looks like a spirit in my direction, almost hitting one of the women on the head. I still can't make out the faces of the sailors, but I have a rough idea of who the four could be.

"Watch where that bottle's flying, Conaire!" One of the women, I know her now as Ethelde, lectures, grabbing the bottle out Conaire's hand and throwing it into the shallow water as they throw the rope back on to the wooden decking. I run hastily onto the wooden planks, waving my arms and hoping the others will notice me.

"Professor! Lorna! Clancy! Conaire!" I call, jumping up and down on the dock. Ethelde raises her hand and the boat stops moving.

"It's Lady Evanie, Professor," Clancy confirms as Ethelde squints, trying to recognise the mysterious figure on the dock. Me.

In its own good time, the boat starts to move back towards me, following the command of Ethelde's hand. I clamber in unsteadily, sitting on the plank next to Clancy. Conaire talks for the entire journey about nothing in particular, his speech slurred and heavy.

"He's an arse when drunk, isn't he?" Lorna whispers to me warily but giggly. I nod silently with my lips pursed. I turn to Clancy cautiously, observing his soberness and then judging he's not quite as merry as his friend.

"Don't ever let him drink like this again, mind," I warn Clancy, laughing with my hand on his shoulder.

"Why do you care?" he laughs jokily, but I give him a serious answer.

"You're my friends, I don't want my friends getting hurt," I say, staring into the glossy sea. It's now completely dark and the light of the houses on Greater Isle reflects warmly onto the water of the narrow passage between the two islands.

We reach the palace all together in a small parade, singing songs merrily and out-of-tune. I don't know any of them but pick the words up soon enough. We are all incredibly hungry as we have not eaten yet today; there had been a promise of a feast this evening but Phyna seemed too occupied with my brother to organise it.

Lorna and Ethelde run into the small palace kitchen and dart out with huge plates of food and cups of water even though Conaire calls loudly for more wine, which is the last thing he needs.

We eat until it is past 9 o'clock and the mantle clock is chiming a low, mellow tune that rings throughout the grand hall. It is at 9o'clock, very shortly after the clock chimes, that there is a knock at the door of the hall. Two figures, one short and one really quite tall, stand shrouded in thick cloaks at the doorway. Their faces are painted with fear and wonder, showing reluctance.

"Excuse me, miss…" the taller figure, the girl murmurs quietly, her words only just audible from across the hall with its tall ceilings and wooden eaves.

"Ah, Lady Leora, Lord Ulric," Ethelde smiles, gesturing for the pair to come and sit with us. She snaps her fingers and plates appear in front of seats next to Clancy and I. "Sorry about the abrupt parting of our parade, as you know-"

"I know, Madam, I know the rules. That is why Ulric and I are here, we would like to ask if there is anything we could do to help," Leora says glancing at Ulric, who is still guiding his gaze around the hall, staring at everything before his eyes with childish wonder.

"Eat, child, and we can get to know you both, then we can assess whether you can help," Ethelde instructs, pouring them both a glass of water and placing food on their plates.

"What house do you originate from, then?" Lorna asks Leora, who is taking a large bite of the meat that has been placed in front of her. "You look Elspethian."

"Right so, Miss," Leora confirms, swigging her water. "No wine around here?"

"I like her!" Conaire declares loudly and triumphantly, cackling with laughter.

"Used to wine at an early age, hm, family a big deal, were they?" Lorna questions.

"Yes, they were," Leora declares proudly. "My mother is the Advisor to the Lady and General herself."

"She's not your Lady and General now," Clancy mutters irritably before turning kindly to Ulric. "And you, my boy, where did you come from?"

"Calia, Fire, sir," he mumbles, frightened, hiding his round face behind the goblet he's holding.

"Scared?" I ask gently, trying to ease his fear with a smile. He gives me an expression that barely resembles a smile. "I think the Little Lord and Lady are tired, could you show them to where they are staying?" I ask Clancy and Lorna.

"You'll be living in the Students' Village, we have houses ready for you now," Lorna tells them kindly, standing and opening the door to the kitchen. "Clancy, would you bring Conaire?"

"Of course," Clancy replies, pulling Conaire up from his chair. "Evanie, could you help me?"

I rush to Clancy's aid, pulling Conaire along in his drunken daydream. I shake my head at Clancy in disbelief as Conaire laughs maniacally, a low and deep sound.

The Student's Village is a small collection of huts, small but well-built and sturdy, just a skip away from the palace. The huts lie on the edge of the forest by the west keep, the plants weaving their way around the smattering of houses on the muddy meadow ground. There are seven or so of the huts in the cluster and when we approach them, Lorna pulls out a ring of keys from her belt and runs ahead to unlock the doors of two untouched huts. Leora's expression drops when she sees the confinement of her living arrangements. Ulric frowns as well, though I detect his upset stems not from the size of his new home.

"Alright?" I ask him as he continues to frown. He nods silently and I chortle. "Not much of a talker?"

"No, Miss," he breathes.

"You'll be fine," I smile, even though his expression tells me he doesn't dare believe a word I say. "Really."

He continues to nod distractedly and timidly as Lorna guides him through the door of one of the huts. He waves her out quickly and I can tell by his red face that he is going to cry himself to sleep. His parents and close family will be here tomorrow to bring his things and say their goodbyes. If they want to. If they care enough. They might, they might not.

"We should put Conaire in bed," I tell Clancy as Conaire snores and rests his heavy and greasy head on my shoulder. I push him away from me in repulsion and he wakes up with a gasp. He pulls his dagger from his pocket and brandishes it at the both of us, eyes alert but staggering about. Clancy glances at me, trying to hold back a laugh.

"Come on then, Conaire, let's get you to bed," Lorna sighs as she closes the door to Leora's hut, leaving her inside.

"I don't want to!" he insists, pouting and crossing his arms like a child throwing a tantrum. Lorna rolls her eyes, obviously used to the situation. Irritably, she grabs Conaire's arm and throws the door to his house open. He's thrown inside with all Lorna's might. Lorna stamps her foot and a canteen of water appears in her hand. She throws it in the door to Conaire and slams the door shut.

"And no, it's not ale!" she exclaims through the thin walls. A loud thump can be heard from inside his home, the canteen obviously being thrown against his wall in frustration.

"Well, it's only eight, we can head back to the palace and clear the dinner things up, though it shouldn't take too long," Clancy says, opening the door to his house. A sign on his door reads four simple words. *Lira Kla Themata Rys.*

"It means 'For Justice, Knowledge finds its way'," he explains, reading my mind, although he may have just seen me scrutinising the sign.

"Wise words," I nod.

"You can come in if you want," Clancy offers, holding the door for me. I'm taken aback. "I have to find a book on my shelf to return to the library or the professor will kill me."

"Oh," I breathe, stepping into the warmth of his home. Usually I wouldn't follow a man who I barely know (alright, perhaps that's a lie, I've spent much time with Clancy in the library over the past month) into his home when he shuts the door behind us both, but Clancy's so kind and genuine that I'm almost certain he wouldn't hurt me and I'm too worried to hurt his feelings, therefore I oblige.

Clancy pulls a chair from his desk for me to sit on. "I'll be back," he says, ascending a rickety wooden ladder to the top of his bookcases. I gaze in wonder at the sheer volume of books in Clancy's home. The ladder leads to a whole other level of books and the first layer of bookshelves is so vast that Clancy can very comfortably walk along the top of them without having to pigeon-step. The bookshelves are obviously not at all organised as there is no distinct pattern in the books. The colours are a hodgepodge of old, faded books with broken spines and torn pages and vibrant, newer ones, albeit still with broken spines and torn pages. I scan the spines of some of the books, reading the silver and gold gilded words that spell out titles of ancient philosophies and modern theories alike. One shelf holds such a variety of titles and topics, ranging from *The Most Noble Magic, the Lightest Magic* to its neighbour, *Famous Centaurs of the pre-Omnian Period* and then on to *Oralee the Great: The East I, Vol. II*. I pause at that specific title.

I ponder whether to pluck it from its place and delve into my own, unknown life. I wonder whether Clancy would be angry, but then erase it from my mind as I'm so hungry for the knowledge that I can feel my head becoming dizzy. I lurch forward and grab the book from where it is, the books next to it falling in on each other with a soft thump. I open the book swiftly, almost tearing out the front page in my excitement.

"Ah, found it," Clancy declares, descending the ladder and smiling widely. "A shame I have to return it, although I'm sure Ethelde wouldn't mind if I made copies of the pages I needed for my project..." He mumbles to himself before noticing me, bundled up in the chair he offered me, trying to focus my eyes in order to read the first few words of my life.

"Found something you like the look of?" he asks me kindly, not a hint of irritation or annoyance in his voice. "You can borrow it to read if you want," he offers kindly, moving my fingers to see the title of the book.

"It's about my life, Clancy!" I exclaim, slamming the book down on my lap swiftly and loudly.

"Not that one!" He shakes his head, snatching the book from my grasp, closing it with a snap and shoving it back on the nearest and most convenient bookshelf to him.

"What? But-" I start as Clancy scans the top row of the first tier of the shelves. He pulls an ancient, damaged volume thinner than the one he took from me. I pout at him, as it's technically about me.

"You'll want to start with Volume I, then you can read that one. I also have volume III but volume IV and V are in the library so when you've finished the first three, I can find them for you, just ask," he waffles, handing me the book. The lettering on the front reads *Oralee the Great:* like the second volume but is then followed by *Princess, Vol I*. I stare at it for a while before turning my gaze to Clancy's kind eyes and smile. It's a handsome smile.

"Thank you," I say. Clancy opens the door and the cold sea air rushes into his house. I hadn't realised how warm and welcoming Clancy's house was. Lorna is standing outside still, scribbling something down in a leather-bound notebook with a feather quill. When we appear in front of her, she stuffs them back into her satchel.

"What took you so long?" she whines.

"Sorry, Lore, it was on my third level," Clancy explains.

"You have a third level?" I exclaim, although the fact hardly surprises me.

"And a few shelves in the library in the palace, I ran out of room last year," he admits as though it's something to be ashamed of.

"That's… impressive," I tell him.

"You should see Ethelde's personal library," Clancy scoffs almost in jealousy but laughs after.

"Like you don't practically have a personal library," Lorna mumbles humorously, elbowing Clancy playfully in the rib.

"I sleep in there as well!" Clancy insists.

"Oh, trust me, you'd sleep in the library if you were given the choice," Lorna reminds him. Clancy is silent for a moment before he nods and chuckles.

"It must be nice having friends like this…" I say quietly, lamenting, I have never experienced a friendship like this before.

"You didn't have friends where you came from?" Lorna asks, jumping gracefully over a stone that blocks her path. I stop to think. It's the first time my home, Earth, has been mentioned since I arrived here. My place of birth, the only home I knew for eighteen years, has been so far from my thoughts and it shocks me.

"N…no." I stutter, still in shock about how much I don't miss home. Not one bit. "I mean… I had Seb growing up, then my sister, Penn,." It's the first time I've talked about Penn since I arrived as well. I should miss her, and in ways I do, but I know she cared little for me and my wellbeing. I certainly don't miss the way she mothered me relentlessly despite me being just four years her junior. Evanie, make your bed. Evanie, you really should be more social. Evanie, Evanie, Evanie. Never once did anything for herself, always had Henry, Seb, either of my parents or me to do her bidding, and I certainly don't miss that.

Lorna nods at my answer. "I understand," She smiles. "I didn't really have friends in Elspeth either."

"Oh," I exclaim. "You're from Elspeth?"

"Well… no and yes. I grew up there but I'm not from there. My parents came from Myrie, a land to the very south of here, and they left me with a family in Elspeth when they left me. In Myrie, girls are regarded as nuisances. Many families just kill their daughters or sell them to brothels. I was one of the lucky ones," she explains, pausing. She kicks leaves in the air and catches one with her hand, tearing it up into hundreds of tiny, flaky pieces. "Unlike many people in Elspeth, the Gullies were kind and they cared for me. They were important enough for me to qualify for choice day. I was officially their daughter, I suppose, but I still never was treated as well as their own sons and daughters. I was to be a lady-in-waiting for Mira, their youngest daughter. Their eldest daughter was Isoletta, the current Lady and General of the House of Water. Of course, I hated the idea of being a *Lady*, I wanted to learn, you know? So, when it came to choice day, I jumped at the idea of being able to study Scrutiny of Light."

"Your sister is Isoletta?" I question. She nods and then shakes her head.

"Again, yes and no. She disregards me as any relation of hers, adopted or otherwise. I was not invited to her wedding; I have never had the pleasure of meeting that bastard Daileass." She mumbles the last part as though she's a child trying not to be heard. Although, from what I have heard from all Seraphyna and Clancy have told me about Daileass, I think that 'bastard' is a suitable word to describe him. I saw Daileass briefly on Choice Day, he didn't say or do anything significant apart from sighing loudly when a young girl tripped over a stone on her way to kneel on the wishing stone. I got the impression he saw women as mere objects rather than his equals.

"Everyone's quite close-knit here, aren't they?" I ask.

"Well, people who move houses are generally the ones who can afford to get to Holynest and are deemed important enough to prove their loyalty and train their magic. Those who aren't rich or important and take part in choice day are ones who have shown distinct talent at an early age," Clancy explains. "So, apart from those that are actually talented, we stem from families with status and as I'm sure you know, important families have a wicked tendency to inbreed and make as many connections as they can with one another."

"Even where I come from the royals are horrifically inbred," I tell them.

We approach the kitchen doors to the palace and Clancy holds the door for Lorna and I. "Ladies first," he smiles.

I step into the kitchens confidently, grabbing an apple off the side and taking a bite from it. The room is quiet and I can feel tension residing within the air. Confused, I open the door to the Great hall, where Ethelde is still sitting at the table nursing a mug of water.

"Oh, Lady Evanie," she sighs in relief, standing to curtsey to the three of us.

"What's the matter, professor?" Clancy asks, noting her awkwardness and fear.

"They've been arguing for the whole time you've been gone, if she gets too angry, she's likely to lash out!" The professor says, alarmed words tumbling from her mouth.

"Woah, professor, slow down," Lorna breathes calmly. "Who's-"

"You cannot act like there was nothing between us back there! You're acting like there was nothing! Nothing at all!" Seraphyna's sharp and furious words shoot through the Great Hall from the Entrance Hall where she and Seb are standing, stern expressions matching perfectly.

"Please, do something..." Ethelde pleads, looking at me desperately. I nod concisely before entering the warzone...

"I'm not pretending! I know that something happened, you're the one who's being irrational!" Seb replies.

"I'm being irrational? I'm being irrational! Honestly, Seb, you're nothing like the man I had faith that you'd be!" Seraphyna yells, raising her hands above her head in insane anger. She moves her hands peculiarly, like she's clawing at the air in hope to cling on to something. I lurk in the doorway, watching her every move, remembering what Ethelde said '*If she gets too angry, she's likely to lash out...*'

I try to run in and stop Seraphyna from injuring my brother, but she swipes her arm through the air, smacking me in the face with air as she does. Seb is knocked to the ground as she looks upon him coldly. I debate who to rush to, whether it is to aid Seb or to calm Seraphyna. I choose Phye, who is hyperventilating and shaking. I grab her arms and stare her in her changing eyes. The look she gives Seb, as she still focuses on him behind me, shifts from fiery rage to shock, dread and mortification. She tries to lurch forward to his aid against my grip, but I continue to stare her down as she still isn't calm, she still breathes heavily and shakes uncontrollably.

"Phye, Phyna, calm down," I plead as her breathing slows. Out of the corner of my eye I see Seb pull himself from his position on the cold stone floor of the entrance hall. He doesn't utter a word, he just darts towards the stairs in disgust. The look on his face is plain, clear and blinding: betrayal.

ENDS OF THE EARTH

Because it is late, Seraphyna goes to bed as well, only shortly after Seb. Clancy, Lorna, Ethelde and I all go to the library to read by candlelight. I start reading the book Clancy kindly lent me whereas Lorna and Clancy write on either their scrolls or notebooks.

"I think that perhaps in a year or two when I'm messenger, we can actually carry out the experiment we've talked about, Clancy," Lorna suggests confidently, showing Clancy her notes she made in her notebook.

"We can't do it here, maybe Herminia could find us some land in Berr for us to conduct the experiment in?" Clancy points out and Lorna shrugs.

"Moving on," Lorna concludes, "Professor, why were Phye and Seb arguing?"

"I have a bad feeling Seb started it," I admit, closing my book.

"He did," Ethelde confirms. "There was something about he was unhappy here, how he felt pressured, how he had no choice whether he could come here or not."

I shake my head in shame. It was my fault Seb ended up here, it was my choice to bring him here. If I didn't bring him here, though, he'd be dead and I'd be living a life of nurses' uniforms, dying men and nagging from Penn without the reminder he's just at the other end of my pen.

"And then Seraphyna said something about how she just wanted him to stay because she needed him and she felt something towards him," Ethelde continues, winding up her scroll to tie it with a piece of string. "Then the argument escalated into something more intense... you could tell they were trying to hurt each other with each word that left their lips. It was as though their feelings for each other meant that the argument meant more to them. It was... it was serious."

"And Phye got so angry she lashed out, she couldn't control her hands," I tell them.

"Sounds like love to me," Clancy laughs, dipping his peacock quill in the ink. "Just you wait."

*

We do wait. The night is long and I barely sleep for I am reading the book Clancy lent me until the early hours of the morning. When the sun finally rises, I sneak down to the kitchens to find something to eat. The corridors are empty and eerie as the curtains of many of the windows are drawn.

When I reach the great hall, I see that I have been beaten there. Seb, Conaire and Clancy are sitting at the long table there, seemingly deep in conversation.

"Hello, Seb," I greet, taking a seat next to my brother. He smiles warmly at me, as though nothing happened last night. "Conaire, are you feeling better?"

"I have a terrible hangover; my ankle hurts from where I stumbled into the boat and I've run out of Karta. I'll have to go and get some more in Olympia when Old Davisham finally lets me use the ship again. So, no, I'm feeling rather awful and it's all my fault.

Thanks for your concern though, Evanie." Conaire explains, rubbing his head.

"Karta?" I question.

"Strong-smelling Calian medicine that's used to treat Star Fever, but it's also a very strong alcohol and can be drunk *very sparingly*," Clancy tells me, glancing smugly over at Conaire, who hangs his head jokily.

"Hey, Evanie, I'll need to go and get some more Karta next week, Clancy needs some more peacock quills and parchment and Lorna I think needs some uh... oh I don't know what she wants but it's something leather, I think," Conaire says. "You're welcome to come with us next week, I think we're thinking about going in four days' time?"

"Sounds about right," Clancy confirms. "You're welcome to join us as well, Sebastian."

Seb looks cautiously towards me and he shrugs, kindly but casually, at Clancy.

"I'll think about it, thanks though, Clancy," Seb replies. After a few seconds of silence, Seb picks up his plate to take it to the kitchen, seemingly to avoid the quick, light footsteps clicking down the entrance hall. Her pace is very distinctive, so we all know who Seb is hiding from: Seraphyna.

She appears in the doorway, dressed regally as usual, but obviously deprived of sleep. Her eyes are red from crying, dark circles have formed under them, her hair lacks its flawlessness and shine and her face is bare of makeup. Despite her wonderful dress, it's not her best; the fabric hangs loosely and the belt has been tied hastily. She's obviously put herself together very swiftly this morning.

"Is Seb in here?" she asks quietly, shyly even, which is rare for her. She shows no confidence in her posture; no spark resides in her eyes. Seb, even though he is clearly in the room, continues to head towards the door as though she's a ghost, like she's not even there. Her words mean nothing to him.

"Seb, I came to apologise," she breathes, placing her foot over the threshold. The meeting of her foot and the stone flooring of the great hall causes a low echoing sound that forces Seb to stop in his tracks. He turns slowly back towards the table, placing his plate back down on the solid surface.

"I should be the one who apologises," he says quietly, ashamed. He changes direction once more, plodding along the stones until he is close to Seraphyna.

"No," she insists. "Usually, I love winning fights, I love getting the last word, it used to make me feel as though I had power, like I had meaning. Now, as you can see, I had a sleepless night, I cannot stop thinking whether I hurt you, I'm sorry I lashed out at you, I was just so angry, with everything that happened yesterday, with my brother and Melaina and choice day and that kiss…"

"That kiss…" Seb repeats.

"And I've had a lot of time to think, all those years I spent in Domhnall's court locked up… I had a lot of thoughts about love… about feelings. I need you to know that I've never felt this way about anyone I've ever met in my life before. I want to spend every moment of my waking day with you, I want to talk with you as much as possible, I am happy when with you, Seb."

"Phyna, what are you trying to say?" Seb asks, taking another step towards her.

"I want you to know that I'm in love with you, Seb," Seraphyna replies, saying his name quietly and shyly. She emphasises each word, one after the other, so that the message is clear. "I'm in love with you and I couldn't stand hurting you. When you cry, I cry, when you laugh, I laugh, when you smile, I'm your mirror." She bows her head, weight lifting from her shoulders, a secret off her chest. I can't see Seb's expression, but I can tell he's heightened from her words, like his heart has swelled and lungs filled with fresh air.

"All my life I've been overlooked, been put last or first but for the wrong reasons," she continues as a way to damper the pain of Seb's silence. "I learnt to be quiet and not question what the men around me were doing because I was a woman, a girl, and my voice could be silenced. But now, I want to scream, I want to shout, I want the ends of the earth to hear what I have to say, because no matter how hard anyone in the realm may try, they cannot silence my words any longer. They cannot silence me when I tell them that I love you, because I do, it is the one thing I ask you to never forget."

Seraphyna's confession leaves Seb gobsmacked. I wait for Seb to say something back, although I'm sure Phyna doesn't expect a grand declaration in return. Even so, I expected him to say *something* before he runs off, but he doesn't, he darts straight past her and out of the door.

I expect Phye to break down or at least show some form of disappointment, but all she does is smile brightly and freely at the three of us before turning grandly to leave as well. She doesn't follow Seb but goes to sit in the library, alone in the darkness.

"Well, that was-" Clancy starts awkwardly.

"Intense," I finish.

"Should you go and talk to him?" Conaire asks quietly, pouring me some coffee.

"I'll leave him be for a few hours to mull it over," I conclude after a while. Seb has to think on his own. He doesn't need me to distract him.

The sunrise is pleasant and I open the doors to the front lawn so I can watch the final stages of it. The sea is calm and the air carries a gentle and cooling breeze. The silence of the situation leaves me to listen to the sounds of the nature. A bird singing. The ebb and flow of the peaceful, rolling waves and their crash against the rocks. The cawing of crows. The rustling of trees.

"Luke, stop!" I demand, holding my hand out to place on his shoulder. "Don't leave."

The rustling of the trees becomes louder and faster, the waves start to thud against the white cliffs.

"You can't stop me," he spits, snapping around to stare me down. His eyes are the same as mine and they burn the same as mine too, bright fire orange, a peculiar colour, I've always thought.

"I can't, you're right," I sigh in defeat to my brother's stubbornness. He's changed little since we came here. I've changed a lot in those three years. Three years is enough time to change, too much time to not change at all.

"I'll only come back when absolutely necessary," he insists, setting his satchel on the ground. I can feel the pain he's holding within him.

"Don't go forever," I sob, embracing him strongly. He stops for a minute, trying to act shocked at my arms around him, but he embraces me back after a while.

"I'll still be alive," he reminds me. *"Send a Bluejay whenever you need me, Oralee, you know they'll find me."*

"Master of Bluejays," I laugh, tousling his hair, sprayed with sea salt and sand from his journey onto the beach. *"Goodbye, brother."*

"You know why I'm leaving," he reminds me, *"You know why."*

"You know you can't," I insist, my voice becoming hushed.

"I know," he whispers. *"But I still love her."*

My head feels heavy, that way that it feels when you've been running from something for a long time. Heavy, weighty, but light at the same time. I close my eyes and open them to stop the dizziness, and in some of my haziness, I mustn't have seen Seb come and stand next to me. He stares out at the now fully risen sun as I do, but he hangs his head slightly, whereas I keep mine held high.

"I shouldn't have run like that, should I?" he questions quietly.

"No," I tell him bluntly. He shouldn't have.

"Did it break her?" he asks quickly, carefully, because he's almost convinced he knows the answer.

"Quite the opposite," I assure him. "She just needed to get it off her chest, she wasn't expecting a grand speech from you in return."

"I should've stayed," he tells himself, kicking a small stone, the size of a pearl, off the edge of the cliff. "I shouldn't have even started that argument at all. We wouldn't be here in this mess if I hadn't."

"It seemed some special moment you shared yesterday," I remind him, and he nods.

"It was," he confirms, smiling sadly at the horizon. "And I ruined it. I should've told her then. I knew it then, I think she knew it then, why didn't I tell her then?" By now, I think he's just talking to himself, but I know what he's talking about. I can tell the words are bubbling up inside him, working their way up to his brain, from one corner of his heart to the other, to the ends of the earth and back. Finally, the words, simple as they are, reach his mouth.

"I love her."

THESE WORDS

I don't see much of Seraphyna for the next few days. She wanders about the palace tirelessly, avoiding Seb so eagerly and easily that it becomes a talent of hers. Not like Seb tries to avoid her, either, to make it easier for her. In fact, he tries to catch her at every moment they even pass but she comes up hastily with some generic excuse. 'I'm going out riding,' she'll say one day, then 'On my way to Greater Isle,' the next. No matter what Seb says or does, Phye won't give him the time of day. It's only after five days of relentless and painful avoidance that Seraphyna finally agrees to, at least, be in the same room as him.

"Evanie, do you know when Lorna, Clancy and Conaire are planning on going to Olympia?" she asks me quietly, entering the library and trying to avoid the accusing but loving stare Seb is shooting her way. I look up from my book, now volume II of Oralee's life, the one I originally plucked from Clancy's bookshelf.

I ponder her question for a minute, scratching my chin in thought.

"Tomorrow or the day after," I tell her certainly. "I am almost certain, at least, depending on when Old Davisham will give them the boat."

"Well," she starts, looking anxiously towards Seb, who is still gawking at her helplessly, "I was thinking that maybe... well."

Before she can finish her nervous sentence, Seb calmly rises to his feet, making his eventual way towards where Phye is standing by the library door's threshold. Tenderly, he leans down so that his lips are brushing against her pricked ears. He whispers something inaudible to her, which makes her draw back away from him. Embarrassment and euphoria stir around on her face so that the emotion is indistinguishable between the two.

"My... uh, my sister said that... uh, well, you see, I have something really, something really quite important with uh, with Aella, and she, well, she, uh, she invited us to her palace whenever, you know? I've never uh... I've never been there but I've seen paintings and it's a... it's a magnificent pre-Omnian building," Seraphyna stutters. She becomes more and more flustered as she struggles to form a sentence with her mouth that's slowly but very, very surely, curling up at the corners into a wide and euphoric smile.

Seb smirks, his gaze judging her every single move with kindness and adoration.

"Well then," he smiles, so besotted with every single thing Seraphyna says and does. "Looks like we're going on a little holiday to Aella's."

*

After being firmly ordered to fetch the boat from Davisham, Lorna, Seb, Conaire and I sit along the cliff's edge, dangerously close to the substantial drop, with our legs hanging over the grassy verge. We watch the sunrise silently, basking in its calming effect on our resting moods, previously on edge. Right in the midst of summer, the meadow sweeping the cliff's edge like a blanket is more alive than I could ever wish to be. Bees dance from flower to flower, the grass dances merrily in the soft breeze, providing shade for ants still carrying on busily with their workload. Lorna starts picking the silk-white daisies from their clusters by her knee and starts to thread them into a crown, an activity I never in a lifetime would have expected Lorna to partake in. She rests the coronet across her calloused hands, admiring her nimble work. Seb turns to smile at me, making time for Lorna to, silently and attentively, place her creation amongst Seb's sandy mop of hair.

"So, you and Phye have made up then?" Lorna asks, trying to hold back her laughter at Seb's new accessory and status as queen of the fairies.

"Not entirely," Seb sighs, hanging his head so that, unfortunately, the daisy crown slides from his head into his lap. "God, I was such a bloody idiot, wasn't I?"

"She's a good one, Seb, she's hard to hurt, that's all I'll say," Conaire offers, shrugging as he gives his oddly neutral opinion.

"You must be one heck of a wordsmith to break down, pull a love declaration from and win back Seraphyna Lux simply using those words of yours," Lorna concludes, leaning back and throwing her arms beside her. Her braided hair nestles in the grass as she lies down, staring up at the cornflower-coloured sky.

"What did you say to her in the library yesterday, anyway?" I question curiously, for I never managed to hear those all too important words that were whispered into Phye's ears, the ones that made Seraphyna Lux, Lady of Light, stutter and blush, shy away and giggle.

"Four simple words," Seb explains simply, holding up four fingers as he does so, "the feelings are mutual."

"And are they?" Conaire raises an eyebrow.

Seb grins, looking back out to the almost risen sun. "Absolutely."

"Well, they'd better be," Lorna threatens, raising a fist comically from her spot lying in the grass. "I'm not letting her take another hit like that, I'll eradicate all possible sources if need be."

Seb throws his hands behind his shoulders in mock surrender as Lorna mimics shooting an arrow from the bow she's slung back off her shoulder.

"Davisham should be up by now, the sun's practically risen," Lorna tells us, rising to her feet with a whimsical jump on the balls of her feet, the action creating a pattering sound on the moist grass.

We start to walk along the cliff's edge, the four of us like Robin Hood's men, a merry band indeed.

"Where are Clancy and the professor?" I ask as Lorna reaches for a small pebble. She kicks it off the edge of the cliff with no audible landing.

"Somewhere hidden away in the library drafting the peace treaty between the Faithful houses," Lorna tells me. "We'll approve it later, but I'm almost certain they'll do a good enough job for us to be able to pass it off at first glance."

"Who are we going to visit again?" Seb asks, changing the subject abruptly.

"Old Davisham," Conaire says.

"He's a fisherman and sailor who lives on Royal Isle. His forefathers have been wardens of this island for centuries, and whilst he is technically Count of Scylla, he just goes by Davisham. Old Davisham. His daughter's lovely, too," Lorna takes a quick side glance at Conaire, who strokes the nape of his neck uncomfortably. "She's the one who did Phyna's portrait. She's married to Count Ilene so she's usually on Greater Isle. She sometimes visits her father though."

Lorna keeps glancing at Conaire suspiciously, who is becoming increasingly red and uncomfortable.

"She shouldn't be there today, though," Lorna says, almost assuring Conaire of something. I turn to Seb, hoping that he's also as lost as me, not knowing what in the realm is going on.

"Pay attention!" I yell, yanking Seb away from the cliff edge in his daze. "Don't zone out when on the edge of a cliff, Seb! Pay attention!"

Seb jumps, snapping out of his state of practical unconsciousness.

"You starting to sound like Penn," he states bluntly. "Or mother."

"Oh, Saints," I gasp in horror, placing my hand to my mouth. "I am. Saints be damned, I am!"

"Yes, you are!" Seb laughs, prodding me in the shoulder with his elbow. I look up to him angrily, which only makes him chuckle louder.

"You need to tell me at every moment I start sounding like a condescending, overbearing pain in the neck, promise?" I plead, mimicking desperation as I cling onto Seb's thin cotton shirt.

"Yes Ma'am."

We approach the place where the meadow starts to mould into the woods, where the cliffs start to slope down towards the beach less steeply.

"Davisham?" Lorna calls out, approaching the pathway.

A grubby, poorly marked path leads its way up to a shack nestled among reeds and rough grassy patches. Well, to call it a shack is a stretch. Four large panels of wood lean in on each other for support, a scarred roof acting as a useless barrier for rainwater as it bears so many holes it could be a honeycomb. Small holes the size of pebbles litter the wood, weaving their way around too many gaping holes the size of large boulders to be comfortable. All types of vines weave their way around the wood, making ladders for spiders to climb and honey bees to dance on. Tiny, pale pink flowers bloom in patches on the vines, an odd, gentle contrast to the roughness of the shack. Despite its destitute look, however, the shack is of a considerable size, stretching right to the edge of the cliff. So close to the edge, I must say, I'm worried it may topple off at any moment. The area is unkempt and wild, all types of flora sprouting up at various angles from the ground around the building. A washing line made with fishing wire carries moth-eaten shirts in various faded shades of grey or cream, the wire tied around two bare logs itself looking like it'll succumb to the weight of the clothes. The whole scene is so overgrown and ruled by the vines and flowers that it's a botanist's haven.

"Davisham!" Lorna calls again. She continues to walk towards the shack, almost cautiously. Lorna stops in her tracks as a young, fresh-faced girl pops her head out from the door of the shack, a wicker basket of laundry hoicked up on her hip.

"He's just inside," the girl says, smiling at us. "Hello, Lorna."

Conaire steps out from behind the wall that Lorna, Seb and I have created, and as he does, both the girl and Conaire's faces fall.

"Oh, hello Conaire," she mumbles. "Who are your friends, Lorna?" she says, a little louder, changing the subject.

"These are Phye's new friends," Lorna explains.

"Why are you here, Lindera?" Conaire growls, clenching his fists.

"Because Florean's in Berr," Lindera explains matter-of-factly. "Probably seeing that awful Rosaleen again."

"He has to stop treating you this way," Conaire says through gritted teeth. He continues to stare at Lindera angrily, but you can still sense the restless passion and tension between them.

"He doesn't treat me badly, Conaire!" Lindera shouts, shoving the pegs down on the washing she's still in the process of hanging out on the thin fishing wire line. She huffs furiously, glancing towards the tattered door of the shack, which opens and reveals a large, Saint Nick-like figure.

"What's all the noise about?" the man, who I can only assume is Old Davisham, grunts, squinting in the morning daylight. He glances to his daughter who sighs and shrugs. "Lindera?"

"I was just asking Conaire *what in the realm is he doing here?*" Lindera strains, directing all of her petty anger towards Conaire, who stands facing her fully and matching her fury.

"Were they…?" I mouth to Lorna. She nods nervously and concisely. I nod back, turning to examine Davisham in his roughness. He's been beaten and battered by the sea, with scars marking his face wherever you look. He walks lopsided with a rough wooden cane, leaning on it heavily for support with each strong step he takes. His beard is like a white forest, so white it could be sea foam. The hairs twist around into knots and over small particles of food that have become stranded in his facial hair. His shirt is even thinner than Seb or Conaire's summer shirts, making him look as though he is only a poor fisherman or boat mender, not a count or revered figure within the community of the Isles.

"Lindera," Davisham scolds, as though Lindera is five years old and not a grown woman. "Let bygones be bygones and ask them how we may assist."

Lindera pouts momentarily at her father, before turning sweetly to Lorna and smiling at the three of us, completely avoiding Conaire's deathly passionate gaze upon her.

"Lorna, how can I assist you and your new friends today?" she asks, tilting her head calmly to the side, which is a drastic change from her recently rage-filled expression.

"We just came to ask to borrow the boat, Davisham," Lorna explains.

"She's in the harbour," Davisham says, pointing southwards some way. "She's yours to use whenever it pleases our Lady."

"Thanks, Davisham," Lorna says. "We'll take care of her, I promise,"

"I'm sure you will," he replies kindly. "And who *are* your friends, Lorna?" Davisham struts up to where Seb is stationed and sticks out his hand for Seb to shake it.

"I'm Sebastian, sir," Seb tells Davisham.

"He's a fine boy," Davisham laughs, looking over curiously to Lindera, who's angrily trying to busy herself with her washing.

"And you, my dear?" Davisham asks, moving along to me. I smile, taking his hand which he shakes happily.

"Evanie," I remark. Davisham's eyes glisten, surveying me thoroughly.

"No, you're not," Davisham articulates, raising a finger at my reply. "You're Oralee the Great."

"You're Oralee the Great?" the figure questions, breathy voice slicing through the darkness like a blade.

"How did you guess?" I smirk, narrowing my eyes.

"I wouldn't say 'the Great'…" I chuckle as the figure removes his hood. "But how did you guess?"

"I'd know you a mile off, Oralee," he smiles, white teeth twinkling under the moon's white glow.

"Ledan," I sigh in relief, as momentarily Ledan's dark locks and piercing blue eyes made me panic, thinking that maybe he's Donovan, instead.

"At your service, my Lady," Ledan proclaims, bowing his head. His hands flinch upwards towards his cloak hood, but I stop him, his hands flicking back down to his sides at my command.

"Have you considered my offer?" I question. At the mention of the offer, Ledan's shoulders relax as he sighs melodically.

"I have," he states, feet shuffling.

"You know that you're not my first choice as General," I apologize, shrugging awkwardly as Ledan continues to look at his feet. "Luke will always be my first choice but he's gone and there's no way of contacting him."

"He's not gone forever," Ledan assures me.

"I've tried all the Bluejays I can get a hold of," I cry desperately, running a hand through my dark locks. "But every time none of them return."

"As your General, I promise I'll help you find him," Ledan says. My eyes light up.

"So, it's a 'yes' then?" I inquire excitedly, "You'll be my General?"

"It would be my honour to serve the House of Light and you, Oralee," Ledan assures me, corners of his lips curling up into a proud grin.

I extend my hand, the black velvet of my cloak brushing past it as my fingertips meet the cold night air. I thrust the yellowing parchment into Ledan's moonlight-coated hand, which sinks back behind the safety of his robes.

"Protect these words," I command, pointing to the spot that Ledan has concealed my untidy, dark cursive on sour-milk paper.

"I shall guard them with my life, my Lady," Ledan vows, throwing up the hood of his cloak and slipping away into the night.

"Evanie?" Lorna yells into my exhausted ears. "Evanie, can you hear me?"

I return into the darkness also.

"I can hear you," I rasp, my voice dry as tree bark and sand. I massage my eyes with the grubby tips of my fingers.

"Will she be alright?" Davisham asks, his usually booming voice suddenly hushed and gentle. I throw a hand up to my face and signal that I'll be fine.

"Everything'll be just fine," I assure him, beaming widely, which makes me wince from the headache

I have developed in the thousand lifetimes or so I've had to travel through to reach my body and senses again.

"We'll get you back to the palace, Evanie," Seb suggests, ushering me by placing his surprisingly steady hand on my unsteady shoulders.

Lorna, Conaire and Seb refuse to take their eyes off me for one moment as we ramble back towards the palace, staying much further away from the cliff as we did on the way to Davisham's cottage. They push me around every stone, leaf and twig that falls into our path. Any other day, I'd be annoyed by their extreme attentiveness, but since my head weighs a hundred tonnes, I'm thankful that they're being my head for me today.

When we arrive at the palace its white stone walls glisten in the sunlight, forcing us to squint if we want to look in the direction of our destination. The portcullis is open, the grass a few shades greener. When we cautiously approach the courtyard, we see an ancient mule tired up with vines to a decaying wooden post, whinnying irritably as we walk past it without paying it any attention. Flowers with neat, teardrop petals pop up in random places around the barren, dry courtyard in a frenzy of every hue you could imagine, deep plum, azure blue, powder pink and baby blue. You name it, the colour's there, somewhere.

We come nearer to the library once we're inside. The door is wide open to the brightly lit chamber but the area is completely absent of anyone, enemy or otherwise. I start to panic, my head's pain subsiding into worry, until I hear a very shrill but excited shout from the great hall of:

"Herminia!" Lorna gasps, running like lightning into the great hall. She's met by a tall, brunette figure whose locks are shinier than green leaves and practically as green as them, as well. Her braid is adorned with all sorts of flora (and I wouldn't be surprised if there was fauna, as well) that weave their way around her intricately styled hair.

"Lady Lorna!" Herminia smiles, embracing Lorna like she's long-lost family.

"I knew it!" Lorna laughs. "When I saw your mule, I knew it was you!"

"She leaves a trail," Seraphyna explains jokily, taking another sip out of her goblet smugly.

"I do not!" Herminia insists, turning to Phye, offended.

"Well," I start, crossing the threshold to the great hall and approaching the table Herminia, Clancy and Phye are sat at. "Begging your pardon, my Lady, but you do leave quite a colourful trail."

Herminia tilts her head, examining me thoroughly. I feel her eyes scrutinise every feature on my body and face, my deep, polished mahogany eyes, my ringleted hair, even my plain attire of a riding skirt and blouse.

"Oh, Phye, she's lovely!" Herminia exclaims, jumping up once again from her reclaimed spot in her chair over to where I'm standing facing them. She holds me in her arms fondly before pulling me over to sit in a chair, giving me no choice in the matter.

"Oh," Seb exclaims, stopping in his tracks as he approaches the Great Hall's gaping door. "We have guests?" Oh Seb, talking like you're already Lord of Light.

"Oh, Phyna, they're both so lovely!" Herminia sighs, joining her hands in delight. She excitedly gestures for Seb to take a seat the other side of her from where I'm sat. During the distracted conversation between Lorna and Phye about the boat, Herminia turns my head around manually with her hands and undoes my simple bun. She mumbles extremely quickly and lightly about how I should take more care of my 'lovely locks'.

"You really should take more care, though, lass," Herminia sighs, teasing out the many knots in my hair with her skilled fingers. "I use coconut milk on mine every day, although I don't suppose coconuts will ever grow this far up north..." She continues to murmur curses about high winds and how badly it treats long hair under her breath. Phye moves her eyes to set them on our comic little scene and chuckles.

"How is the contract writing going?" I ask. Phye brushes fiery wisps out of her eyes and sighs tiresomely.

"I think we've practically perfected it as of now," Phyna explains, looking to Clancy for reassurance.

"Just might need a spell check here and there, nothing Lorna or Conaire can't rectify for us," he confirms, passing the glance to Lorna.

"I can look over it on the boat ride," she says. "I'm sure Conaire will help me."

"When are we leaving?" Herminia questions, dropping the intricate and thick braid she's woven from my hair. She continues tying the ends together as she's glancing over at Seraphyna.

"Soon, I expect," Phye explains, looking out of the window into the midday sun.

"Is the professor coming with us?" Seb asks as we hear the door to the library slam shut in the high winds. I shoot Seb a look, scolding him for leaving the door open.

"I expect not," Clancy concludes. "She's tired and, besides, she can't stand sailing. She's already signed the document's clauses already, so she isn't needed."

"See!" Herminia throws her hands into the air after admiring her handiwork. I pull uncomfortably at the braid she's weaved, adorned with thin, wispy vines. "This is why I had to come! When I heard that six children were going to be sailing a sailboat across the sea alone, I knew I just had to come and escort you all!"

"We're hardly children, Hermie," Phyna sighs, standing to walk in the direction of the library.

"You'll always be my baby sister, Phye," Herminia pouts at Seraphyna, who doesn't look convinced. "Fine, I just wanted to see you, alright? Aella and I drew lots to see who would come and fetch you all because we both wanted to see you so badly! I won, naturally."

"Well, I'm flattered, but as much as I hate to admit it to you, I'm no child anymore, Hermie," Phye explains desperately.

Herminia hangs her head, embarrassed before looking up at us all again.

"Aella and I... we had to grow up into warriors before we were even women," Herminia looks up to the eaves of the great hall, where a light patter of rain can still be heard. "I wanted nothing more than to save you from that fate but, I suppose, us Omnia women, we have little choice in the matter, do we?"

"No," Phye mumbles. "I appreciate your concern, and I didn't want to sacrifice my innocence or my childhood, either, but when I realised that a whole house was looking to me, a thirteen-year-old girl, for their hope and inspiration, childhood was one of the many things I abandoned and threw out of the window."

We stand in silence for a moment, pondering what Phye just said. Herminia's face has brightened slightly and she starts to smile radiantly. Phyna gestures to us all as she starts to turn the handle of the door that connects the Great Hall and the library. Curiously, we all follow, watching as Seraphyna gazes around the room, crossing the parquet floor to an intricately carved wooden chest with a tarnished silver lock. Rummaging through the extensive collection of bronze, silver, iron and even gold keys that are bunched together in a cluster hanging from her belt, she presents a dainty, rusting key. Unhooking it from the bunch, she inserts it into the lock and turns it. She struggles to lift the incredibly heavy lid of the trunk, straining until she's managed to throw it open.

She plucks a thick wad of parchment from the top of a towering pile of various scribbled-on papers, ripped-out pages of books and battered scrolls. She rifles through the document, nodding approvingly as she does so. Taking a pair of scissors from the great table in the centre of the library, she cuts off a lock of her hair. I'm taken aback, as are the others. Chuckling, she runs the honey-coloured hair through her hands, moulding itself into an exquisitely woven blue ribbon. As she rolls the papers together and starts tying them together with her ribbon, she signals Clancy over to where she's standing. Reluctantly, she holds the treaty out in front of her for Clancy to take.

"Guard this with your life," she tells him. It's not a request, it's a command.

"Of course, your Lightest," Clancy promises, tucking the treaty inside his doublet.

"You know how important every word on these pages are, Clancy," Seraphyna says, "These words are the most important words to be written, to be read, to be heard. They are the history and the future of our realm and they will free every enslaved man, woman and child one day. Their effect will be massive."

She pauses for a moment, glancing out of the window behind her. "These words... these words are our words."

THOUGHTS

"Why don't you let your mule carry your things?" I ask Herminia as we walk down to the harbour. She has various stuffed satchels and bundles bound in rags piled up in her arms as her mule trots along beside her happily, with no luggage at all, not even a bridle or saddle.

"Oh no! I couldn't do that to him, poor darling. He gets tired, see, and I'm just fine carrying all my things," Herminia explains, lovingly glancing sideways at her mule, who's stalling by inspecting one of the rotting wooden poles of the dock. We've all managed to assemble on the dock with our small satchels of belongings and coin purses that hold tiny discs of metal.

"That's it," Seraphyna states, thrusting her hand towards one of the few boats clustered in the dock. Herminia pushes her mule forward gently, helping the ancient thing into the festering wood that makes up the bow of the boat. The rope is fraying and damaged and flops lifelessly into the water when Conaire releases it into the sea away from the wooden post.

The boat is large and well-built but obviously overused and a good few years older than Seraphyna or me. Planks are laid across the structure, acting as benches for potential rowers if the wind doesn't catch in the patched-up sail that's hanging, static, from a long pole stuck in the centre of the boat. There is little wind to accompany the blazing summer sun, but we need not row as when Seraphyna flicks her hand lazily to the south-west, the boat is pushed forward effortlessly as though a hundred soldiers were rowing the vessel.

A pile of fishing and boat-mending paraphernalia are pushed up against one end of the boat, fishing rods and hooks, broken and splintered planks of wood among them. Conaire, obviously still shocked from his encounter with Davisham's daughter, busies himself with the task of organising the disorganisation.

Clancy and Lorna start talking discreetly, whispering about the same unknown topic for the entire journey and rarely leaving their conversation. Seb talks to Seraphyna, who dips in and out of their discussion to ask various vague questions to Herminia

"And how's Dagan?" Seraphyna asks as the image of the Eastern Isles fades into the mist from behind.

"Oh, he's fine," Herminia smiles. "He's hungering for a child, as am I but... well, we're having some issues."

Seraphyna's face falls as she places a pitying hand on Herminia's shoulder. "I'm sorry," she sighs.

"Never mind about me, I'll just depress you all," Herminia says chirpily before turning to Phye again. "We need to talk about something very important!"

"What might that be?" Phyna asks distractedly, focusing on her effortless boatmanship.

"Getting you a husband!" Herminia yells excitedly, the words echoing off the clear waters and back into our ears.

"I don't need a husband," Phye assures Herminia, discreetly looking over to where Seb's twiddling his thumbs.

"Oh, but you'll need a General, a companion, of course, it's important you have someone by your side," Herminia explains.

"My General doesn't have to be my husband, my companion doesn't have to be my husband either and we don't keep Generals in peacetime, you know that, Hermie," Seraphyna sighs irritably.

"Oh," Herminia gasps, her expression filled with worry that she's destroyed Phye's already fragile temperament. "Oh, I'm sorry."

I try to think on my feet, gathering together every idea I have of how possibly to move on the conversation and change the subject to a much less tense one.

"How did you get to the Eastern Isles, Herminia?" I decide will be my question.

"Oh, well I was already in Olympia so I found a ferryman to take me here in a boat. There were so many down on the dock that day for some reason, although I don't know whether that is normal now because people don't have their own boats nowadays. Anyway, out of the two dozen or so ferrymen, there was only one that agreed to bring Orphrey, but he didn't want to talk much on the journey despite the amount of questions I asked him. Shame, really," Herminia rambles.

"Orphrey?" Seb asks and Herminia laughs her honeyed laugh.

"This little darling right here," Herminia explains lovingly, tickling her mule under the chin as he whinnies fondly. Seb and Phye look over to me awkwardly as I chuckle at Herminia's unconditional love for the ancient, flea-ridden animal munching on hay in front of her.

"Hey, Evanie?" Lorna whispers, tapping me on the shoulder. I turn away from Herminia and Orphrey to face her.

"Yes?" I answer.

"Do you think that maybe you'd want to go with Conaire around the market?" She suggests, shrugging as though she doesn't care although I can tell she does. "He's just still a bit shocked about seeing Lindera this morning. Clancy nor I can even get him to talk about it or open up and, well... he seems to like you and maybe you could ease him out of being so..." she struggles to find the word.

"Heartbroken?" I propose. Lorna nods sadly, glancing to where Conaire's swatting Clancy's concerned words away from where he's still tidying.

"Yeah, he's still really caught up about Lindera and Clancy and I are going to buy parchment and quills anyway which he *hates* and please make sure he doesn't buy too much of that awful stuff..." she pleads.

"Karta? Of course, he'll be safe with me," I promise.

"Look! There's Mt. Altuma, the famous home of the Valkyries!" Clancy points out excitedly, gesturing to a blue peak rising gradually from the valley of her sister mountains that surround her.

"Oh, and Highest Point, that must mean we're close to the bay!" Seraphyna explains, moving her head fluidly to try and catch a glimpse of the first signs of civilisation we've seen for the last hour.

To say the markets of Olympia are bustling would be an understatement. Everywhere you look or turn, a new, alien thing is happening. Grumpy men or young, clean-shaven merchants guide horses and carts filled with a small fortune's worth of grain or odd items. The bay circles round the market in a wide, clear port that is home to both cloud-grey dolphins and mud-brown boats unloading several barrels or crates marked with runes being closely inspected by merchants or sailors. The cobbled street that works its way around the whole market is being trampled on by at least a thousand people as they stomp around to the various quarters in gaggles or groups, or even alone if they're unlucky enough. Various corridors of stalls branch off the main bay, many vendors building their stalls with vermillion or azure blankets draped over splintering, spindly sticks stuck in the soil. Exchanges and purchases are being made left, right and centre, small coins in copper, silver and gold being pressed into hands at nearly every stall, so that the market has a constant jangling sound added to its already foreign and wild atmosphere. We clamber out of the boat when we're able to find a post to tie to, having to dodge carts and horses flying at us from all directions. The cart drivers are relentless, shouting at us to move out of the way rather gruffly. Others don't notify us of our danger, as they're perfectly happy to just run us over if we're unlucky enough to fall into their path.

When we're finally safe from carts and horses, we find a tiny nook of the market that's, miraculously, not already occupied by another, for our crowd to assemble. Seraphyna does a quick head count, not counting Orphrey, and nods in satisfaction of our safety.

"You'll have until probably dusk to go around the markets. I'd advise returning to the palace before that time, though, as my sister's throwing a banquet for you all, and unless you want to turn up at her table dressed like you are now, I advise you give yourselves time to freshen up. I trust you'll all be punctual, but just in case-" she starts, gesturing to Herminia. Herminia pulls a bunch of wispy vines from a bunch of greenery hanging from her belt and hands one to each of us.

"When the vine withers, that means you should come back to the palace," Herminia states excitedly, handing one to Seraphyna despite her having no need for it. Seraphyna brushes the vine away from her face. Sneakily, Herminia tucks the vine into Seraphyna's braid, making it grow so that the vine weaves its way through Seraphyna's fiery locks.

"Are you going with Clancy and Lorna?" I ask Conaire quietly, who's fiddling with his vine, trying to attach it to the leather belt fastened around his midriff.

"They're buying things like parchment and quills but I just need some Karta and I'll be fine. I'll be bored but I don't mind that much," he explains, sighing in frustration as, once again, the vine falls onto the dusty cobbles after a failed attaching attempt. I pull one of the many pins out of my hair that are holding my braid together and reach down to Conaire's belt, pinning the vine on with the help of the sharp metal.

"I need to get some fabric and jewels, maybe you might want to come with me?" I offer, glancing over at Clancy and Lorna who are waiting eagerly for Conaire's verdict.

"Alright, that sounds like a good idea," Conaire decides. He waves distractedly to Clancy and Lorna, who charge off in the direction of the parchment and quill quarter.

When Seb, Herminia and Phye have also left us by the glistening bay, Conaire and I decide to head to the corridor of food vendors, as neither of us have eaten since before we left for that fated trip to Davisham's.

The corridor isn't as covered as the others; many of the stalls are just lopsided tables laden with stewing pots of unrecognisable meats or large baskets of over-ripe apples. The aromas weave their way around Conaire and I, as well as the many others who are seeking something to quell their assumedly roaring appetites. I pause at a few stalls, inspecting the endless baskets and cauldrons of sweet or foul-smelling food they have to sell. A particular smell guides me to a table laid out with various cups and beakers holding generous portions of stew, but none of the cups are the type you'd expect to hold a thick, lumpy, brown liquid and chunks of meat. I pick up one of the cups, choosing not by the quantity of the stew, but at the beauty of the goblet that contains it.

I stretch my hand over the table in an effort to pass two silver coins to the vendor, a shrivelled, ancient man who has to pull himself from a barrel acting as a stool using a spindly walking stick to fetch his payment. He slides the coin out of my hand, greedily pocketing the money as he retakes his place on the splintering barrel behind the table. I look around, unable to find Conaire. Confused and worried, I push my way to the end of the corridor only to find Conaire arguing with a vendor over the price of meat.

"You're a scammer and rouge!" Conaire insists, brandishing a furious finger at the terrified girl behind the table.

"Conaire!" I yell, pulling his arms behind his back so that he doesn't attack the poor girl, who's backed up against the wall behind her. I grab Conaire's face, turning him so that his fury is directed at me.

"Conaire..." I breathe, using all my physical strength to restrain him and to calm him down from his rage. "Conaire, please, calm down."

It takes him a good amount of time for his expression to soften and for him to rub his cooling eyes agonisingly before turning to the girl and grimacing.

"Sorry, girl," he mumbles, handing her a silver coin in exchange for one of her legs of meat, laid out in neat lines along a tartan table cloth. The girl inches forward nervously, snatching the coin swiftly from Conaire's hand before sinking back into the shadows. I reach my hand out to take Conaire's, guiding him out of the darkness into the daylight of the bay.

I keep my fingers crossed that the light will calm him down. I gesture to a wide, bare log that sits in the middle of the now less crowded street and Conaire sits down uncomfortably on its splintering surface. The view is calm, the clear, turquoise water sparkling like crystals in the midday sun, fins of grey dolphins poking slightly over the surface of the sea. The boats continue to come and go, the birds continue to chatter garrulously. I continue to glance over at Conaire, whose face softens more with every glance. He finishes the meat he's holding and throws the porcelain white bone into the sea. I scrape the last of the stew out of the bottom of the cup and Conaire inspects the goblet curiously, beckoning for me to pass it to him. As he traces the intricate patterns of the goblet with his fingers, I lean into him. Conaire turns the goblet upside down, showing me the hallmark that's branded on the silver base.

"Real Calian silver," Conaire murmurs. "Could be worth a good deal of silver or gold. How much did you pay for the stew?"

"Two silver coins," I tell him, and his brow knits comically.

"For stew? Well, if you sell this then you'll most likely get triple your money back, but that vendor probably just found this in one of the dumps behind the palace," Conaire sighs, shoving the glinting silver in his satchel after wiping it down with his grubby handkerchief. "I can't believe he tried to charge you that much for stew!"

"I can't read runes so I just gave him a tenth of what I had. I thought that was reasonable enough," I explain.

"Well, you chose well, the goblet's beautiful," Conaire assures me. "For a beautiful lady, that is."

I turn an embarrassingly deep shade of scarlet. Conaire chuckles and stares back out across the bay, looking pensive. I tilt my head, my eyes tracing the shape of his exquisitely defined brow.

"Are you alright?" I ask him nervously, observing his thoughtful state.

"Alright? Why wouldn't I be? I'm perfectly fine," Conaire insists, his eyes drooping and his gaze directing to his fiddling fingers.

"Your words say that you're fine but your eyes tell a different story altogether," I sigh. "Seeing that girl this morning, the way you looked at her with such a mix of hatred and love, I can tell something's wrong, Conaire."

"Lindy? No, it's not her," Conaire tells me, mumbling awkwardly.

"I thought her name was Lindera?" I question, my inquiry only making Conaire jerk his head away from me further.

"I loved her once," he grimaces, almost as though he's admitting a crime. "And I thought she loved me, but maybe our parting was for the best."

"What happened?"

"I wanted to marry her," he explains. "We were young but it felt right and I had Phye's blessing. But Lindy... she's always been ambitious. Being heiress to her father's title of Countess of Scylla wasn't enough for her. When that awful Florean Ilene arrived on the island after two years of naval training she jumped at the chance of being Countess of Ilene. Left me in the dust like I was some kind of statue. It was like what we had turned to ashes in that moment."

Conaire pauses, brushing fair wisps of hair from his eyes. He looks back at where I'm still willing to listen.

"He doesn't even treat her well, you know?" Conaire continues. "He makes trips to Berr almost every full moon to see the Professor of Earth, Rosaleen. I heard through the grapevine he even has a child by her. He doesn't love Lindy but it doesn't bother her in the slightest. She lives in as much luxury as she could wish for. Worst part is, it's been a year and I still can't stop being hung up about all of this."

"Maybe you just need to move on?" I suggest, raising an eyebrow. "Find someone else? Make her jealous?"

Conaire sighs, chuckling lightly. He shakes his head in disbelief. "Maybe..." he whispers.

The silence that rests in the air feels dense, as though it's guarding and hiding a hundred secrets. I glance at Conaire, whose fists are clenched and knuckles are white with tension. He turns his head, eyes meeting mine with a cheeky grin painting his face.

"Penny for your thoughts?" I ask. Conaire's eyes twinkle as he leans in closer to me, breathing lightly. He smirks, mouth twitching as he asks, "A kiss for yours?"

I inhale sharply from shock, immediately wishing I hadn't. Conaire takes my inhalation as rejection. He turns his face away from mine, embarrassed and deflated. He looks to the dirty floor, at each hoof mark that stains the stones. Instinctively, I place my hand on his cheek, as though I'm begging him to face me again because I want this.

Don't go. I plead silently.

I tell him all I'm feeling through just the contact of our flesh. Slowly, his milky eyes meet mine, and I ask with my eyes for him to come closer.

Conaire obliges, our lips meeting softly, silently.

I could've sworn I was falling for Clancy but this... this is something else. Conaire's arms wrap around my torso as I nestle into his thin shirt. He smiles ecstatically, standing and reaching out his hand for me to take.

We walk in uninterrupted bliss, chuckling fondly at each other as we advance towards the fabrics corridor. The atmosphere is loud, with bargains being negotiated at nearly every stall, whether they be selling buttons or entire bolts of thick winter wools. Most of the vendors around the area are young women, all similar-looking with blonde hair and pale faces dotted with clusters of freckles. I peruse some of the stalls that sell fabrics that I know Phye would approve of, which are hard to come by as most of the styles are more suited to Aella's court of greys and blues. Most of the fabrics that are cream or pale yellow, however, are thin and badly made, which is the opposite of what I need. I continue looking for a thick, well-made cream fabric. I pause at a table laden with various bolts of material, one of them being a weighty cream and grey brocade that's still on a full bolt. The vendor notices my interest and snaps to attention, acknowledging me slyly.

"Looking for a lace, my lady?" she asks me cunningly. She's blonde like all the other girls around her, but her hair is so yellow it's borderline obnoxious. She glances at Conaire who chuckles with genuine amusement.

"Not quite yet, I don't think," he laughs, throwing his strong arm around my shoulders. I look up at him, bemused, as he towers over me. I continue to run my fingers along the edge of the brocade that caught my attention, my hand shifting over to a golden net that shimmers effortlessly.

"These two?" I suggest to Conaire and he shrugs.

"Wonderful choice, my lady," the blonde says, anxiously glancing at the House of Light stamps that emboss our satchels and Conaire's beautifully carved scabbard. "The total will be 19 silver."

I furrow my brow, as does Conaire. Rummaging through my coin purse that's hanging from my belt, I only have 18 silver and I still need to buy gems.

"Listen here," Conaire starts, raising a finger at the vendor, who's stubborn and smug expression doesn't budge from its place on her narrow face. "Just because we're courtiers of the House of Light doesn't mean we're bathing in gold like the Air courtiers or Water students you're used to. Six silver, that's what I'm offering."

Pouting, the blonde scratches her head irritably, making an agonisingly slow decision.

"Twelve," she shoots back simply, crossing her grey-clad arms.

"Nine silver and a penny for your troubles," Conaire offers, refusing to budge. "And you're not even losing money at those prices,." The blonde's face twists, her nose twitching like a rabbit. After a considerable amount of time, she sticks out her hand, commanding the money into it. I scramble around in my coin purse, presenting nine silver coins piled on top of each other and sliding them into her palm. Conaire pulls a tiny bronze disc from his pocket and drops in amongst the collection of silver ones, eyes glinting with a hint of stunningly rich mischief. The vendor takes a pair of worryingly sharp scissors that could do a considerable amount of damage and cuts the lengths of fabric unevenly, balling them up and throwing the bundle into my arms with a mean smile. Conaire offers his hand to me once more and we wander down along the corridor into the daylight.

The end of the corridor opens out into a lively square, with people crossing over each other from all directions, emerging from each corridor and entering a new one. Conaire gazes around the square, furrowing his brow and pausing once he glances behind him, to where two very familiar faces have emerged from the fabrics passage and are now standing right behind us.

"Clancy? Lore?" Conaire questions, tapping Lorna on the shoulder as she's still in conversation with Clancy. She jumps, almost dropping the bundle of odd items gathered in her arms. Several bolts of fabric in colours that I've never seen someone from the House of Light wear. Some of the fabrics I see, I could swear I wore dresses made out of them when I lived in Hertford. She also holds thin planks of wood and a good number of dazzling necklaces are hanging from her wrist as she struggles with the load.

"Saints, Conaire, don't make me jump like that!" she scolds, hitting Clancy in the midriff with a protruding plank as she turns towards us.

"Sorry, Lorna, but I thought you two were going to buy quills and parchment?" Conaire's brow knits as Clancy turns to reveal a backpack stuffed with at least a dozen rolls of parchment and double the number of quills from all kinds of birds sticking out from the top of the burlap.

"We did, but we had some spare time so we came to buy supplies," Lorna explains.

"Phyna won't approve of those fabrics," Conaire reminds her, shaking his head as he runs his rough fingertips along the edge of the material.

"All part of our plan, it's a surprise!" Lorna chuckles as Clancy's eyes widen in horror.

"Plans? We don't have any plans! Lorna, I said we had to keep it a secret!" Clancy whines, snatching some of the bolts that are escaping Lorna's arms for him to carry himself.

"Don't mind him, he can't keep a secret to save his life. Anyway, we must be off," Lorna sighs, pulling on Clancy's arm for him to follow her towards the bay. They disappear behind stalls and carts and we watch them bicker as Conaire turns to me.

"Where to next?" I ask Conaire as we walk along a breezy cobbled street, straddled by two corridors of lively stalls and crowds of people looking to buy vendors' wares.

"You said you needed jewels?" Conaire says. I nod as he points southwards to a front of deep grey fabric making a door for one of the corridors of the market. "This way then…"

The passage of the market dedicated to jewels has been completely covered with cloth so that it has been shielded from almost all sunlight. For the first few moments I step into the corridor, I'm confused by the lack of the glorious daylight, but once I see how the abundance of gems glow in the darkness, I understand completely. Every stall has tables laden with clusters of jewels that stand out in the dark like starts in the night sky. Most of the gems are fiery orange or yellow and red. Rarer ones come in cooler blues or greys but even fewer mix the tones completely, with azure or sapphire blending into caramel gold or mustard yellow.

Many stalls have huge piles of common orange stones that glow dimly and are simply the size of raisins. The sights of these ordinary piles, some even the height of the length of my forearm, are extremely common, so I stop even glancing at the towers after a few minutes or so of them being all I see. Some tables have one or two rarer gems to sell, but even then, they're tiny, no bigger than a baby's fingertip. I linger at a stall near to the end of the corridor, a splintered table holding just a few beautifully hued and sized gems. A boy, no older than 10 or 11, sits on the table with his legs swinging tiresomely, a bored expression drawn on his face. I smile at him warmly as I approach the stall. The woman, who I assume is the boy's mother, jumps to attention and takes her attentive place behind her table, aligning the gems so they're all in a straight, neat line.

"They're beautiful," I smile, toying with a few grey ones that are clumped together at the front of the table.

"Not to Sheevian quality, I'm afraid, my lady, but they're from around here in Olympia, from our own land, and they're unique," the woman explains in the centre of the fabric and ties the little parcel with the string his mother hands him.

"What do you say?" She asks, stopping Alarick from handing the stones to me.

"Well, two and one and two is five," Alarick starts, his eyes squinting in concentration, trying to figure out the total. "And three and four is seven. So, that'll be five silver and seven copper, Lady, please."

His mother nods proudly and approvingly as I hand the total to her. She plucks one of the copper coins from the pile and hands it to Alarick.

"Go and buy yourself a candied apple, Al," she tells him. Eyes widening, he runs off happily, waving the coin in the air like a trophy.

"I've been trying to teach him," she explains, moving her head around to keep an eye on where Alarick is heading. "But I do worry about him sometimes."

"I do worry about him sometimes," Hestia sighs, gazing out to where Erich is crouched at Xanthe's feet, pouting.

"Well, you have nothing at all to worry about," I assure her, waving as Conaire ushers me away.

"He'll be fine," I tell her lightly, waving my hand. "He's my son, it's not your place to worry."

"That's why I worry," Hestia jokes. "Because he's your son."

I laugh, first at Hestia and then at the comical scene of Erich's mirth as Xanthe throws the ball across the field for him to run after, giving in to his adorable pouts and pleads. Caspian tentatively passes me a goblet of wine and I thank him happily. We continue to gaze out at the meadow, where Xanthe's now chasing little Erich around the small grove of ash trees that stand behind the palace.

"Isn't he wonderful?" I ask Caspian, who laughs as loudly and as happily as me.

"Absolutely," he insists, throwing his arm around my shoulders.

"Have you heard from Luke recently?" Hestia asks me quietly, pulling my elbow and ushering me aside.

"I've sent all the Bluejays I could find, I had to ask Ledan to travel to Berr and ask the Duke of Earth to find him as many Bluejays as he could get his hands on. Every single one of the birds came back to me with no message or dead. I'm starting to think maybe Luke's in danger," I explain desperately, resting my heavy head in my hands. Hestia places a supporting palm on my shoulder.

"He'll be alright," Hestia assures me.

"It's been two and a half years since I last saw him," I sigh. "And all I've received is a fistful of parchment containing an untidy scrawl simply describing his health and how he misses here."

"Just order him home, he has to follow your orders," Hestia suggests. I ponder the thought before shaking my head profusely at the selfish thought.

"No," I tell her, grabbing the carafe to pour Caspian more wine. "I don't know what or who he has wherever he's gone. He might have married the woman he couldn't, he might have a child by her. He might've been crowned a King of an unknown Kingdom, for all we could know."

"You've always been an optimist, Oralee," Hestia laughs, trying to hide her sorrow. She misses Luke, too. My head starts pounding and I reach up to hold my *head, trying to dampen the stabbing from the inside of my head. My knees give, I fall to the ground.*

I massage my eyes, making as much effort as I can to locate the dull pain behind them. Suddenly, I lose my balance and wait to hit the cold floor. Gladly, Conaire is behind me to catch me.

"Oralee?" Caspian asks, grabbing my arm in concern. "Oralee, can you hear me?"

"Evanie, can you hear me?" Conaire questions, holding me sternly in between his strong arms.

"I can," I reply weakly. "I'm just... I'm just incredibly tired, Conaire."

"Can you stand?" He asks.

I assure him I'm fine, but my head tells me I'm not, it still throbs like a thousand swords have pierced my brain. "I just need to lie down."

Conaire pulls me along, escorting me into the daylight. We emerge at the very back of the markets, at the foot of a grand and dominating mountain. Carts and carriages are individually working and winding their way up the narrow mountain path, where a sturdy and picturesque palace hugs the summit, which is snow-capped and bluer than the cornflower sky. Conaire tries to wave down every cart that passes us, but none of them stop. I still focus on closing my eyes as often as possible, as I find comfort in the darkness. Wait, no. Seraphyna would kill me if she ever heard me say that.

Conaire stands in the middle of the street for a good two and half minutes before a cart stops to ask him what he needs. Conaire explains the situation to the cart driver, a young man in a straw hat to shield him from the strong afternoon sun. He pauses for a moment, before begrudgingly saying he's heading to the palace anyway and gestures to the cart for us to clamber in. Conaire and I sit in amongst large sacks of grain and rice, which provide ample comfort for me to lean against.

Despite the journey being dangerous and winding, I start to feel a lot better during the ride to the palace. We approach the Palace of Air, which is an incredibly grand and pale building, at least a dozen times the size of the Palace of Light. Even the portcullis is a dozen times larger, stretching the entire height of the palace. It's open and welcoming us into the courtyard, which has a stable built into one side of it and ten separate doors on the other side leading to various rooms. There is a huge main door straight ahead leading from the courtyard, which is bolted shut by a large number of tarnished silver locks. The cart driver mumbles for us to get out of the back of his wagon. Gratefully, Conaire flips him a silver coin and the cart driver catches it, close fisted, in mid-air.

Stationed in the middle of the courtyard, it's eerily quiet. Even the cart driver had ridden off to begin the palace. I start to wonder if anyone's actually here yet until I see Orphrey in the stables, wildly attacking the hay net he's been provided. I turn around, surveying the entire courtyard until the opening of one of the small doors on the wall opposite us.

"Is my brother here yet?" a girl asks, standing in the threshold of one of the doorways. It takes me a few seconds to register who the girl is, but I could've known even if I've never seen her before. Clancy and his sister, Aviana, share the same dark hair, the same brown eyes hidden behind the same round spectacles and the same slim figure.

"Avie," Conaire sighs as she saunters over to the middle of the courtyard where we're standing. "No, he's not here yet, I think he needed to get some more things in the market."

"Shame, I was wanting some real quality big brother time," she chuckles.

"Where's my lady?" Conaire asks, obviously referring to Phye.

"Looks like yours is standing right next to you," Avie points out smugly.

"I'm Evanie," I tell her. Avie is really quite young, her legs skinny and underdeveloped. Realistically, I wouldn't guess that she's older than fourteen. "And could you show us where Lady Aella and Lady Seraphyna are? I'm ever so tired and I would like to be shown to a room so I can rest before the banquet this evening,"

Avie scrunches up her face in thought. "I *think* that they're in the library, reading over some document I'm not allowed to sign," she explains bitterly. "Because I'm too young,"

Avie beckons for us to follow her inside to a dimly lit, dead straight corridor that has several doors coming off it from each side. It's only when we reach a door that's adorned with brass and silver shields and outlined by a crumbling but charming stone arch. Avie knocks on the panels.

"I swear to the Saints, Avie, I told you-" Aella sighs, answering the door begrudgingly.

"It's not about that, Aella, I'm not *that* persistent, I have some visitors for you," Avie explains, stepping aside to reveal Conaire and I standing behind her awkwardly.

"Ah, Conaire, lovely to see you again," Aella nods her head, beckoning for us to step inside the library. The library of air is one thing that doesn't belittle its counterpart in the Palace of Light; the rooms dedicated to scriptures and books are, surprisingly, around the same size. However, this library has one difference: scrolls are more prevalent than books. Cases with glass fronts hold a hundred scrolls each and two dozen outline the room completely. In the very middle of the room is a broad dark oak table laden with inkwells and blank scrolls. Seraphyna is sitting at the end of the table, the empty chair at the head of it I assume was Aella's chair before she rose to answer the door. Herminia is next to Seb who is across from a dark-skinned, curly-haired man I know as Dagan, Herminia's husband. Another face is around the table that I don't recognise as well, but I can match it to a name – Corentin, Aella's husband. His face is scarred, the true face of a General. One scar even covers his right eye to the point that it's closed shut.

"You're back early, Evanie," Seb points out, rising from the table to embrace me.

"My lady, if I may, I'd like a room to rest in before your graciously thrown banquet this evening," I ask Aella, who nods understandingly.

"Aviana's brother, Clancy, sent me a letter asking if I knew anything about flashbacks and how to prevent you from tiring so much when fading back to this world. I'm afraid there is nothing else I can do, my child, except offer you a room to sleep in for a few hours," Aella explains. "Sebastian, you know where the rooms are, please choose one near to yours and my sister's room that's grand enough for Oralee the Great."

Seb smiles warmly at Aella, which is easy to do as, like her two sisters, she is an incredibly warming presence within her own palace and, I assume, elsewhere. Seb ushers me out of the library as I say goodbye to Conaire, who stays inside the library and starts looking over the peace treaty placed on the table in front of him. I am led up a grand, grey carpeted staircase to a corridor with doors to several grand bedrooms.

Seb chooses one halfway down the corridor, opening the door cautiously.

"Definitely alright?" he checks, waiting for me to enter the room.

"I'm fine, just a bit dazed, that's all," I assure him, before saluting him a goodbye and sinking into the room.

I don't even bother to take my dress off, all I do is slip off my muddy boots and sink under the covers so I can just sleep as I'm so exhausted, I'm starting to see every star in the night sky right in front of my eyes. When I sleep, I don't dream, I just relive Oralee's life so many times I forget I'm Evanie. I see every smile everyone has ever given her, every fall, every giggle, kiss and embrace. I hear every word she's ever spoken and every word she's ever heard. I die, I am born, I give life to a son and watch all I love crumble before my eyes hundreds and hundreds of times. It's not until I feel a jarring pain in the small of my back that I wake and become Evanie once again.

"Evanie! Wake up!" Lorna yells, elbowing me in my back. I roll over gingerly, pouting at her well made-up face. It comes at a shock. She notices my bewilderment at her hair and makeup. "Don't ask," she mumbles. Pulling me out of bed, Lorna signals for Clancy, who's standing behind her to leave the room but tells him to stand outside. Avie, who is also in the room for some reason, ushers him out of the room irritably, sarcastically yelling nervously. Conaire pokes his head out from behind me, also smiling at the boy whose eyes still dart around the area to try and provide him some entertainment. Conaire reaches over from behind me, making a small pile of selected stones in front of me. A smoky grey one, one that is clear but twinkles like a star and one that blends turquoise and gold seamlessly as though the two colours were made to exist together, trapped in this gem only. All I can say is that Conaire chose well, and I wouldn't choose any differently.

"How much?" I ask and the woman glances at the boy expectantly.

"What do you think, Alarick?" she asks her son and his eyes light up with the prospect of something to do. He inspects each of the stones Conaire selected carefully.

"Well," Alarick starts, rubbing his pale and smooth chin like an old man deep in thought. The image makes me chortle quietly. He points to the blue and gold stone. "I like this one a lot, Pa found that one and it's really big, too, so I'd say that one's worth two silver. They grey one is really nice as well but it's a bit small so maybe that one's only worth a silver and four copper. The clear one is the best though, I found that one and Pa said it'll fetch a lot at market so maybe that one's worth… two silver and three copper?" Alarick looks to his mother uncertainly.

"No, that's right, well done!" she assures him, ruffling his hair lovingly.

"Thanks, Ma," he mumbles happily, presenting a square of white cotton from the inside pocket of his torn doublet. His mother takes a ball of string from one of her pockets, cutting a length of it with a pair of silver scissors laid out on the table. Alarick places the stones that she loves him into the corridor. Even from in here, I can hear his comedic sigh. Lorna runs over to the ceiling-height wardrobe behind Avie, rummaging through the racks of grey and pale blue dresses. After working her way through the entirety of the two rails, she presents a stunning grey ball gown with a silk bodice and lace skirt that juts out at the hip. Lorna thrusts the gown at me, brushing off my obvious confusion.

"Just put this on," she orders, starting to unlace the corset of my grubby day dress Phye lent me this morning. I take off my stockings, my bodice and my skirt as well as letting my hair out of the now scraggly braid Herminia crafted in the great hall back at the Palace of Light. I slip the dress over my head and it's a little tight around the hips but gaping around my chest. Avie and Lorna tilt their heads almost in unison, inspecting the dress and its imperfections. Lorna knocks on the door of the room from the inside.

"Clancy, can you go to the kitchens and get some saffron?" she yells through the closed door. Clancy mumbles back that he'll return imminently. It takes him less than five minutes for him to open the door and pass the saffron to Lorna before being shut out again.

"You can leave now, if you want!" Avie shouts, chortling. She turns to me, holding a finger up. I notice that Avie, whose fashion sense is similar to Lorna's (whatever fits) is also wearing a floor length gown and has her hair teased up into an updo adorned with grey pearls. She takes the bowl of saffron from Lorna and holds it up to her face to inspect it.

"Now close your eyes, don't open them, alright?" Avie tells me, gesturing down for me to close my eyes. I do and as I do, I feel as tickling sensation on my head and down my back. She's poured the saffron all over my head. I blow the saffron that's landed on my lips off them subconsciously.

"Stay still," Avie says.

Now instead of tickling down my back, I feel a cool stream of water and my hair wetting spontaneously, as well as the soothing patter of rain on the parquet floor of the room. When the pattering stops, I start to peel my eyes open but before I can fully regain my vision, Avie flaps her arms frantically in front of my face.

"I said don't open your eyes!" she sighs, shouting at me. I raise my hands in apology, trying to murmur a simple 'sorry', but I don't know if the word ever came out of my mouth as I'm deafened by the roar of wind brushing against my ears. When the wind stops, I feel soft hair against my back, which the dress has exposed. Either Lorna or Avie, I don't know which one, steps forward and places something amongst my hair.

"Right, now you can open your eyes, Evanie," Avie says. I do and as I do, Lorna starts inspecting the structure of the dress as it still doesn't fit right. Gesturing with her hands, she pulls the dress in at the chest and lets it out at the hips effortlessly without even touching the fabric.

"All good now?" Lorna asks and I nod gratefully. She hands me a pair of golden shoes which I slip my feet into. Surprisingly, they fit just fine. Lorna and Avie admire their work as they spin me around to a tall mirror on the back wall of the room. I let out a small gasp. The dress I am wearing flatters me in all the right places and is now completely dyed a gentle saffron colour. I wear a gold coronet on top of my half-braided and half-wavy hair, which has no knots or tangles at all, a rarity for me, even on good days.

"What do you think?" Avie asks me nervously, glancing at Lorna approvingly.

"So, you poured the saffron over my head, dyed the dress with rain you just produced out of nowhere and then styled my hair and dried my gown using wind you produced out of nowhere?" I ask Avie, she nods. I point at Lorna. "And then you just made the gown custom to my size using just your hands?"

"Uh-huh," Lorna replies, sticking another hairpin into her hair.

"I look… decent," I conclude quietly, snapping to attention after hearing a knock at the door. Avie runs to where the door is and pulls down the silver handle to open it. Conaire stands in the doorway holding a bunch of dainty flowers and dressed in a creaseless clean doublet and shirt.

"Wow," he exclaims, the sound escaping his lips involuntarily.

Maybe I look a little better than just decent.

"Thanks to us, I'll have you know," Avie tells him sharply, but that doesn't mean Conaire takes his eyes off me. My already reddened face deepens further as he holds out the flowers to me and I take them gratefully, placing them in a vase by the door.

"So, stop gawking!" Lorna cackles. Clancy is lurking behind Conaire and, as I link arms with Conaire, he offers his to his sister who rejects him at first, jokily mumbling something about how that would be incestuous, but then after she jokes, obliges. Conaire and I, Clancy and Avie as well as Lorna, who doesn't need anyone to lead her, all travel down to Aella's great hall together. The Palace of Air's foyer is larger than the great hall of Light's, making enough room for Aella,

Seraphyna, Herminia and Sebastian to have already assembled there and be in a vague conversation about the ridiculous price of flagships.

"Finally," Seraphyna sighs. "You all look lovely, now come on, let's take our places for the banquet."

I start to move behind Sebastian, but Seraphyna stops us both.

"Wait here," she tells us. I glance at Seb, confused. "It'll all make sense, I promise."

Seraphyna tails the small procession before winking at us both as she goes to shut the door to the great hall, which must take some effort as it's gigantic.

Seb and I stand in the foyer awkwardly. I stare blankly at the huge door of the great hall, my eyes following the pattern of the markings carved into the wood.

"Aviana and Lorna did an amazing job," Seb says kindly after a long pause when the chaos of glasses clinking and indistinct murmurs from inside the hall start to die down.

"Thank you," I smile. "Whoever dressed you did one hell of a job making you not look scruffy for one in your life."

"Seraphyna," He laughs at my joke heartily.

"Naturally," I reply. "Only a miracle worker could make you look decent."

"Love you too, Evanie," he scoffs.

"Welcome, my friends," we hear from inside the hall after a shrill tap of a knife against a wine glass makes the remaining murmuring die down completely. Aella's smooth but booming voice reaches us even through the thick wood of the door. "Tonight, we have some very special visitors, the guests of honour, even, to our banquet this evening. Not only are we joined by my beloved sisters and members of their faithful courts, but we have two extraordinary members of the House of Light."

I turn my head, glancing nervously at where Seb has taken up my stance of staring at the door.

"Please welcome Lord Sebastian and Lady Evanie of Light!" Aella announces as the doors open and we're revealed to her entire court. Their heads turn in unison, all eyes of every man, woman and child dig into us like swords as we nervously walk down the middle aisle of the great hall. When we reach the table Seraphyna, Herminia and Aella are sat at, they all rise.

"Lady Evanie and Lord Sebastian," Seraphyna says, obviously uncomfortable with the formalities. "You play two of the most important roles in my house yet just hold the mere title of courtier. I'm afraid I have no more land in my territory to gift you to make you a count and countess, but there is a title I could give you both."

She pauses momentarily, looking to Aella and Herminia for help.

"As you know, the title of baron or baroness of a house usually goes to the uncrowned brother or sister of a Highest Lord or Lady of a house." Herminia explains. "But there have been cases in the past where this title has been awarded to members of a house who are particularly loyal or important to the Highest Lord or Lady."

"Therefore," Seraphyna continues. "As an act of thanks for all you have and will contribute to the House of Light, my sisters and I have agreed to bestow the titles of Baron of Far Off Lands to you, Sebastian and to you, Evanie, the title of Baroness of the Unknown Realms. Do you accept these gifts from your lady?"

"Yes," Seb nods, smiling lovingly at Seraphyna, who nods concisely to put him at ease. I pause.

"And you, Lady Evanie?" Aella asks me, raising an eyebrow.

"My Lady," I declare, addressing Seraphyna, "It would be my honour."

PORTRAIT

The banquet goes on until we can see the sun of the next day. After hours of fine eating, heavy drinking and casual flirting, Aella declares regally (she was still incredibly regal in her drunken state) that the banquet and ball were over and we should all return to our rooms. Seb and Phye slope off somewhere, I don't see where, but I manage to find Conaire in the crowds exiting the great hall. He's next to a tankard of ale and slumped against a gilded pillar, cradling a goblet of a dark brown liquid. I sigh and pull him up onto his feet, tossing the goblet aside.

I drag myself back to my room sluggishly, my head heavy from the surplus of wine I consumed throughout the several hours I spent dancing, chatting and eating. Conaire follows on my heels half passed out, to the point that I have to take his arm and drag him along.

"Which room is your room?" I ask him, my speech slurred in an ugly way. Conaire doesn't answer straight away as it takes him a while to process the question through his drunken mind. Eventually, he giggles and shrugs casually.

"Dunno," he slurs, collapsing even more onto me. I sigh, frustrated and exhausted, opening the door to my room I left twelve whole hours ago. The room is still empty, still grander than Buckingham Palace and still warm thanks to the crackling fire lit in the fireplace placed in the middle of the expansive space. The bed is still pressed up against the wall, except the curtains are now a grey in the dimmer light instead of the pale blue they were in the daylight. I still have Conaire's weight pushing against my shoulder, and my arm that is holding him up and protecting him from collapsing on the floor is starting to ache immensely.

"Conaire," I whisper, closing the door behind me with my foot, sealing us in. "Conaire!" He continues to ignore me in his drunkenness.

Ugh. I think to myself. What am I going to do now? Because of my state that goes slightly beyond tipsy, my brain doesn't think as quickly as it usually does. All I can think of is getting Conaire off my arm. Frustrated, I waddle over to the bed, stumbling as I approach the corner of a huge fur rug. As I trip, Conaire jumps into consciousness, awaking with a small grunt.

"Evanie?" he calls into the darkness, frightened and dropping to the floor with a rather loud thump. I sigh again, finally engaging my strength enough to pull him up off the floor and on to the mattress of the bed. The action tires me out completely (Conaire isn't the smallest of men) and I have no more energy to even take off my coronet or unlace my corset. I simply plunge face first into the covers with my legs dangling over the side.

I have no idea what time I wake up, but I've managed to shift my body to the other side of the bed so that my head actually manages to touch the pillows rather than merely brush against them. Conaire is still in the same position I placed him in when I mustered my strength and dumped him on the bed last night. His doublet is undone and missing a button, which I see glinting on the rug below the bed. His hair is wildly tousled and his eyes are circled by crescents of darkness from the lack of sleep he must've had last night. The curtains that were drawn when I arrived in my room in the early hours of this morning have been opened, light flooding in from every inch it can find available. I throw my feet over the side of the bed, noticing one of them is still concealed by a, now rather dirty, golden pump, whilst the other is caught up amongst the furs and duvets that adorn the bed. I rub at my eyes as I stand. Only once I am on my feet, I notice my pounding headache that is almost as severe as the one I experienced yesterday. I see that the door to the bathroom has been left wide open and, curiously, I make my way towards it.

In the centre of the room is a huge bathtub built into a platform you can reach by ascending several steps. In fact, I'm not even sure that that bath is a bath, it may even be a miniature bathing pool. There is a large cloud of steam erupting from the surprisingly full bath, swirling around the room. Several empty buckets sit in the corner next to another fireplace, which is also roaring and crackling, the sounds echoing throughout the chamber, which has wonderful acoustics as all four walls are tiled with squares of what could be mermaid scales protected by glass. As I go to slip my single shoe off of the only one of my feet that isn't as cold as ice, a dark-haired head pops itself into my view from behind the bath.

"Morning Evanie," Avie smiles, giving me the fright of my life.

"Saints, Avie, don't you know how to knock?" I gasp, clutching my chest.

"I did," she sighs, pouring another bucket of water into the bath, "but you were fast asleep, as *was*

Conaire." She sniggers and glances out of the door, where Conaire is still face down in my covers.

"Nothing at all like what you're thinking," I insist. "He was so drunk he couldn't walk and I had no other choice but to dump him on my bed. It was either that or leave him in the corridor to be trampled on by all the other drunk occupiers of rooms in this hall."

"Right…" Avie says disbelievingly. "I'll let you carry on," She reaches to a side table next to the bath, grabbing a clear bar of rose soap and lobbing it at my chest, which I catch, fumbling.

"At least it's not my brother," she mumbles, striding out of the bathroom door and crossing to the bed mischievously. She grabs a pin out of her extremely messy updo and pokes the back of Conaire's hand with the sharper end of it. He jumps awake, rolling over and sitting up abruptly, gazing around the room bemused and shocked.

"Evanie, where am I?" he asks me.

"I am just going to take a quick bath, Conaire," I smile at him warmly and the alarm on his face increases.

"Evanie, what happened?" He raises his voice further. I chuckle as I close the door and see him fly off the sunken mattress and run over to me. He pounds on the wood. I wait a few seconds for effect, before answering the door sweetly.

"Yes?" I answer.

"Did…" He stammers, rubbing his eyes as though he has a headache. The amount of wine and ale he drunk last night, though, I wouldn't be surprised if he had a particularly persistent headache.

"Nothing happened, Conaire," I assure him, but his face doesn't fall with relief.

"Really?" he asks uncertainly.

"Yes, Conaire," I sigh, closing the door in his somewhat settled face.

The bath is unbelievably warm, a relief in the cold Olympian breezes that blow the shutters of the palace violently, even at the end of summer. I use the soap to wash all of the makeup that cakes my face from last night, including the lipstick that's smeared halfway across my face. I throw my beautiful dress in one corner of the bathroom, wondering if I'll ever be able to wear it again. I could've been done in the bathroom in a matter of minutes but stay in the warm water's embrace for longer than I needed, ducking my head in and out of the water. I only stop and snap out of the heat-fuelled trance I'm in once I hear a sharp rap on the door of the chamber.

"Conaire, tell whoever it is I'll be out in a minute!" I yell through the bathroom door, and I hear Conaire's sluggish, hungover footsteps patter their way to the door. I can't quite hear what he's saying, but the sprightly tone the caller speaks in tells me that he's clearly talking to Lorna.

"Hold on, Lorna!" I shout, jumping out of the bath and pulling on a silk robe that hangs lifelessly from a peg by the bathroom door. I fly into the chamber, noticing that Conaire has very kindly lit the fire and made the bed.

"Morning, Evanie," Lorna says, welcoming herself into the room and taking her place down on the grey armchair Avie sat on yesterday by the fire. "We need you down in the library."

"Let me get dressed first," I tell her, grabbing the hairbrush to start to tease the thousand knots that make my hair look like a lazy bird's nest. Lorna holds up her finger, shaking it in the air and grabbing my arm with her other hand.

"Don't change. Just come down as you are," she tells me, opening the door with the brass handle and pulling me along the corridor by my wrist. Several courtiers pass us and I pull my robe tighter around my body. My hair's still damp and my palms still wrinkled, my feet still leave water marks on the carpet as I'm dragged down the stairs. We approach the library, which has its door open and is alive with excited murmuring coming from inside. However, when Lorna steps into the dimly lit room, it's only Clancy, Seb, Phye and Aella sat around the table, no one else.

"Ah, thank goodness you're here, Evanie, we can start," Clancy says, escorting me into a chair he pulls out for me.

"Right," Lorna starts, pulling a roll of parchment from her jacket pocket. "Seb, Evanie, we have a surprise for both of you."

"Surprise?" Seb question, raising an eyebrow at me.

"I pulled you and Evanie away from your lives in the darker realm," Seraphyna hangs her head shamefully as Seb reaches out to tell her that it's fine. It is fine, we mean something here, whereas on Earth, we were just another two neutral faces in a crowd of millions.

"Well, after some investigation, we found that your sister, Penelope, is now living in your Hertford estate with her husband Kurt and three children, Margret, Kingsley and Lydia. She is now thirty-five and it has been exactly ten years since she thinks Evanie disappeared and Seb died," Aella explains. "She's ill, we think she may die, but we want you two to go and visit her and take this cure." She holds up a vial of clear liquid that shimmers in different colours as it catches the light of the candles suspended from the ceiling by dainty chains.

My eyes widen, hearing of Penelope. I've often wondered in that half-awake state you're in before you fall asleep if she survived the war, if she's happy.

"And Henry?" I ask.

"Dead," Aella replies sadly. I don't expect to cry, but a tear escaped one of my eyes. I never cared fully for Henry as I saw so little of him, but he always seemed to be the only one of us who was certain to make it through the war. But he's dead.

"When can we leave?" Seb asks eagerly. "And how?"

"Wait," I stop him before Seraphyna has a chance to open her mouth. "We can definitely return safely? You're not sending us away?"

"No, of course not, and you are practically guaranteed to return safely, so don't worry, either of you," Seraphyna assures us. She signals for Lorna to open the chest behind her. Lorna pulls out a perfectly made dress that looks incredibly familiar and similar to something I would've worn in my early teenage years.

"We have no idea what the fashions are like in the current times in Hertford, but you'll look more at home in clothes ten years out of date than ones that are from a different realm entirely," Aella sighs, moving a room divider across the room and handing me the dress to change into. She also hands me a hairbrush and I thank her before sinking behind the room divider to change out of my robe and slip on the dress. It fits perfectly to my body, and the fit is so familiar it's almost like I'm wandering the streets of London as a fifteen-year-old once more. I smooth out the creases in the skirt with my hands before attending to the forest of knots that is my hair, dragging the hard bristles of the brush through my chocolate-brown locks. I emerge from behind the canvas screen, pulling the long sleeves of the dress down to my wrists. Seraphyna drops a pair of leather pumps at my feet, which I slip into gratefully. I smile at Seb, who's ready as well. It's strange, now I realise it, he'd been ready and in the clothes he's wearing now when I arrived in the library, but I'm so used to seeing him in the high-collared shirt, well-made waistcoat and pin-striped trousers he's wearing at the moment, I didn't even notice. He pulls a long, heavy suit jacket from the unlit candle holder it was hanging off, and smiles back at me, pulling it on over his arms. I hand him the vial Aella gave me and he tucks it in his trouser pocket.

"How are you doing this?" I ask Phye, but Clancy steps into the conversation and answers for her.

"Well, you know how one of the first things I said to you when we met was how Lorna and I were going to set up an experiment to go to the Lightest Realm, the next Realm along from here?" he asks and I nod, recalling fondly how eager and curious he looked when we ascended the cliff side the day Seb and I first arrived on the Eastern Isles. "Well, we found out the experiment would be successful, but the spell we made has enough power to return two people to the Darker Realm for a few hours, when, if we went to the Lightest Realm, we'd only be there for a few minutes, which is little use."

"Well, how did you send Seraphyna to the Darker Realm when she went on that journey to find me?" I ask.

"Well, she cast that spell herself, and it didn't come without sacrifice, we had to burn off the power of several important scriptures for her to muster that much magic to send herself to the Darker Realm for that long. This method is much safer and more viable, as well," Clancy continues.

"You two must get ready, quickly, now, because we'll run out of time, the weak spot here between the realms will fade," Seraphyna starts to panic, placing Lorna, Clancy and herself is a semi-circle around Seb and I.

"You both remember the spell?" Lorna asks Clancy and Phye and they signal that they do.

"Close your eyes," Clancy tells us, and glance at Seb before shutting my eyelids closed, concealing my eyes from the dim light around me. "And Evanie?"

"Yes?" I answer, not opening my eyes.

"Safe travels," he says, and I can tell he's smiling. I smile, too, although I don't know if it's in his direction or not.

"Thanks," I whisper.

I forgot what the sensation of being between realms feels like. Every part of my body tingles madly, making me twitch and lurch in all directions. The winds of time rush through my ears, and every now and again I catch snippets on everyday conversations, in all languages, and I can't understand many of them, but I recognise some words further on, some as French, some as Spanish, some as English, in fact, all I hear in English is:

"Mummy, why are you crying?"

I open my eyes, the sun hitting my face in the pattern its light makes through the trees.

"I'm just upset, Lydia, dear, that's all." The girl's mother asks. I can hear their continued conversation through the trees as I come to fully. It takes me a while to recognise the house I can see through the patchwork of branches in front of me.

My childhood home.

The front-door is a different colour, that's the first thing I notice. It used to be brown, but now it's a sickeningly bright red. More vines have grown up the trellises my father put in place just a few months before the war, and the vines have started to sprout dainty white flowers I know my mother would have loved. The beds in front of the manor that used to hold various roses my mother cultivated every morning relentlessly for a good five years are gone. Instead, they're replaced with a black, glistening automobile with a shiny badge on the front and leather seats on the inside. The red brick has started to fade even more, which, I suppose is expected, as the manor dates back all the way to the times of the Georgians. I peer through the grove of trees I've found myself in the middle of. I have to squint, my eyes adjusting the low levels of light. There she is. Penn. She's grown tremendously, not in height, but in manner and elegance. Her hair is a lot longer than her usual shoulder-length, straight-but-messy style she wore out in her teenage years and early twenties. She looks much more mature. The girl on her left is as short as her hip and clings on to Penn's hand in a way only a daughter would to her mother. They linger by three trees, placed in a neat row by the side of the house, Penn clutching the fabric of her bodice sorrowfully, holding back her tears for her daughter's sake. I turn away from the scene as Penn's daughter, my niece, I realise, pulls her mother happily back inside the house.

It doesn't take me forever to find Seb, as we meet in the middle of the grove whilst looking for each other. I embrace him, happy we've completed the journey safely. I whisper, telling him to approach the house. He removes his jacket, as it's the summer solstice, after all, and the air is buzzing with all kinds of flying creatures and pollen spores that reach my nose, making me sneeze lightly.

"Bless you," Seb smiles at my watering eyes and red nose. He's never had to suffer from hay fever. I sneer jokily as we emerge from the trees, checking that no one will spot us through the open drawing room window that opens widely and has a view over the grove of trees we've just emerged from.

We approach the front door apprehensively, in the end running towards the porch and up the steps so that my hand is paused over the knocker. I survey the scene behind me, checking for anyone, even animals or gardeners. I sigh, glancing nervously and anxiously at Seb, who raises his thick eyebrows at my hesitation.

"The door's red," he mumbles. "I can hear Grandmother rolling in her grave now."

The comment makes me explode with stifled laughter. Once I stop laughing, however, I impulsively grab the door knocker and rap it against itself sharply, twice. Seb and I stand shoulder-to-shoulder in the doorway, waiting for someone to answer. It takes around thirty seconds before we hear the surprisingly familiar pad of footsteps down the grand staircase that opens into the foyer of Hertford Manor. We hear several locks click and a key being turned in the huge keyhole that we can see from the outside, the one I used to peer through when Seb, Penn and I were playing hide and seek in our young years.

Penn is occupied as she answers the door, trying to shake off the small girl that clings to her skirts.

"Margret, stop," she sighs in the open doorway, before glancing out at Seb and me. Her face falls.

"I... I'm sorry, who are you?" she stutters. The little girl, Margret's face, lights up and she points an accusing finger at me.

"Mummy, it's the lady from the mantelpiece!" she chirps excitedly and Penn turns towards her in frustration, shooing her away from the door.

"Run along Margret," she sighs, glancing nervously at me and Seb more than a few times. "Go and play with Daddy."

The girl pouts momentarily, before Penn gives her a stern look that's all too familiar to me. Margret turns angrily, before descending the few steps into the drawing room.

"I'm sorry, I don't buy on the doorstep," she says angrily but apprehensively, starting to close the door.

"Penny," I stop her, in a hushed tone.

"No," she shakes her head in disbelief. "No, no."

"It's me," I whisper as Penn still continues to shake her head and close her eyes, trying to wake up from the nightmare she must think she's in.

"Penelope?" Seb offers his hand. She refuses to take it.

"It's me, Evanie, and Sebastian," I tell her, although I'm positive she's completely aware of the fact.

"No, you went missing ten years ago to the day," she points an accusing finger at me, before moving on to Seb. "And you, I buried you, you're dead and buried in the graveyard down the road."

"But you never found my body," I remind her.

"But I searched the whole of Abbeville, the whole of France, I even went to Germany! I searched for years hoping that maybe you were alive until I finally accepted that you were gone," Penn explains desperately, before shaking her head and biting her lip to hold her tears back, a mix of angry, desperate ones and ones of humiliation and sorrow. "No, what am I doing? Is this some kind of cruel joke? Is Henry going to pop his head around the corner now, as well? Or am I going to find my father in the library smoking his pipe and greeting me like he hasn't been dead for five years? Or maybe my mother will emerge from the greenhouse and start fussing over the roses in the flowerbeds or my hair?"

"For someone who's denying everything she's seeing, you seem pretty convinced it's us, Penn," I sigh, taking a step towards her. Penn defensively places her arm across the doorway to block me out.

"How?" she breathes, looking me up and down. She stares me right in the eyes, same as hers, forgiving and deep brown, wide and curious.

"We can tell you," Seb offers, placing his hand on her arm. Penn flinches. "If you let us in."

Penn gives in, dropping her arm from the doorway but holding up a finger that tells us we can't come in yet.

"Kurt?" She yells up the stairs.

"Ja?" a voice shouts back in a thick German accent.

"Take the children out for a walk around the garden, will you?" she asks.

"Of course, *meine Liebe*," he replies. We stand awkwardly in the doorway for another few minutes as we hear the various happy squeals or bored moans of the three children. Once we hear the back door close with its sonorous thud, Penn looks around behind us nervously before letting us in, ushering us quietly into the drawing room. The room is now painted white instead of grey and the wine cabinet has been replaced with a huge commode made from a wood that doesn't even match the coffee table. The drapes don't even match the armchairs, either. Penn gestures for us to be seated on the sofa, much more faded and dustier than I'm used to, but still the same one with the same cushions and covers.

"Tea?" she asks, fussing over the cushions on the armchair she's nearest to.

"I think we'll be fine," Seb replies and I nod, agreeing with him.

"I should've known not to ask you for tea, Sebastian, are you sure you don't want anything? Coffee? Evanie?" Penn questions, the shock she's endured obviously still making her nervous.

"I'm fine, really," I tell her, pointing to the armchair to tell her to sit down.

"I'll wake up soon, anyway, so it's probably for the best," Penn mumbles.

"Penny, this isn't a dream," I assure her, but she shakes her head profusely.

"Evanie, even in dreams you're impossible, you went missing ten years ago, and even if you were here, it's impossible for Seb to be because I buried him," she sighs.

"You told me once that you believed in magic," I remind her. "Do you still?"

"I was a silly girl when I was young," Penn insists. "I think that a whole war and five deaths later I realised that if magic was real then I could've stopped all of this if I tried."

"Did you?"

"Of course I didn't!" she exhales angrily and shakes her head in a way that only Penn or my mother could've. "It's not like I could've waved my hand and flames erupted from my fingers and I just lit the Germans on fire! You have always had a dangerously over-active imagination, Evanie, that's- that's one thing I bloody miss about you! When you just disappeared off of the face of the earth I didn't believe it, I'd still wake up every morning and make breakfast for two because I forgot you weren't there, I'd still take out books I thought you'd like in the library because I forgot you weren't there and when the war was over, a whole two years after you just vanished – I booked two train tickets home because I forgot that I was returning to Hertford alone. I searched for you. I did. When I'd reached the borders of Abbeville that first week – that week I actually had hope you might come back – I searched as far as Paris, Marseilles, Brittany, I searched everywhere! I spent a whole year in France and Germany just looking for you, chasing a memory I just wanted to ignite once more. But that's all you are, Evanie, you're just a portrait on the mantlepiece and a cluster of memories at the back of my dusty mind somewhere. And I miss you, I do."

"You're talking about me like I'm just a figment of your imagination, Penn, I'm not, I promise." I assure her as I kneel down in front of her chair and take her hands. My eyes start to tear up as she refuses my grip.

"I dream of you too often, you know," Penn says quietly. "But you never talk to me. You just sit across from me, and smile. You have a wonderful smile."

"And I'm talking now, Penn, does that help you realise that I'm real?"

"A little," She admits, working up the courage to face me.

Make sure to give her the vial. A little voice in the back of my head prompts. I turn behind me and gesture for Sebastian to come over.

"We heard you're sick," I tell her and she nods sorrowfully.

"The children don't know. Kurt can't really understand enough English to know exactly what's going on, and the doctors say that I don't have long. Trouble is, I feel fine most of the time, except for this rash I get and this odd mark on my stomach. I had a fever for the longest time, but to be honest, I feel just as well as I usually do at the moment," she explains, pointing to an area around her abdomen. Seb extracts the vial from his waistcoat pocket, handing it to Penn tentatively. I notice that a small square of parchment has been pinned to a ribbon around the vial.

"What's this?" she questions, taking the vial from Seb's hand. She turns the parchment over, reading Seraphyna's criminally tidy cursive that patterns the paper.

"Star Fever?" Penn widens her eyes. "What's Star Fever?"

"All I know is that if you drink this, you'll be cured," I tell her.

"Is that all you have to tell me? Usually at this point you leave." Penn sighs. I shake my head as I make my way back to the sofa with Seb.

"We're not leaving until we have to," I promise. "We have some time to talk, I haven't seen you in three months, well, ten years for you, tell me, what's changed in your life?"

"Oh," Penn says, obviously taken aback by my casual curiosity. "Well, the war went on for another two and a half years after you disappeared. I thought that Henry and I would be the two who would make it out alive, but maybe just a month before the war ended,

Henry was shot by some bloody German somewhere in Flanders and he died a few hours after that. That was when I realised, I was alone. Mother died in a train crash shortly after father was conscripted, they became so desperate for soldiers they forced anyone to fight that they could find, in the end they even stopped throwing out the women and boys that snuck their way onto the front, everyone had just died."

"Mother and Father died during the war?" Seb asks, looking absolutely horrified. Penn nods sadly, rubbing her eyes with her pristine fingers.

"I couldn't find a way to get home, all of the trains to Calais and boats on to Dover were held up, and if I miraculously found one, I couldn't find the other. I'd handed in my notice at the hospital, because I had to get home to Hertford, but no. I tried for a month, whilst I was in Calais the war was won and that's when I decided that I'd go home for a month and then return to France to look for you, Evanie," Penn explains, looking out of the window longingly. "I did, I actually had some fun travelling around France. I lodged with friends in Paris, soldiers I'd treated in Abbeville, and if I didn't have Hertford Manor to come home to, I would've stayed there. I became engaged to one of the soldiers in Paris, but then I found out that he'd gotten some poor girl pregnant whilst we were courting each other, and so he was sent along the road with a few hundred shouts and swears. Anyway, the girl I befriended, she knew nothing about me, and well, she died giving birth to her poor daughter. Oh, I fell in love with the child, Evanie, I couldn't just abandon her, her father left Paris for Bruges and he wouldn't answer the girl's mother's letters, so I knew that she would only have one chance at a life, and that was with me. I travelled to Germany, to the Alsace, I travelled all around the borders of France and Germany, all with a darling little girl. It wasn't until I had no money and went to travel to Bern University to see if one of Seb's friends was there."

"William De Prevue?" Seb asks eagerly.

"Yes, him and his brother, whom from your letters I knew were happy to receive guests," Penn confirms.

"You never told me you had a Swiss friend," I tell Seb, furrowing my brow.

"He's not Swiss, otherwise he wouldn't have fought in the war, would he? He's French, he studied at Bern University with his brother before he signed up to the war to impress some girl. Don't know who, but he's French, lovely chap, glad to hear he lived," Seb mumbles, talking to himself more than anyone else.

"Anyway, whilst at the university, I met a certain Kurt Schultz who lent me money for a train home with one catch – that he accompanies me and the child, Lydia I named her, to Calais and on the boat and ride to Hertford," she sighs, smiling for the first time since we arrived. "It was an odd request to me at the time, but it was the only way I was going to get home, therefore, I obliged. I married the man not four months later. He graduated from Bern and came to live here, with Lydia and I, and then Margret and Kingsley were born. He makes me incredibly happy, he's criminally clever, but hasn't been able to grasp English well enough to speak it in public, but I'm gradually teaching him the proper vocabulary. He has a wonderfully quirky habit of using under-used adjectives for common words, he says 'ecstatic' instead of 'happy' and 'splendid' instead of 'good' – bless him, I've never had the heart to correct him because I love it so much."

"So, you're happy?" I pose the question and Penn dwells on it for a while. I can hear the conversation going on in her mind, one side of her brain saying she is and the other says she isn't. Eventually, she lays her hand in her lap and comes to a conclusion.

"Very," she assures me. "There was a time I thought I would never be anywhere remotely close to happy, but now I am very much content, despite my past."

"Then that's all I need to hear," I tell her. Penn smiles, so do I. I glance at Seb and he's grinning like a fool too.

"Tell me about you!" she insists. "What's gone on in your lives?"

"We're part of something that's larger than all of us, that's why we had to leave and can't stay. Seb's found himself a rather wonderful lady," I smirk and Seb turns a pale shade of pink.

"And you?"

"Me?" I point to my chest. "Oh, well, I'm studying daily, you'll be happy to hear, I've made some great friends."

"I didn't think that you'd ever say you'd be studying daily, Evanie," Penn sighs, obviously remembering all of the times she tried to tutor me on the books of the bible or the exact order of the kings of England.

"Well, the history of our new home is much more exciting," I smirk, glancing at Seb who agrees. "And they have a wonderful library."

"Scotland?" Penn guesses, I shake my head, chuckling.

"Much further away than that," Seb tells her gently.

"India?" She speculates again.

"Colder," I inform her.

"Siberia?" It's become more of a game than anything else now, and we're all chuckling quietly.

"I can't exactly tell you."

"But you're happy?" Penn questions.

"Extremely," Seb assures her.

"Life is scary at times, but we're needed and loved, and that's all that matters, right?" I add, to be met with an agreeing nod from Penn.

"I just can't believe that I searched France when you were even further afield," Penny sighs.

"You wouldn't have found me even if you tried your absolute hardest," I tell her solemnly.

Evanie, you have to go, you don't have too much time to say goodbye. The same voice speaks in my head again, and I look nervously over to Seb, who's none the wiser as he sits, staring at the artwork that caresses the faded walls.

"Seb, we have to go, *now*," I insist and he jumps to attention.

"You're leaving?" Penn asks, shocked.

"We have to," I admit to her. "I'm sorry."

"I have one last thing to ask, Evanie," Penn speeds up her words desperately.

"Yes?"

"We used to play a game, when we younger, where I was a Fire queen and you were a Light queen and we had to hide from Henry, the Darkness king," she tells me, my eyes widen. "Was that just a game, a product of your over-active imagination, or was it something that was more real than it should've been?"

"Once upon a time, I would've said no, Penn, but the story of Hestia and Oralee was real. More real than the sun in the sky," I smile, watching her reaction shift from wonder to disbelief.

"Goodbye, Evanie," she grimaces, embracing me warmly.

"Goodbye Seb," she continues, moving onto him.

I don't have the chance to say goodbye, the cool colours of the drawing room mould into an odd blend of light and darkness. My eyes don't work. I move them to one side, the view is the same, I move them to the other, constant light and constant darkness.

Nothing else.

STARS

The cold water hits my face like a harsh, freezing punch. My first instinct is to breathe in deeply, but the truly awful taste of salt attacks my nose and mouth. I gag, not daring to open my eyes as I don't want them to sting like hell too. After a while of flailing my arms around, most likely looking like an absolute idiot, I manage to float to the surface. The light that hits me when I open my eyes is almost as shocking as the water and salt, as the sun's rays reflect off of every inch of water that surrounds me, which, as I look around, is everywhere.

No land, no boats, nothing. For all I know, I could be in the middle of the Atlantic. My hair clings to my face in uncomfortably thick clumps and my legs tire as I continuously tread water. It's not until I look down at my feet that I notice I'm still wearing the robe I put on this morning. However, seaweed is tangled up in the silken belt and the white material is floating around me. Just as my eyes start to droop from exhaustion and my consciousness ebbs and flows like the waves around me, the tide starts to cradle my body, moving my arms and legs for me and embracing me like an old friend. The mon starts to rise as I lie on my back, staring up at the sky and the stars that litter its landscape and paint a thousand pictures. The moon is a silky white and the glow reflects off of the ocean around me, rippling slightly as the tide continues to hug me and protect me.

My state of mind means that I don't think of Seb and I don't worry about where he might be. Drowned? Dead? Safe? Alive? I don't know and I don't ponder on the thought any more. I only snap awake when I hear a loud, ringing bell that cuts through the calm that coats the inside of my mind like a thick blanket. I open my eyes and, even though they are covered by clumps of my hair, I see a great and really quite intimidating flagship floating along the water. The flags that adorn the masts are painted red and the sails match their colour. The ship is lined with rows of cannons on every deck and the top deck is alive with men running around and pointing at where I'm floating along the surface of the ocean. Suddenly, the sea drops me and I plunge beneath the waves and choke from the pressure of the vortex that's been created around me. My world goes black, the night becomes darker.

And all I see is stars.

*

I pry my eyes open, exhaling painfully as I do. I'm bundled in blankets, a washcloth pressed to my forehead. The walls of the room I'm enclosed in are a drab brown and smell of damp wood. A woman, with green eyes so piecing they are all too familiar, sits in the corner and traces her finger along lines of a battered book of ancient runes. I sit up in alarm as I see a roaring fire in the middle of the room, that is just sitting there as though it were a dog, but doesn't dare spread anywhere, and its flames don't tarnish the wood or burn a hole in the floor.

"It won't hurt you, dear, don't worry," the woman mumbles, not even looking up at me or the fire. "It's all under control,"

I push myself into the corner where the bed meets the salty wood of the cabin walls, pulling the covers over my damp robe. As I draw back, the fire ceases as the woman signals for it to stop. Her eyes dart around the cabin and then they survey me, watching me intently with every move I make and every breath I take. She smiles a toothy smile at me, almost too sweet and sickly to be genuine. Those same eyes dart to the door continuously. It's only when I start to observe her closely that I recognise those eyes, and who she must've got them from and who she must be.

"You're Eithne," I croak as she chuckles and nods her head. *Ethelde's daughter.*

"In person, my dear," she replies, smiling. She calls me *my dear* but she's barely even twenty-five and has a face as fresh and dewy as Seraphyna's. She certainly has the look about her that tells me she was born in the Eastern Isles, brown hair so light it's practically blonde and eyes bright and fiery. Then it hits me. Fire. I'm on Fire's ship. Aidan's ship.

I'm in a deep hole of danger.

"Do you know who I am?" I ask her cautiously as she closes her book.

"I have a few ideas," she tells me. "You're either the daughter of the pirate captain Lannick George, a runaway from a Myrien brothel or that new baroness my sisters-in law have appointed in Light's court. I could be wrong, but no one else would've survived the sea like that for how long you were out there. You could be from Water's court, but I have no idea how you crossed the border through the ocean, so it's much less than likely, dear."

I crane my neck to watch the door, waiting for it to fly open and someone, anyone, to come and save me. Seraphyna, Clancy, Lorna, Conaire, I don't care, just anyone.

"Do you need some fresh air, dear? I can get someone to walk you around the deck if you need," she offers, standing to open the door. As she stands, I notice that she's heavily pregnant and waddles uncomfortably to the door.

"Does your mother know that she's going to be a grandmother?" I question quietly. Eithne's hand is suspended over the door handle.

"So, you are from Light's court," she mumbles. I widen my eyes in fear, having just given myself away. I stare her in the eyes for a few seconds, a quiet plead being sent to her to not go and get her husband. Please.

"I'm prepared to strike a deal with you, dear," she tells me quietly, sitting back down in the chair again. "I'll take you back to Olympia if you tell me how my mother is and give her a message from me."

I pause for a moment, reluctant. All Eithne wants is to tell her mother about how she's loved and how she's going to be a grandmother. All she wants is for me to play messenger.

"Your mother is thriving, somewhat," I whisper, "but she misses you, she's always obsessing over books about the court of Fire, and she mumbles and sits alone in her house in the Students' Village."

"I caused a rift to open between my mother and father, they're all but separate people now, when I was a lass, they were inseparable as the shore and sea. But ever since I was chosen for fire, they took it out on each other, my mother blaming my father and my father blaming my mother for my defect to fire," Eithne's eyes settle slowly towards her fidgeting hands. She looks up swiftly towards where I'm still hunched up with the covers in the corner.

"You know," she continues, "I never in a million years would've guessed I would be chosen for fire. When I was maybe just a lass of six or seven, I turned the candle in my bedroom into smoke with just my hand and I was so proud because I thought I could control the light. But no, I was controlling the fire, wasn't I? When I arrived in Calia I was so terrified, I was maybe fourteen? Fifteen? I can't even remember, I haven't the best memory, but I was bundled up into a small house into a village an hour's ride from the palace. I worked at the mines there for years, and I was somewhat content with my life, I suppose, although I ached for the smell of the sea when I awoke in the mornings and the cool breeze running through the open windows of brick cottages. Then, one day, we were told that our Highest Lord would be coming to visit our mine to see how everything was going, but we all thought it was a lie or a fable made up by the foreman to make us work even harder than we already were. A month later, a huge precession rode through the village, and all of the miners were grovelling at the feet of a rather short man, I must admit, who was literally *cowering* away from them and refused to ride a horse. He saw me as probably the most intimidating one, with the eyes and my stature, but he still tried to spark an incredibly uninteresting conversation with me. He asked for my hand in marriage the day he left and foolishly, I left with him, because who was I to turn down Aidan Omnia's proposal of marriage? They say the only reason he proposed was because I can control fire better than anyone any of his advisors have ever seen and before the palace tarnished me. I was apparently a rather captivating beauty."

"Well, you look positively glowing now, Eithne," I assure her.

"I get that from my mother, of course. She's one of the most beautiful women I ever knew," Eithne explains lovingly. I ponder on the thought momentarily. Ethelde isn't the kind of woman I'd imagine to be *beautiful* but now that I think about it, she must've been stunningly gorgeous in her youth. She's as tall as a giant but has a regal air that could just about match Seraphyna's, if that's even possible, Ethelde would be the only one to do it. Her eyes match Eithne's piercing leaf green ones, and her hair, although now steely grey, still has a leftover essence of shining caramel locks.

"She's going to be thrilled about being a grandmother," I smile.

"I'm not so sure about that," she sighs, rubbing her eyes irritably. "The fact that they're Aidan's won't please her, they may be half mine but they're half coward, too."

"They?"

"I'm so big the doctor thinks it may be two, and ever since then I'm sold on having twins or maybe even more. Trouble is, I'm not even sure that they or I will survive, see, as the physician in the Palace is incredibly old and has an incredibly old and really quite backwards way of thinking. He'll save the male heirs, not usually care about the poor girls or the mothers, even if she's his lady," Eithne pouts. It's a pretty pout, I'll give her that, but she's obviously pondering something quite deep at the moment, so I don't interrupt.

"Aidan's much less than thrilled, too," she continues irritably, biting her nails harshly after she says it. "Of course, he's already a father to I don't know how many bastards, but he's just anxious about actually having an heir and having to be a present father. Once in his life, he can't run from something, and the utter coward within him is panicking with every ticking moment closer to their arrival."

"So, you're not too keen on him?" I question, although I think I know the answer.

"He's an absolute coward above all other things," she sighs. "I suppose you'd quite like to meet him morning come, dear," I don't know how to answer the question. Seraphyna has never spoken too much ill of Aidan, not as much as her other brothers. I don't dread meeting him as much as I expect I would've, but I'm certainly not looking forward to it.

"Do you have any food or water?" I question quietly, waiting for her reply with bated breath as my stomach groans with ravenous hunger.

"Of course, my dear, we're not barbarians, I'll find you something from the galley," she offers, standing with some difficulty due to her size.

Eithne returns a few several minutes later with a plate of menial rations and a man standing behind her holding a leather bag.

"This is Lord Ambustian, he's kindly agreed to look over your state of health, my dear," She tells me, passing me the plate and signalling for me to eat and then for Ambustian to enter. He sets his bag down against the wall of the cabin and reaches for a flask. He takes the cork from the neck of it and hands it to me.

"Here," he offers kindly. "It's just water, child," he reassures me after I pause with the bottle at my lips. Gratefully and thirstily, I drink, downing the entire bottle as the coolness soothes my salty throat. He gestures for me to stand up and I throw the covers off my legs as my feet meet the damp and splintering wooden floor. I no longer wear my robe but find myself sporting a loose cotton gown in a deep wine red. Ambustian lifts my arms one by one, inspects behind my ears and hands me another vial for me to drink from.

"This should warm you up," he says, noticing my shivering legs. He takes my hand in his, smiling at me kindly. He turns my hand over in his to inspect the back of my hand. His face falls.

"My Lady," he turns to Eithne frightfully, face white as a sheet. He drops my hand as he glances at it again. I widen my eyes at him. Staring at my hand, I notice that it's almost as though someone had taken black ink and spilled it on my hand in the shape of a star.

"She's cursed," Ambustian mutters under his breath, throwing the door of the cabin open wide and ushering me out violently. Eithne follows behind me, staring at me in disbelief.

"Aidan!" Eithne yells across the deck we've just walked onto. A man with light blonde hair and deep brown eyes, who I couldn't believe is Seraphyna's brother by looking at him, turns towards the calamity of Ambustian, Eithne and I charging towards him at full speed.

Aidan isn't the most regal-looking man I've ever seen. His eyes are tired and surrounded by dark circles and his lips are dry and flaky. The deep brown of his eyes and flaxen colour of his hair offset each other, making him look as though he's been patched together using spare parts from other people. His cape reaches an awkward point halfway down his skinny legs, his scabbard empty and his shirt is ripped in the top corner. He does look more like a sailor of Water than the Highest Lord of Fire as his hair is slightly damp and his breeches are a dark navy blue, which doesn't match the flaming look of his cape at all.

"Is this the girl?" He asks gruffly, looking at Eithne as more of a nuisance than a wife.

"Yes, she's another Myriean runaway, she's asking to be dropped off in Olympia," Eithne explains to him as Aidan pulls uncomfortably at his cape.

"You think that that woman will let me further into her territory?" Aidan retorts bitterly, finally giving in before removing his cape entirely and thrusting it vigorously at a servant behind him.

"Aella is not that kind of person," Eithne sighs. "And you know I hate it when you refuse to name any of them, they're your sisters, Aidan, not objects."

"But, alas, my enemies also, my *dearest wife*," Aidan replies with a cunning smirk that only makes Eithne frown further.

"But, my Lord, if I may," Ambustian pipes up, raising a finger and emerging from behind Eithne. "Look at the child's hand."

Aidan tilts his head, examining the back of my hand. His eyes trace the outlines of the star carefully, his expression altering ever so slightly but not significantly enough for it to mean anything.

"Throw her overboard, the stars have cursed her," he orders casually, as though the words are so normal to him.

"Oh, Aidan, no!" Eithne insists, shaking her head profusely and deepening her expression of anger.

"You do not tell me what to do, Eithne, it's her death or all of ours, she'll die within the month, anyway," Aidan thrusts a furious finger in Eithne's face, not acknowledging me at all. I send a confused look in Eithne's direction and she gestures for me to come over.

"Listen, my dear, you have Star Fever, some people call it a curse, others just think it's a disease, many think it's a mix of both. If you aren't treated, my dear, you will die, it's not a might, it's a will. You will die if you don't fight this," she explains to me. I start to shake my head in fear, my eyes pooling as I do so. "We're not even an hour from Holynest, Aidan, send her there and the founders can attend to her,"

Aidan doesn't answer, he just pouts and turns his head away from us.

"Please," I squeak, mustering my courage to say it.

"Change course, we're detouring via Holynest, Captain," Aidan announces to the man by the ship's wheel. The man reluctantly and irritably agrees but turns the wheel towards the east and changes the course of the voyage. Eithne gestures kindly for me to follow her, nodding in thanks to Ambustian. We reach another door to another cabin. Eithne ushers me inside.

"We're safe in here, my dear," she assures me, sitting on the edge of a grandly-carved and covered four poster bed built into the cabin, the posts nailed to the floor and fitting around the wine-red carpet that covers the otherwise rough floor.

"Thank you," I murmur, "for assuring my safety."

"My dear, the fate of the realm is in your hands. If you were to die, then there is no hope for any of us," Eithne explains solemnly. "The founders will not leave you alone, my dear, I promise it."

"I can't seem to find this power I'm told I have," I admit, rubbing my eyes with my wrinkled fingertips.

"Well, if you can't find it, it'll find you, my dear," she smiles.

"Evanie," I tell her. "My name is Evanie."

"A pretty name," Eithne states. "I've never heard of it before, where are you from?"

"A far-off land, no one has heard of it," I insist.

"I am the daughter of the professor of Light, my dear, try me," Eithne challenges. I smirk.

"Britain, England specifically," I tell her.

"Darker Realm?" Eithne guesses. "Never heard of that place before, but it sounds like a place from the Darker Realm, that explains a lot, then."

"I.... I... uh…" I stammer, struggling to form a sentence in my disbelief.

"Oh, don't be so surprised, we're always watching what's going on down there in the Darker Realm, dear, your lives are sometimes quite entertaining," Eithne laughs.

"That's how Aella knew about Penn," I mutter under my breath before turning back to Eithne. "Why are you sailing through Aella's territory when you could be back in Calia?"

"Because Aidan said so," she spits his name bitterly. "Because I have to do what he says because *woe betide those who meddle with fire, Eithne,*" her nostrils flare and she pouts, crossing her arms.

"How does he treat you?" I question.

"Not as badly as I expected, surprisingly," she says. "He has countless mistresses but he's never once raised a hand to me, probably because he's too scared too, however. He doesn't lock me up or forbid me from any material possessions or friends, so I suppose I don't have it the best and I don't have it the worst. Poor dear Melaina, Domhnall's wife, she's mistreated more than a hunting dog, bless her, she's locked in a wing of the palace much of the time, her son was sent to the other side of Shee and she only sees him once a month, poor boy. Daileass' wife, Isoletta, however, is worshipped by her husband, he never even looks at other women. They say he's not that bad, in all truth, but he's just wants the throne so badly it's twisted him into a bloodthirsty man. That's what war does to you, though, I suppose."

"Why did anyone even challenge Domhnall for the throne in the first place?" I ask. "It's not that I think he should be king, but doesn't he have a perfectly legitimate claim to the throne?"

"Ah, yes, you would think so, but it is practically accepted by everyone that Domhnall killed his father, mother and Seraphyna's mother once he became bored of just being prince. The law states that you can't become the monarch if the founders frown upon you, and I'm sure the founders frown upon murderers. The Sheevians were all too happy to accept him as their highest Lord, but Daileass wasn't just going to let Domhnall take the throne even if there was the tiniest speculation that he might be eligible for it instead. Of course, no one has proved who killed Domhnall XXXIV and his two remaining wives, but we all know it was Domhnall, despite how much he denies it. So, because of the uncertainty, the fight goes on. Aella and Herminia joined only because their professors and previous Dukes pressured them to, and then they couldn't withdraw in later life, so they just signed that treaty with Seraphyna to change their cause of fighting to abolishing the throne altogether. Aidan joined because, well, I'm not even sure, to be honest, but he had a small chance to be king, so, naturally, he grabbed it with both fists, head on," Eithne explains wearily.

She takes the teapot from the rack in the fireplace, dipping her hand into the flames as though it were just water, and withdraws her hand from them completely unscathed, fingers clasped around the teapot handle. She pours the infused water into a gilded teacup resting upon a matching saucer and draws it to her lips.

"Please, help yourself," she offers, and I oblige, craving some more liquid running down my scalding throat. Once I take a sip I realise my mistake, as the tea is so hot it burns my throat more as I gag, spitting the boiling contents of the cup into my lap.

"Oh, sorry, my dear, I forget that most people can feel heat," Eithne sighs casually, passing me her handkerchief to mop up my dampened skirt.

"You can't feel the heat?" I ask in disbelief.

"No, not at all, not if I don't want to, my dear," Eithne assures me matter-of-factly. "Although I'm not a huge lover of the magic of my house, it does have its benefits, I'm sure you can see-"

Eithne is just about to call me *my dear* once more, which I am quite sick of if I'm being honest, before she's interrupted by a sharp rap at the door. She murmurs for the knocker to come in. We wait apprehensively as the hinges creak open and the man at the door enters the dimly lit cabin.

"The captain says that we will reach Holynest in a matter of minutes, my lady," the man says, before bowing swiftly and closing the door behind him.

"We'd best prepare you for landing then, Baroness Evanie," Eithne suggests, standing to examine the extensive contents of her wardrobe, robes in shades of red from ones almost bright orange to ones closer to purple than red.

"You…" I pause, surprised at her finally calling me by my name and title, one which I have not possessed for very long, but still, I am a baroness.

"This is the letter for my mother and there is enough food in there to last you a few days. I think I have some rope in there as well, although I'm not sure if it's the strongest kind," Eithne starts, handing me a wax-sealed, yellowing envelope and then a leather satchel that she drapes around my shoulder.

"Thank you," I reply meekly. "You could've just killed one of your husband's greatest enemies, but instead you listened to me, and I thank you, Lady Eithne."

"It has been a pleasure to be in your presence, Lady Oralee," Eithne nods, and it's not until I'm outside the door I've realised what she said.

*

The captain agrees to let me take one of the lifeboats to the shore of Holynest alone, gruffly barking orders at me not to rock it as they lower the vessel into the water. Aidan smugly throws an oar down into the boat after me, squinting in amusement at my sheer irritation of his existence. I grab the oar with both of my hands so tightly that my knuckles turn white as I drag the wood through the crystal ocean, away from the unwelcome smattering of red in the midst of the blue behind me. The last and only other time I arrived in Holynest it was by carriage through a parted sea, and even then I never even remembered arriving on the beach and climbing the mountain as Evanie. I waded through the shallow waters and clambered up the crumbling rocks as Oralee, in my white dancing shoes and cape, with a pearl tied around my neck. The area around me is so quiet it's almost eerie. The only noise I can faintly hear is the sand swilling around on the beach in the mellow summer breeze that rustles the reeds and ripples the water that laps up against the shore. I drag my belongings out of the boat as well as the oar, as it can be used for firewood quite easily and I have no idea how long I will be here.

I spend most of the day hauling logs from the undergrowth onto the beach to start a fire as well as looking for stones to start it as, despite it being late summer, I know that the nights will be cold and the weather is already starting to turn. I make sure to stay on the beach in the cooling shade of the mountain where I lay my satchel behind my head as a pillow and lay to rest as the sun sets.

I stare up at the night sky, the patterns all too familiar to me, so recognisable to my mind they could be the freckles on the end of my nose. They litter the sky like flour on a black tablecloth, they consume the sky so much with their brightness it wouldn't be hard to believe they're all just one group of light. The moon is absent from the night sky, but I can still see the reflection of the constellations in the twinkling ocean shore and the way the escalated breeze is ushering the sand along hastily with its blustery fingers. I exhale deeply, waiting for sleep to finally consume my mind. As I do, I lift my hand to my face, examining the black star printed on it closely. My fingertips trace the outline of the shape, seemingly permanent in its horrifyingly dark shade that paints my pale skin.

Again, I dream of the stars. I float among them on a wave of darkness, it cradles me like the ocean as I reach out, further and further towards the light. My fingertips are the tiniest fraction of an inch away, it would've taken no time more to clutch the star in my hand before the Darkness pulls me back again.

"*Lara di Baroness*?" A gruff, bearded man pokes me awake with a stick. He stares down at me cowering away from him, rolled in sand and filth and dressed in my blood red dress I didn't even agree to wear. It takes me a while to realise what he's asking me and in what language.

"Va," I reply, using one of the only words of Old Omnian that Clancy and Ethelde taught me. *Va means yes, Ovi means no.* It's one of the few things I remember them telling me about the harsh language. I don't completely understand the phrase the man asks me, but I can just about make out what he's asking me. *Are you the Baroness?* Yes, I am the Baroness.

"Ah, Lady Evanie, your brother and your Highest Lady will be elated to know you're alive," he sighs, stretching his bony hand out for me to take and clamber onto my feet as I stumble amongst the damp sand.

"Where is Lady Seraphyna?" I ask him.

"In the boat just there," he tells me, pointing to a small ship anchored on the shore as he starts gathering my things into the satchel and handing the bag to me by the fraying strap. His accent is thick as he mumbles to himself, shuffling along the sand as he drags his staff behind him.

"Who are you?" I question once we've nearly reached the point where the shore meets the sea.

"I am Horus, Professor of Air, Lady Evanie," he says, staring out at the sea. He waves his staff once in a large circle around our heads, lifting us both off of our feet as we do. I widen my eyes as I stare down at the rippling waves below me as I float through the air like a bird. I place my hands over my eyes, not opening them until I am confident that my feet are stable on the deck of the boat.

"Evanie!" Seraphyna flings herself at me, her arms thrown around my neck in a tight embrace. "Oh, Evanie, I thought you were dead!"

"I'm alive, Phye, don't worry," I smile, holding her at arm's length.

"What happened?" Aella questions, strolling over to me and handing me a handkerchief to wipe the blood from my face from a wound I had sustained somewhere between floating in the ocean and being thrown off of Aidan's ship.

"Honestly? I don't really know. But Fire's ship found me floating in the middle of the ocean somewhere off of the coast of Olympia and then Aidan's wife figured out who I was."

I see Phye cover her face with her hands in defeat, shaking her head as she does.

"But she agreed to not tell Aidan who I was if I told Ethelde how she was and that she's going to give birth to possibly multiple children any day now," I explain.

"But then they told me I was going to die or something awful and then Aidan tried to drown me but Eithne just said to dump me on Holynest and let 'the founders attend to me'."

"Eithne's pregnant?" Aella questions. "And you're going to die?"

"Star Fever they said, I think," I shrug simply, extending my hand for Phye to examine the star that paints the back of it.

"No," She murmurs.

"Evanie," Aella breathes, placing a hand apprehensively on my covered shoulder. "I think you may have little chance of survival."

"Nonsense," Seraphyna sighs, staring out at the water as she commands the ship forwards with the tiniest strain of her hand. "She's Oralee the Great, Aella, she'll pull through even stronger than before, I'm certain," she assures us both.

"She'll need a great amount of care before she slips under, Phyna," Aella reminds her. "And no one who has never had the curse before can't go anywhere near her."

"Clancy and Avie had it when they were young," Phyna tells her. "I'll send for them. I think that's everyone, so you'll have someone at all times to keep you company at least, Evanie."

"I don't understand what's going on," I whine. "Am I going to die or not?" The words come out louder than I wanted them to, but I wanted to make a point and no one was listening to me.

"No, of course not," Phye assures me. Aella raises an apprehensive brow at her. "She's not!" she insists.

"If you say so," Aella sighs.

"Thank you for your hospitality, sister, I plan on seeing you in the not too distant future, please do me a favour and send my court back to the Eastern Isles," Phye says, nodding her head at Aella before preparing to leave. I go to say something, opening my mouth to ask Phye what we're doing, where we're going, but I don't think that the question needs answering. I don't have time to ask anyway as my body gives up and the darkness consumes me.

*

"You've been spending an awful lot of time with her considering she's been asleep for three days, Clancy," Avie sighs, sitting on the end of my bed. Neither of them notice me open my eyes and look around the room. I'm home. Finally. The curtains are a warming yellow that turn the room into one with a welcoming glow of gold and cream. The bedsheets of my bed are white and crisp and cradle me gently, which is a relief as every part of my body aches viciously. My head has a washcloth laid over it, my arms are wrapped in soft linen and my hand that bears the great black star is bandaged clumsily. I breathe out, letting all of the tension in my body escape.

"Evanie?" Clancy questions. "Oh, Evanie, thank the Saints."

"I'll leave you two alone," Avie smirks. "And go and get Phye."

"And Seb?" I croak hopefully.

"Sorry, Evanie, it's a risk to you and him for him to be near you," Clancy sighs.

"Then why can you and Avie and Phye be here?" I grumble, crossing my arms. I haven't seen Seb since we left the Darker Realm, and I'm sure he wants to see me as much as I want to see him.

"Because we've all already had Star Fever and you can't catch it twice. You know, it's very interesting, Star Fever, as it is one of the most common diseases in the realm but it rarely reaches Omnia because we all have so much power. It's fought off not by your body, but by your magic, and that's what makes Star Fever so interesting and deadly to the elders and children and those with no power," Clancy explains excitedly. Even through my pain, I chuckle at his excitement.

"You mean people without power like *me*?" I ask after panicking slightly.

"No, you're not powerless, Evanie, you're Oralee the Great and she practically defeated an army of darkness all on her own, you'll be fine, I promise," Clancy soothes, handing me a cup of water that resides on the nightstand next to me.

"Thank you," I say. I start to take a big gulp of the water to cool my burning throat.

"You'll have some nastier symptoms than this in a few days, I'm afraid," he carries on, scribbling something down in the leather-bound notebook that is resting in his lap.

"Oh, Saints," I sigh in disappointment.

"But once you get past that stage, it all gets better, I promise," Clancy assures me, resting his hand on my shoulder.

The lock on the door clicks and I hear a low chatting voice from outside the door.

"Yes, I'll make sure to, Seb," Phye sighs from outside. Seb's low tone continues to mumble and the door bangs a few times.

"No, you can't see her, Seb, I'm sorry," she apologises.

"Hey, Evanie," Seb shouts through the wood.

"I'm alive, don't worry!" I shout back.

"Good to know," he yells, and I can hear him chuckling even though the noise is incredibly faint. The door opens, Seraphyna standing in the threshold and holding a fresh lit candle.

"I could finally light a candle, Clancy," she announces proudly, sheltering the flame to protect it.

"That's a surprise, Aidan never lets you," Clancy replies, gathering the various torn pieces of paper that litter his lap into his notebook and tucking the feather quill into his belt.

"Strange," I murmur as Seraphyna flies at me.

"I'm so glad you're alright," she sighs, hugging me awkwardly and with difficulty as my arms won't support my weight to pull myself up.

"So am I," I reply with as much of a smile as I can muster.

"I'll take over, Clancy, don't worry," Seraphyna tells him, pointing to the door distractedly. She turns to me joyfully and enthusiastically. "So, what do you want to do?"

"I don't exactly think we could take a walk around the island, and I don't know what games you play around here, so maybe you should choose," I conclude, finally mustering the strength to pull myself up so my head is leaning against the headboard.

"We could play cards," Phye suggests, pulling a small wooden box out of a pocket in her dress.

"Oh, I love playing cards, I used to play with my sister all the time," I tell her, sliding the box open and inspecting the rectangles of parchment that are piled inside the case.

Phyna starts to lay the cards out on the bed, and the symbols that splatter the paper aren't the ones I'm used to.

"These ones are stars, these are moons, those are rivers, those are flames and those are roses and the last are clouds," she explains, making piles of each of the card sets.

"One for each of the houses," I nod, picking up a stars card and tracing my fingers over the beautifully inked designs.

"Yes, well observed," she nods in approval. "I'll reach you how to play Rose Garden. It's a wonderful game."

"How do I play?" I question.

"I was getting to that," she sighs, dealing the cards into three piles, one for me, one for her and one in the middle. "You'll start with a hand of cards; you have to find pairs of either the same number or same suit. You play your pairs onto the pile in hope of getting a rose from the pile, and your aim is to have all twelve roses by the end of the game. It's pretty simple, but there are some laws that I'll tell you as we play."

We play Rose Garden for a few hours. Phyna wins the majority of her games, hoarding all of the roses before I even have my chance to place my pairs in the middle. The games are usually short, but, surprisingly, they don't become boring as I enjoy looking at the designs on the cards. As there are six suits, there are many cards to look at, as every single one is unique. The stars cards are my favourite, as the numbered cards depict constellations with that number of stars in it.

Instead of a King, Queen and Jack, each suit has just a Lord and Lady.

We play until the clock chimes three times and Avie comes in to sit with me. She hands me some parchment and a quill without saying anything. Satisfied, she sits back in the armchair on the other side of the room and places her hat over her eyes to sleep.

"Thank you for coming all the way from Olympia, Avie," I whisper into the room.

"No problem, Evanie, I get to spend quality time with my brother which I haven't been able to do for a while, just an excuse to get away from my mother, I suppose," she mumbles, her voice muffled by the hat placed over her face.

"I'm glad," I smile, and I am. Clancy never really talked of his sister before we met her in Olympia, but he seemed to enjoy spending time with her the few times I've seen them together.

"He talks about you a lot, you know," she smirks, removing the hat that's covering her face. "Do you want me to get the book you've been reading? Clancy made sure to get it from your room in Olympia. He told me all about how much you're enjoying it. I could even tell you what page you're on, if you want."

"Thank you for the offer, Avie, but my eyes are a bit tired, now, I'm afraid, so maybe later," I apologise, setting the parchment and quill aside onto the nightstand.

"Clancy!" Avie yells all the way down the hallway, and I'm certain most people on Greater Isle could even hear her shout for her brother. Clancy comes bursting into the room just a few moments later, looking flustered and worried.

"Good," Avie nods, standing from her chair to go and leave. "You can take care of your lady and you can read her that book you were telling me about," she runs out of the room, not even glancing back at Clancy standing breathless and pale in the doorway.

"Really, Clancy, it's fine, it looks like you were in the middle of something there," I have to force myself not to chuckle, as Clancy is still brandishing a sword in his left hand.

"Duelling... with... Conaire," he gasps, placing a hand on his chest from breathlessness. He catches his breath, stumbling over to the armchair Avie just jumped up from and drops his sword next to it.

"I'll go and get that book," he concludes after a while.

"Thank you," I call after him as he descends the stairs, heading towards the library.

Clancy returns a few minutes later with the leatherbound chronicle gripped tightly in his hand. Kindly, with that wide and welcoming smile of his, he sits on the edge of my bed and opens the book to the exact page I stopped reading the night before we travelled to Olympia.

"Where in the book had you stopped?" he asks me awkwardly, closing the book in embarrassment but keeping his hand on the page.

"That exact page around about the paragraph about Erich, I think," I recall, trying to reassure him in his embarrassment.

"*Oralee's husband, Caspian, was a doting father to their son, Erich. The boy was born when the Morning Moon rose that year, but he was a very sickly and powerless child, which came as a surprise to all members of Light's court as Oralee and Caspian were extremely talented in their magic and expected their son to be the same. When he was just a small boy, Erich caught Star Fever, the source unknown, and despite his lack of power, fought for a long time against the illness in the care of his half-sister, mother and father, who all caught the illness from him during this time but fought it off easily and without struggle. After five whole moons of the boy being cursed, the illness finally took his life, much to the devastation of his whole family and court. His funeral was attended by every member of his mother's court, his father's family and his Aunt Hestia's family from Calia."* Clancy reads, his expression not changing. He pauses, shuffling his feet on the carpet awkwardly as we both listen intently to each other's breathing.

"Probably not the best passage to read, considering the circumstances," he grimaces, closing the book and setting it aside, cringing.

"I disagree," I tell him. "In fact, it was quite reassuring."

"Really?" he asks, "how?"

"Well, Oralee survived Star Fever once, so she'll survive it again," I assure him, although I'm more trying to reassure myself more than anyone else.

"I suppose you're right, Evanie," he nods happily.

"What's the Morning Moon?" I ask, changing the subject and recalling a term from the passage I didn't recognise.

"We have two moons in the Lighter Realm," he explains. "The Night Moon, which rises every evening and sets every morning, and is as silver as an old professor's beard, and then the Morning Moon, which is lilac and cream and only rises once a year in the morning and stays all day until midnight. They say those who are born under it are blessed. It appears at different times every year, although they've started to predict when it will be. The professor is almost certain that the day of the Morning Moon will be in the next week. Everyone watches the Morning Moon rise and set, and those who don't are cursed," Clancy explains. His explanations are always thorough. I love hearing him so excited when talking about different parts of history or even scrutiny he's studied, like he's just happy someone will listen to the information he has.

"How long until I can get out of bed?" I quiz, raising a brow as I lift my lips to the glass of water in my hand.

"About a week and a half - oh. Oh," Clancy stutters.

"I think I'm already cursed enough, is there a way to get me out to see it rise?" I ask sweetly, batting my eyelids comically.

"Depends how you are, Evanie," Clancy admits nervously. "I'm sure Phye would rather have you cursed than dead."

"I suppose you're right," I shrug.

"You look awfully tired, maybe it's best for you to go to sleep now, Evanie," Clancy suggests. "I'll get Conaire to come and sit with you." My ears prick at the mention of Conaire's name. I haven't seen him since I dragged him back to my room in a drunken state.

"Settle down and he'll come in a few minutes," Clancy tells me, closing the door behind him.

Sleep evades me. I toss and turn in the glorious sunlight that pours through the open window to my right, pulling the cover around me in a tight cocoon of linen and cotton. I listen to my slow breathing, a constant and welcome reassurance that I am still alive.

*

The next few days are increasingly painful, to the point where every joint and bone and muscle in my body aches, my head throbs, and I can't keep any food or water down without it coming right back up. I blink drunkenly, watching the uncertain movements of Clancy as he scribbles in his notebook in the corner. He can't be getting much work done, however, as every few seconds he looks up and across at me in concern, raising his judging brow at the terrible state of my health. My tongue is as dry as the desert, but I daren't drink water because that would make me feel much worse.

"Clancy," I rasp, and he looks up expectantly. "Can you read me more of Oralee's life?"

Clancy grimaces apologetically, closing the notebook and making his way over to me.

"I'm sorry, Evanie, I'm not leaving you alone like this," he insists, shaking his head. "I would get Phye or Avie or maybe Conaire to fetch the book, but Avie and Phye are on Greater Isle, looking for something from the physicians and Conaire, well…"

"He won't come anywhere near me," I sigh sadly. Even though Conaire's had Star Fever before, and fought it off quite well, he refuses to sit with me or even come upstairs in the palace for the fear of 'breathing the same air as the cursed'. He thinks that, because his power is now hindered by his heartbreak over Lindera, he could catch the curse and die. Even though Phye, Avie, Lorna and Clancy have all assured him that catching Star Fever more than once is almost impossible, he won't take that chance to see me. In the moment that Phye hung her head and told me the fact, I lost all respect for that man. I cursed his name to the wind. I thought he cared about me. I cared for him, after all.

But, no. Won't take a chance to just see that I'm alive and well. Now I'm starting to understand why Lindera married Ilene instead.

"I could tell you another story instead, if you like," Clancy offers.

"Anything but sleep," I throw my heavy hands up. Faces of foes have been haunting every dream every night I have been sleeping. I see Domhnall silencing Melaina with just a wave of his hand. I see Aidan threatening to throw me over board into the ocean. I see Donovan, raising his hand to kill Oralee...

"I often look to the night sky when the weather is clear. Every star and the pattern they make tells a story. We have many constellations, as I'm sure you know, and the most famous one I'm certain you know the story of. The temple of the eastern sun is six stars, Star Oralee, or the Eastern Sun in the middle, the brightest and largest star in the night sky, surrounded by one each for her brother, her General, Ledan, her son, Erich, her stepdaughter, Xanthe, her sister, Hestia, and one for her husband, Caspian. There isn't much of story around that constellation, I'm afraid," Clancy tells me, eager.

"I'm glad to know Oralee always has her loved ones with her," I smile weakly.

"However," Clancy starts. "The Constellation of Rea, the maid, has a very interesting story behind it."

"Go on," I urge him.

"One of the first Omnian kings was Atwell of Water, who had three sons and a daughter. His eldest two sons lived with him on Royal Isle, but his youngest son, named Atwell himself, lived with his mother and sister in Elspeth. The boy had many girls swooning over him, left right and centre, but he only ever had eyes for one girl, a mermaid who lived in the Crystal Lake. His sister's name was Rea, and she was a kind-hearted girl who despised her father and her magic of water but loved her brother and mother with all her heart. One night, when Atwell was praying to the founders to bring him and his love together, Rea heard his desperate pleas that hadn't been answered. Rea asked her mother, a very talented holder of Water magic, to cast a spell of transformation on her and Atwell's love. The spell dictated that for mermaid to be turned to human, a human must be turned to a mermaid, and Rea offered herself as the sacrifice. When, that evening, Rea went missing and Atwell's love appeared on the shores of the Crystal Lake and could speak to him in perfect Omnian to tell him what happened, Atwell ordered his courtiers to search the Crystal Lake for his sister, who he said he owed his life to. They never found Rea, until one day when Atwell's father and brothers were visiting the lake and a mermaid jumped from the water. She gave one of Atwell's brothers a shock, so she was cut down on the shore by his sword. Rea lay dead on the shores of the lake, killed by her own brother. The mermaids that had taken her in placed her body in the night sky, so she was forever immortalised as the constellation of Rea, the maid," Clancy says.

"Mermaids? You have mermaids here? I thought that mermaids were things of story books and children's tales," I furrow my brow and Clancy raises his at my comment.

"You can't be that ignorant to think that it's just humans and animals who inhabit this realm?" Clancy asks in disbelief. I shrug, "No, we have mermaids, centaurs, water nymphs, forest nymphs, all sorts, really. Generally, they act as messengers for each house. Water has water nymphs, we have mermaids, although most of them do inhabit the crystal lake in Elspeth, and Darkness has centaurs, they're incredibly good at intercepting messages, Air has Valkyries, I suppose you saw some of them walking around Aella's court," I shake my head.

"Very tall people, mostly women, always dressed in armour, all have very long hair. Avie's father was half-Valkyrie," Clancy explains to me.

"That explains the very long hair then," I realise, thinking of Avie's incredibly long, dark hair. "You're only half-siblings? You'd never guess, she's practically the female version of you"

"Our mother isn't the most honest person in the world," Clancy admits, pinging the sleeve of his shirt awkwardly. "She married my father when they were young, along came me, but then Avie's father came along and took her attention, my father never knew, but even as a small child I wasn't stupid, I knew what my mother was doing. My father only found out when my mother had Avie and... well, it would've been impossible for it to be his, let's just say."

"And your father now?" I question.

"Oh, I stayed with him for a while when we were in Olympia, he and my mother aren't married anymore, and my new stepmother brings him a lot of joy. Avie lives with my mother, but when she turns sixteen, she'll be able to move into the students' village, which I know she'll do in a heartbeat," He chuckles.

"Don't tell her I told you, but she said she enjoys spending time with you," I whisper.

"I'm not surprised, we spend the majority of our time together in the library, and why wouldn't she love that?" Clancy laughs. I glance towards the window, streaks of the setting sunlight streaming through the window and giving the room a golden glow.

"I wish I could see the stars tonight," I sigh.

"So do I, Evanie," Clancy laments.

*

Eventually, I start to feel better. My sleep is no longer plagued by images of Domhnall and Donovan. I dream of stars, the patterns they make with their twinkling eyes that litter the sky. I'm still unable to get out of bed or be seen by anyone other than Clancy, Phye and Avie, but my body stops aching violently, more just gently. My head no longer spins when I read, so I am able to read some of Oralee's life to Clancy, rather than just him reading to me.

"I never knew Oralee was born on Holynest," Clancy tells me, nodding in approval.

"It was one of the things Hestia told Oralee when they arrived on the island the day she was chosen for light," I recall to him. "'*Welcome home, Oralee, we were all born here,*' she said, Oralee loved Hestia very dearly."

"Well, that fact is often documented in the chronicles, they had a very close relationship to the point that Hestia spent more of her time in the Eastern Isles than in Calia for a few years before her children were born," Clancy throws his hands up.

"Does Fire have a constellation story?" I ask eagerly.

"Blight, the candle, is their house constellation. It doesn't have the most exciting story in the world, but the basic story is that the only queen we've ever had of fire, Eira, used candles to light her palace during the winter, and one night her whole palace burnt down because of a fire and she banned candles altogether. The royal candlemaker from Calia went out of business because no one was allowed to use candles so he starved to death. His star is the fire's very tip. Every one of the stars is a candlemaker who died from the candle ban and the constellation reminds Calians of Eira's tyranny."

"Was she a tyrant?" I question.

"Absolutely not," Clancy confirms. "They just hated her because she was a woman and the Calians don't like having a woman in charge. They'll find any reason to avoid putting a woman in power and tearing her down if she falls into the position, I'm afraid."

Clancy looks up at me. "That reminds me," He says, raising a finger. "I made something for you, stay here."

Clancy stumbles out of the room before I have any time to question his abrupt departure, what he's leaving for and where it is. He returns clutching a roll of parchment tied with a rough length of string. Expectantly, he extends his hand and the roll for me to take it. Untying the knot, I unroll the thick paper across my covered lap.

I gasp.

"Did you make this?" I question in disbelief, staring down at the sight before me. Clancy has gifted me a scroll painted with every star in the night sky, every constellation and element annotated, the sky in the back ground the most glorious shade of blue.

"Well... yes," he admits, as though it's a crime. "When we were talking about how you wanted to see the stars but couldn't because you were bed-bound, I felt awful that I could gaze upon such beauty and you couldn't."

"I don't know what to say," I breathe, my fingers pulling themselves over the grooves made by Clancy's pen on the page. "I love it, thank you, so much."

"My pleasure," he replies.

Clancy and I talk for hours as I'm not tired and he says that he isn't either. He tells me about several of the constellation on the map, the stories behind them, the names of each of the stars and his favourites. We laugh about memories that seemed to have happened years ago, although they were just weeks in the past. We talk about his childhood, my childhood, our respective siblings, our love for them, our hatred of them and everything in between. We talk for so long, in fact, that it gets to the point where the light outside starts to shift into the dim moonlight of the tiny hours of the morning. A sharp knock sounds at my door.

"Evanie!" Seraphyna calls through the wood. "Wake up! The Morning Moon is rising and you can't miss it!" She opens the door apprehensively and silently at first, but then sees that my candle is still lit and Clancy still by my side.

"Oh, you're awake anyway," she sighs. "You'll have to go to the window."

"Are you sure that's wise, Phye?" Clancy asks nervously as Phyna goes to pull the covers off of my legs. The cool breeze hits them like a shock of cold water as she guides my feet onto the floor. It's been a week since I've properly left my bed, and my feet don't welcome the feeling of the cold tile against them. Phyna pulls me up, and I'm surprised by her strength, as she manages to guide me over to the small window of my room just in time.

The sight is unfamiliar but breath-taking. The silvery, crescent moon I'm used to hangs in one corner of the sky, letting off dim, milky moon beams into the night, reflecting off the ocean. However, in the other corner of the wide expanse of stars and darkness sits another milky crescent, a cream and lilac face hiding amongst twinkling diamonds. Its beams are almost as bright as the sun's, they reflect off every surface, the Morning Moon dazzling in the sky like a thousand Night Moons.

The light reflects in my eyes as the Morning Moon bathes amongst the stars.

PROMISE

"Erich?" I question, turning my head towards the door. Caspian shuts it behind him, sighing deeply. I can tell the news just by his expression. Opening my arms, I step over to him, meeting him in a desperate and sorrowful embrace. We sob together for what feels like hours, our eyes eventually running out of the bitter, melancholy tears they have shed so many of.

"I promise everything will be just fine," I lie. Caspian raises his head, his gleaming eyes meeting mine in pain and disbelief.

"He is -was- our son," he sobs, pressing his hands to his eyes.

"Don't," I plead, his words stabbing into my heart so sharply it makes me double over in pain.

"Why?" is all Caspian says in reply. He says it so quietly I barely hear him, but he shrinks in defeat. "Of all the people in the world, why did the stars choose him?"

I shrug lightly, sighing. Caspian stands to leave, but I don't try to stop him, as we both just need to be alone.

"Caspian," I alert him quietly, just as he goes to shut me in.

"Yes, dearest?" he replies.

"Don't do anything rash," I ask of him.

"I can't promise you anything, Oralee," he sighs.

"Caspian!" I shout, jumping to my feet and attempting to chase after him. "Caspian!"

I try with all my might to open the door, I even try magic, but nothing works at all. He's locked me in. He saw the star that painted the back of my hand.

Curses.

*

I'm still not allowed out of my room, but I'm all but healed and well now. Clancy keeps me company most of the time, and Avie and Phye are with me quite a lot of the day. Leora, who is also immune to Star Fever, sits with me often too, when Clancy, Phye and Avie are all occupied. As hard as I try, I'm still unable to get Conaire to even pluck up his courage to come in and see me.

"What are you reading?" Leora demands gruffly, sketching in the glorious evening light that pours through the window.

"A book about the stars," I reply, rifling through the remaining pages I have in the book.

"You read a lot," Leora sighs, attacking the page violently with her pencil. "For a handmaid."

"You talk back a lot for someone of your age," I shoot back. "And I'm not a handmaid, I'm a Baroness."

"Yes, but I'm a student," she replies. "And you're not even from here."

"Neither are you," I mumble.

"I know absolutely nothing about you, Baroness," Leora mentions after a while.

"Not very many people do know much," I respond distractedly.

"I worry that you and Lady Seraphyna resents me and Ulric," she admits.

"And why might that be?" I look up at her, she's staring out over the ocean and twiddling the pencil between her pale fingers.

"We're part of the reason the imperial academy fell," she laments.

"Certainly not," I assure her, standing to walk over and comfort her. "You and Ulric are the reason the house didn't fall, because at least we took in powerful and valid candidates on choice day, ones that further the house and not pull it back. Seraphyna would never resent someone for something they cannot control, and you and Ulric had no control over who the founders chose for Light."

"Thank you, Lady Evanie," she smiles.

Seb doesn't bother to knock, he just bursts in. His presence takes me by surprise, as I haven't seen him in just over two weeks. He hasn't shaved recently, there is the faintest sight of flaxen stubble on his face. His brown eyes are thrown wide in a state of half-madness.

"Seraphyna said that you're fine, you're healed, you're all good and not infected!" he laughs, throwing his arms wide for me to embrace him.

"Oh, Seb!" I exclaim, wrapping my arms around his torso and smiling up at his kind face.

"It feels like it's been forever," he sighs, and I nod in agreement.

"Seb?" I mumble.

"Yes?"

"You'd better shave that beard off before I see you next," I tell him, shooing him out of the door.

"Yes, ma'am," he chuckles.

I change from my nightdress into a light gown, and it's a relief to finally look presentable. I glide down to the great hall, everyone there to greet me. Lorna, Phye, Seb, Clancy, Avie, even Ulric, are all sitting around the banquet table in the great hall.

"Evanie!" Lorna exclaims, running towards me as I enter the hall. She embraces me happily, guiding me to the table and passing me a glass of wine. Raising it, I salute to them all before sitting opposite Clancy.

Leora follows me a few moments later, sitting next to Ulric.

"Where's Conaire?" She quizzes Clancy quietly, but I still hear her ask. Clancy shrugs, not saying anything.

"Why?" I question as she leans back over to talk to Lorna hastily.

"I wanted to talk to him," she replies swiftly, not looking me in the eye. "I'll tell you later," Leora finally looks up, her dewy, watery eyes meeting mine. I can sense she just wants to let whatever secret she has hidden inside her off her chest. I send her a small smile, which seems to calm her slightly.

"Phye?" I ask, glancing over at her briefly.

"Yes, Evanie?"

"Am I definitely cured?" I try to keep my voice low. "I still have this star on my hand," I hold my hand up, the back of it facing her observing eyes.

"No, you'll have that mark forever," she assures me. "You're absolutely fine, Evanie."

"But you had Star Fever when you were young and you don't have a mark," I say, furrowing my brow.

"The location of one's star mark is different for everyone, Evanie," she tells me, drawing back her hair from behind her ear. She turns her head sideways, showing off the black star resting alongside her hairline.

"Yours is a little more discreet," I sigh, raising a brow.

"Yet yours is noticeable, a clear battle mark that we can see," she offers. At this moment, Conaire enters, shuffling his feet along the floor irritably. He looks up at the table, our eyes meeting briefly. He doesn't call out my name in glee, running to me and muttering about how he missed me, he doesn't even smile at me or say 'hello', he just sighs deeply and takes a seat next to Clancy, staring at the empty gold platters pensively.

"No food?" he mumbles, staring at his twiddling thumbs.

"No, not quite yet, it's not even midday," Avie sighs. "Saints! You haven't seen your lady in what, two and a half weeks, and you don't even utter a word to her? Some man you call yourself."

"It's all right, Avie," I smile, holding my hand up to stop her yelling. I expect Conaire to finally muster his courage and look at me, but he just grimaces angrily and exhales.

"She's not my lady," he murmurs, picking up his knife from its place on the table, gripping it in his large palms worryingly tightly.

"You can say that to my face," I growl, raising my voice. "You can't hide from me forever, Conaire, I just want to talk."

He still refuses to raise his chin and I'm fighting the urge not to do it myself. Shaking my head, I sit back down, as, in my anger, I have somehow risen to my feet and bent over the table as though I'm interrogating Conaire.

"Conaire," Leora pipes up, looking shaken and taken aback. "Conaire, is there something you'd like to tell Evanie? Something you'd like to tell me?"

"Women," Conaire mutters under his breath, pushing the table away from him, crushing Seb, Phye and I in the process. He storms out of the great hall, the sound of his hobnail boots pounding against the flagstones echoing through my ears. I'm sure that if he could, Conaire would slam the door behind him for effect, but the doors are so large it takes two strong men, or someone with magic, to close one of the doors.

"Evanie, can I talk to you in the library for a minute?" Leora asks quietly, placing a hand on Ulric's shoulder, as he's quite shaken by the conflict.

"Of course," I reply, standing to follow her through the small door leading from the far wall of the great hall into the library. I slide the lock, opening the creaking wooden door as I do, and Leora steps in meekly.

"What's the matter?" I ask once the door has closed behind us.

"I didn't know you had a relationship with Conaire," Leora admits, whispering as she collapses back into an armchair behind her.

"What are you trying to tell me?" I demand, starting to become suspicious.

"I am not a good person, I never have been, I don't know if I ever will be, even though I am trying," she continues, not answering my question.

"Just get to the point!" I exhale in irritation.

"I think I'm with child," she blurts out, covering her mouth right after she says it. "Conaire's child."

"Leora, you're sixteen!" I exclaim. "Oh Saints, what are you going to do?"

"I don't know," she admits. "I really don't know."

"Why did you tell me first?" I ask, before realising. "Oh."

"That's why Conaire has been avoiding you, Evanie, because he felt guilty," she sobs, wiping her eyes with a handkerchief she pulls from her pocket. "I cannot tell you how sorry I am."

"It's not your fault," I growl, locking my jaw in anger and clenching my teeth so hard I'm surprised they don't shatter.

"You don't sound like you feel so," Leora whispers, reaching her hand out to place it on my arm in sympathy.

"Leora," I sigh, trying to be calm. "We all make mistakes, some bigger than others, but you aren't at as much fault as you think you are. You've obviously gotten yourself het up about the issue and into a right state."

"I cried for days," she discloses. "Conaire doesn't know, he doesn't need to know until I feel that it's appropriate."

"Of course," I agree. "But he doesn't deserve to walk free of responsibility or shame that he messed us both around and treated us like objects to be played with."

"I don't care if you confront him about that, I'm absolutely fuming as well, I never knew about you two," she shakes her head and throws her hands up in irritation.

"It never went very far," I tell her. "But it felt real, I suppose, although I was a fool to think it."

"We're talking about this like this incident happened months ago, but it was only two weeks," she concludes. "Please don't tell anyone about this, Baroness, I confessed to you in confidence."

"Your secret is safe with me," I assure her, winking slightly.

*

After dinner, I walk with Leora back to her house with Clancy, Avie and Lorna. Leora tells them about how Conaire has done us both wrong but doesn't go any further.

"Conaire and his women, eh?" Lorna sighs, rubbing her eyes with frustration. "That man can be impossible sometimes."

"Sometimes?" I question, which makes Leora chuckle lightly.

Clancy and Avie decide to head back to the palace to sit in the library all night which doesn't surprise me in the slightest, and Lorna says goodnight and shuts herself in her house for the rest of the evening. I stare at Conaire's door for a while after Leora goes in as well, debating whether to confront him now or whether it can wait until morning. My hand hovers over the knocker, my mind still debating with itself on what to do. Finally, my hand makes the decision for me. I beat the knocker against the wood several times, probably more violently than appropriate. Conaire's footsteps are apprehensive and angry, his pace sluggish. He answers the door with a beetroot face and an irritated expression. I frown as his eyes meet mine and he goes to shut the door.

"Don't you dare," I mutter under my breath, extending my trembling hand to stop the door from closing. I push it open so that our faces are level again. Taking a deep breath, I smile a phoney grin.

"Conaire," I sigh, "May I come in?"

"You're not going to let me say no," he replies grouchily, pulling the door open with his strong hands "So, by all means."

I step purposefully over the threshold, crinkling up my nose at the strong smell of ale. Conaire's house is so different to Clancy's it could be a different world entirely. There are no books in sight, not one. However, a bookshelf is pressed against the far wall, but it holds shelves and shelves of half-filled ale jugs and bottles of Karta. A messy blanket is laid out alongside a cluster of pillows that litter the floor under a dangerously loose hanging candle that's lit dimly and sits among several burnt holes and scorch marks on its surrounding wall area. The walls remain unpainted, the planks are incredibly grubby and every single item within the house has a thin layer of grime or dust coating it.

"I know what you did," I disclose quietly, waiting for my anger to bottle up inside me.

"Well, you see, I did several things over the past few days that you may be angry about, Evanie, so you'll have to be a little more specific," Conaire explains, slurring.

"You're drunk, aren't you?" I question, sitting him down against the wall, fuming.

"Well observed," he chuckles, reaching across the room for one of the several full jugs of ale. I knock it out of his hand immediately.

"Listen, Conaire, sober up, because I want you to remember everything I say," I sigh.

"Write it down if you're that desperate."

"I can come and wake you up at five in the morning if you continue to refuse to cooperate," I threaten.

"Fine," he gawks, standing up, dragging his back against the wall and placing his entire weight against the flimsy planks, making the hut shake as though there's an earthquake.

"I thought that you cared for me," I shake my head.

"I'm not denying that I do, Evanie!" Conaire shouts. "I suppose this is about Leora."

"Yes, it's about Leora!" I growl, pointing a judging finger at him. "I thought you cared about me, and then you refuse to see me because of the almost non-existent risk I was hoping you'd take to see me, so that I could see you, so that you could know I was alive!"

"It just... it... uh... it hurt seeing you ill," he stutters, making up excuses.

"Don't play that card with me, Conaire," I huff, thrusting my finger further towards him. "Not only did you disrespect the feelings I falsely believed were there, you have practically broken Leora."

"She's at fault, too!" he insists, throwing his arms up above his shoulders in frustration. "She accepted my advances."

"She wouldn't have done so if she knew about us," I point out. "Honestly, you can't go on like this, thinking that treating other people this way is acceptable,"

"And since when did you have the right to tell me what to do?" he questions furiously.

"Since you took my heart and shattered it," I spit, turning to leave.

"Evanie, wait," Conaire pleads as I go to open the door. I don't answer nor look back at him, though I know the look on his face will be pained and desperate.

"At least now I know what a broken heart feels like," I reply sadly.

"I love you, Evanie," he whispers.

"I wish I could say the same, Conaire," I breathe, shutting the door of his house behind me.

The muddy ground below my feet is now sodden as the rain and lightning pour down on the grass. My hair becomes more and more matted and damp, but I stop caring as the only pain I feel is the one stabbing from the inside of my heart. Sinking down against the side of the house, I pull my knees up to my chest and sob into my skirt. How dare he. *How dare he.*

"Evanie?" someone questions through the darkness. Through the dark veil of night, a hand sticks out, pleading for me to take it. I wrap my fingers around the helper's palm, pulling myself to my feet and wiping my eyes with the hem of my sleeve.

"Clancy," I sigh, catching the glimmer of his deep brown eyes. Their caring depth comforts me.

"Seraphyna sent me out here to get you," he explains, wrapping his cloak around my shoulders.

"Why?" I question.

"You'll see," he sighs, but the words aren't said with a smirk or with cunning, they're said with apprehension and worry.

The library's table is laden with scrolls and maps pinned down with golden pins in the corners. Seraphyna is resting her head in her pasty hands and sighing, analysing the table before her. Lorna is scribbling more furiously than usual and the professor is pacing the far edge of the library frantically.

"Ah, Evanie," Phye nods, not looking up when Clancy and I enter the room.

"Where's Seb?" I ask.

"Sending word to Old Davisham," she replies distractedly, pulling one of the books closer to her, tracing a few lines of words that pattern the yellowing pages.

"Word of what?" I question, alarmed and panicked.

"We received a tip-off from a source at the Court of Fire that Domhnall is planning on storming the Eastern Isles and left two weeks ago," Phye sighs, becoming more and more worked up by the minute. "No, this one's no use. Clancy, do you have a new copy of *Frigates and Galleys*?"

"I'm not familiar with that one," Clancy laments, which surprises me as Clancy knows all the books. Maybe it's just the pressure putting a strain on his memory.

"I think I have one, my lady," Ethelde offers, producing a tiny key and unlocking her personal library door, which not even Clancy is allowed in.

"Thank you, professor," Phye replies. "Also, in the letter of tip-offs, several other things were mentioned, like how Aidan's Flagship abandoned a Myriean runaway on Holynest because she had Star Fever."

"Oh," I nod, taking a seat as Clancy does, moving his head around, trying to catch a glimpse into the Professor's library as she searches for Seraphyna's required book.

"And we discovered why they were in Aella's ocean territory, too," Seraphyna continues.

"Really?" I widen my eyes in wonder, as I really have been wondering why they were casually gliding through the water off the coast of Olympia.

"They were running away," Seraphyna smirks wickedly, her eyes alight with well-meaning mischief.

"Why would they be doing that?" Clancy questions, shutting his notepad abruptly.

"Uprisings," Seraphyna explains simply. "Uprising after uprising. I knew that the Calians hated Aidan, but I had no idea that they wanted him dead. They tried to put someone else on the throne. They plotted to put their favourite member of Aidan's court on the throne of Fire."

Ethelde emerges from her library, shutting the splintering door behind her with a defiant thud. She brandishes a shiny, newly covered and silver-gilded book at Phye.

"Who might that be, my Lady?" Ethelde asks, reading Seraphyna's neat cursive from over her shoulder.

"Your daughter, Ethelde," Seraphyna tells her matter-of-factly. Ethelde takes a step back, mouth agape, eyes wide open.

"*Eithne?*" She questions. "No, not Eithne."

"The tip-offs also said that Eithne gave birth under the light of the Morning Moon to a boy and a girl. They are all doing well and are currently residing on a ship off of the coast of Shee. Aidan has returned to Calia's capital but refuses to join Domhnall in his fight against me," Seraphyna explains.

"Honestly, you'd think Domhnall would force him to fight," Lorna sighs, throwing page of her notebook she tore out over her shoulder.

"Aidan is nothing more than a coward," Seraphyna tells her. "He reaches for his neck before reaches for his heart or his hilt."

"And is Daileass going to be here as well?" Clancy questions.

"I'm not sure," Seraphyna admits. "But I have a feeling that tensions between Domhnall and Daileass could mean that they refuse to work together, even against a common enemy."

"But even without Daileass' help, Domhnall's army by far outmatches ours," Clancy points out. "There's no hope."

"Of course there is hope," Seraphyna smiles. "There is always hope."

*

We spend a long night planning for any forthcoming battles and receiving messages from Aella and Herminia. Several times in the early hours of the morning Seraphyna, Seb and I have to walk down to the beach to receive the messages transported by the mermaids that live by the dock. It gets to sunrise, and the adrenaline of the situation means I am still raring to go at any moment. Seraphyna and I sit on a low ruined wall at the back of the castle.

"Seraphyna?" I ask quietly.

"Yes, Evanie?"

"Can I confide in you?" I say, turning my head away from her as I ask.

"I would've hoped you didn't need to ask. I'm your friend, of course, I'm always here for you," she replies kindly, placing her hand on mine, which is resting on my knee awkwardly.

"I have a struggle. I'm trying to choose between two men," I tell her, not specifying who the men are.

"Clancy and Conaire?" she guesses. I nod in embarrassment.

"When we were in Olympia, Conaire and I shared a... moment. We kissed and I really started to fall for him. The problem is, Clancy had been so nice to me up to that point and I really thought that maybe there was something between us, but then I focused on Conaire,. Then, he developed a relationship with Leora behind my back, and my heart broke, but that only makes me think that actually I did love Conaire. I cared about him enough for his betrayal to break my heart, after all. But Clancy's always there for me, always listening, always caring, but he's never struck me as exciting," I explain desperately.

"And now you're stuck with the age-old dilemma. Brains versus brawn," Seraphyna says, tilting her head and sighing sympathetically. There is a long pause as we stare out at the sunrise and sit in silence.

"You look at them as equals," she points out after a while, "But I can tell you love one more than the other,"

"I…" I stutter, hesitating. "Well…"

"The question is which," Phyna finishes.

"I don't know," I give in, shaking my head in fervent despair. "I really don't know."

"I think you do," she concludes. "But I'm not going to tell you who it is, because you'll just disagree with me and go off with the other."

"I won't," I promise. "I value your wisdom, Phye, please tell me."

"I don't need to," she smiles knowingly and hops down from the wall, "you'll know eventually."

"You know me better than I know myself," I lament as I step down from the wall and start to follow her inside.

"Oralee? Yes," Phye confirms. "Evanie? No."

"I barely know this side of me, Phyna, I just… I'm not Evanie Harley anymore, I'm Baroness Evanie of the Unknown Realms, Mistress Oralee of the Eastern Sun, I have moulded myself around this realm and I refuse to look behind me," I tell her.

"Lorna?" Seraphyna calls into the palace as the back door closes behind us.

"Phye, I think you'll want to see this," Conaire runs in an alarmingly fast pace down the stairs, not daring to look me in the eye. Engulfing me in one of his strong, guiding arms, he leads me to the window that looks out over the meadow.

Darkness fleets towards the palace so slowly it's barely moving. Whether it be in the form of twenty-thousand or so men marching in synchronisation, the black saddled mares and stallions in a line straighter than the soldiers or the standard bearing Domhnall's arms, it is fairly obvious to the three of us watching in horror.

"I'll need a General," Seraphyna utters quietly after pausing in shock and thought. Naturally, Conaire straightens his posture, smiling as he expects the title to be his as student of wielding, despite having not cast a spell in a year and a half.

"I'm at your service, my lady," he announces proudly, a thin smile working its way across his face even after the shock and worry we're all enduring.

"Thank you, Conaire," Phye replies, distracted and still staring straight ahead over the meadow in terror. "Fetch the General's standard for Evanie, will you?"

I turn in mild disbelief to Phyna and then Conaire. Phyna's expression still does not change. On the contrary, Conaire's does, drastically as well. His face is warped into the ugly offspring of shock, hate, embarrassment and anger, first towards Phye and then directed entirely to me. For someone who told me they loved me yesterday, he stares at me with such loathing I feel small as a candle flame.

"But, Seraphyna," he argues.

"I'll have none of it, Conaire," Seraphyna finally faces us both. "Ah, Lorna, good."

"I gather you've seen-" Lorna starts as she approaches us from the library.

"Get me Sebastian," Phye orders, gesturing up the stairs for Lorna to leave. Lorna nods understandingly, running up the stairs towards Seb's room. Conaire lingers awkwardly, mumbling curses under his breath.

"Conaire," I urge. "Go, please."

Staring at me in loathing, he saunters away, pouting. I sigh loudly at Seraphyna once he's out of sight.

"Thank you," I nod at her in gratitude.

"You really think I would've chosen Conaire?" she asks me, raising a questioning brow.

"Sebastian, at least," I admit, shrugging.

"As much as I love Seb, you are the best for the job of General, and I hope you won't disappoint me, Baroness," Phye smiles knowingly at my nervousness.

"I have something for you," Phyna tells me, leading me towards the library.

"You're not worried about the battle?" I question, alarmed.

"It's not an attack," Seb intervenes, gliding down the stairs, pausing in the library doorway to kiss Phye on the cheek. "It's a siege."

"Right," Phye confirms, "If they were preparing for battle, they'd have their cavalry at the front, not their archers. They're starving us out."

"Why?" I ask.

"To see us dance," she smirks.

"Well, if they came for a show," I conclude, "we'd better give them one."

"Most certainly," she agrees.

No one is in the library as we enter, so I assume Clancy and the professor have finally tired themselves out and retired to bed.

"What is it you have to show us?" Seb asks, turning the corner of bookshelves as Phye leads us to a dark corner of the library.

"You'll see," Phye laughs knowingly as she reaches into her pocket of her skirt and pulls out a key. She digs the old, rusty thing into the lock of a cupboard suspended from the ceiling by ropes.

"Melaina gave me these the day I was chosen for Light. Domhnall had them in his possession even though they were supposed to belong to Light and whoever is leading Light, so maybe Melaina knew something I didn't on that day. As she handed them to me before I left for Holynest, she said, 'Only you can strike down your only foe'," she reminisces, prying the creaking, mahogany doors of the cupboard open. As they open, they start to reveal a set of three magnificent weapons. A sword made out of the shiniest silver and purest gold and opals I've ever seen. A bow strung with what looks like spun silver paired with a leather quiver full of shimmering arrows tipped with silver heads and ended with crisp, white feathers. The last weapon is a beautiful dagger with a hilt more bejewelled than a queen's neck. I trace my fingers over the hilt of the sword, the gold weaving patterns of fireworks around the stones.

"They're beautiful," I gasp, retracting my hand away from the cabinet as Phyna uproots the sword from its place in a plume of dust.

"Ancient, too," she tells me, pointing the hilt in my direction. "They have an extensive history in the house.

The sword, the Sun Sword, was used by Oralee in all of her battles and conflicts throughout her life. The Star Knife only joined the Sun Sword when it was given by the Duchess of Air at the time to Oralee. The Moonbeam Bow was forged later than the sword but was used by my own mother as she grew up on this island," she smiles, running her index finger down the string of the bow.

"You never talk about her," Seb points out.

"I never really knew her," she admits sadly, "She died when I was three, and then I was shipped off to Shee to live in Domhnall's court under the care of Melaina. She was the one who raised me and tried to keep my mother's memory alive. From what I know about my mother, she was the last of my father's six wives, and she was his wife at the same time as Adrienne and Tess, Domhnall and Aidan's mothers. Her name was Arista and she was born on Greater Isle, her mother was of Darkness and lived in Shee, but her father was of Light and so she lived here. When her choice day came, she was chosen for Darkness and then married my father not long after. They say Domhnall killed her at the same time as his own mother and my father."

"At least Melaina kept her memory alive," I offer.

"Melaina is the closest to a mother I will ever have," Phye shrugs. "I was confused when she gave me these before we left for Holynest. Domhnall never knew of course, but I was young and attracted to anything pretty, so I accepted them gratefully, not knowing what important relics they were,"

"She gave them to whom she knew would become their rightful protector," I smile.

"I suppose so, yes," Phyna nods, shrugging as she brandishes the Sun Sword at me. "Go on, take it."

I reach out and grab the hilt, the weight feeling perfect and the shape of it fitting wonderfully in my palm. I go to turn it around in my hand until I look down and it's not my hand clutching the sword at all.

Small drops of my blood splatter onto the battlefield as I wipe it off my forehead. Swinging the Sun Sword violently at those in front of me, I manoeuvre the reins to avoid the cannonballs that fly in the direction of my troops.

"Ledan, retreat!" I yell at Ledan and he nods. I watch as the few soldiers not lying dead on the ground or practically the same turn away from the battle and start running back towards the palace, now wounded more than myself, bearing many gaping holes and crumbling gashes. Caspian still sits on his white stallion, stationed next to me.

"Go," I urge, shouting as he is revealed further by the retreating men.

"No, I'm staying with you!" he insists as his horse rears up on its hind legs as Donovan's army advances further towards us.

"Fine," I sigh, not having the effort nor time to argue with him. "But be careful!"

The Dukes of Water and the Duke of Fire, Hestia's tyrant of a husband, advance at a slower pace to Donovan, who trots along calmly a few dozen yards ahead of his army.

"Oralee, Highest Lady of Light, we have come to claim your territory and the Sun Crown in the name of the noble houses of Darkness, Water and Fire. Surrender the Sun Crown and the Eastern Isles and you shall not

die," Donovan declares loudly as the Dukes trot up to where he is sitting high on his saddled mare. The one he raised from a foal, Mika, who he found wounded in the royal woods one winter's eve some ten years ago. His eyes were as aglow with mirth and laughter then as they are now, although now, it's a different kind of laughter. The evil cackle of a tyrant.

"Never!" I swear, placing my scarred hand over my heart, "If I die, I will not have died in vain!"

"Just try and stop me!" he snarls, steadying his horse.

"So be it then!" I announce when Donovan and his army refuse to budge. I swing the Sun Sword in the air and watch as the sunlight catches on the silver effortlessly. A Valkyrie soars ahead, crying out to friends. The Duchess of Air, I see, is amongst them and clinging to the mane of a griffin that bows its head meekly. Out of the corner of my eye, a dark bloodwood and silver arrow shoots through the gap between Caspian and me. The Duke of Earth heads a crew of rouge centaurs and wood nymphs, none of which I recognise, until a familiar face peeks its way from the front of the crowd.

"Luke," the word passes across my lips like a shadow, and I almost believe I'm hallucinating for a moment. But no, he's there, in full glory, ready to fight alongside me. The Duchess of Air lands her griffin so gracefully it's as though she's riding a swan. Wisps of golden locks flow behind her and as she lands it floats above her head in a plume of shimmering ribbons. On her belt is a minute scabbard, so faded in colour it could only house one thing, the star knife. As Luke and the Duke of Earth approach her, she tosses the covered *dagger their way, Luke catching it, close-fisted in mid-air.*

"The battle has begun," Ledan whispers as he canters back up to my side. My army is once again behind me, ready for the second attack.

"Indeed it has, Ledan, it certainly has," I reply, smiling over the meadow, raising the Sun Sword in the air as the light beams out over my army. My hand drops to the side of my horse, but as I stare at it, it's not my hand.

It's mine.

Gasping for breath, I swing violently on my feet and blink vigorously. Seb takes my hand nervously.

"Don't," I plead, raising my hand to thank him as I release my grip. "Phye, I've touched this before, I mean Oralee has. There was a battle and I-"

"The Battle of the Six Houses, about ten years after Oralee was chosen for Light and a few months after her son was born. Light's most desperate hour," Phye tells me, "Yet also its finest."

"Light won?" I ask, amazed, after seeing how outnumbered the army was.

"Don't be so amazed, Evanie, the Faithful houses had both Luke and Oralee during that time, and now, we have you."

"What difference do I make?" I question.

"More than you know," Seraphyna laughs, "So, Evanie, will you lead light to another victory?"

I look around the library, at the books decreeing Oralee as 'the Great' and a hero. I stare at the portraits of the leaders on the far wall, at how they look to me for salvation. I look around at this realm, the realm that isn't mine, the one I must save, the realm I love so dearly.

Valiantly, I slam my sword into its ornate scabbard, the clink of metal a soothing assurance of balance.

"Where do I start?"

*

Seraphyna leads us down to the stables, propped up against the palace and collapsing slowly into the dry ground. Rows and rows of stalls are empty, it's only when we reach a cluster of stalls holding beautiful horses that Seraphyna pauses and turns to me kindly.

"Melie should serve you well," Seraphyna assures me, opening the gate of stables and stroking the head of a tall, exquisite mare, obviously built to carry soldiers through a battle.

"Thank you, Phye," I smile, brushing my calloused fingers over Melie's mane of chestnut hair.

"And Sebastian, Blight will carry you truly through this." Phyna promises, gesturing to Melie's stable mate, another chestnut horse, a stallion this time, with a white crest on its forehead.

"Thank you," Seb says weakly, embracing Seraphyna passionately. "Be careful, my darling," he whispers in her ear.

"I will be," she promises him, placing her trembling, pale hands on his chest as he rests his forehead on her left shoulder.

"Phye, he's here," Lorna pants, running into the stables. "They're here."

"Evanie, Seb, mount your horses," Seraphyna murmurs calmly

"Oh," I remember, reaching to return the Sun Sword to Phyna.

"No, keep it," Seraphyna insists. "You'll need it." Slinging the scabbard back over my shoulder, I nod and climb on to Melie's back.

"Lorna, I need you to find Ethelde, Leora and Ulric. Ask Ethelde to escort them to safety. If Leora insists on fighting, let her, but not Ulric. He has to be hidden," Seraphyna instructs opening the gate with a flick of her hand.

"What of Conaire? Clancy?" Lorna questions.

"They're men now, and we're women, they too can fight, live or die, win or lose, just like the rest of us."

*

I ride next to Seb, him and I both trailing at Seraphyna's heels. She looks amazing in battle armour, long hair braided down her back like a ladder from her horse all the way to the rim of her silver helmet that weaves its way in thick vines of metal and thin streaks of dust around her head in a shape more like a crown than armour.

The army of Darkness sits in uniform rows and columns patiently in front of the palace. Domhnall stands in front of it all, not even on his horse. His General, Darsey, is mounted on a beautiful horse similar to Melie, chestnut in colour, tall and regal.

Conaire and Clancy are stood by the walls and Lorna guards the drawbridge. Ethelde must be halfway to Greater Isle with Ulric and Leora, who decided not to fight, as I'm sure she's thinking about the baby.

Everyone behind us, including the Earls and Counts, their wives and even some of their sons, watch anxiously as Seraphyna rides closer and closer to where Domhnall's army still stands and waits, silent but ready to kill at any moment.

"What is she doing?" I whisper to Seb, but he shrugs and carries on trotting behind Phye.

Sliding regally from her horse's back to touch the soft ground with her riding boots, she still wears the clothes suitable to that of a royal, a long train of fabric trailing behind, leaving a gap at the sides and front, for where her riding trousers and boots are visible.

"You always wanted anything I had, I suppose, brother," Seraphyna snarls, stationed but seven feet away from where Domhnall is, arms crossed and smirking as though he's already won. "I have the attention of Melaina, all of a sudden, you want it too, I have a room overlooking the barren passage, now you want that room instead," she pauses, waiting for a reaction that is not given. "I have the Eastern Isles and the Sun Crown and you want even those trivial things. I'm flattered you think so highly of me!"

"This is not about flattery, baby sister," Domhnall sneers. "This is war, go home. Gather your silly scriptures and your people and leave. Do this and no one important will die."

"Everyone who belongs to my house is important in my eyes," Seraphyna shoots back and it makes me sit a little taller on Melie's back.

"Well, aren't you good at playing lady mother of light?" Domhnall laughs. His cackle is matched by a few chuckles from Darsey and the front archers.

"You will never have the Sun Crown, or the Eastern Isles, or the title of king. I will die fighting against you,"

Seraphyna insists and Seb flinches uncomfortably at the mention of Seraphyna's death.

"So be it," Domhnall declares. "Darsey, set up camp here and tell Hiram to prepare the army for a prolonged stay, we may be setting up camp here for some time."

"W... what?" Seraphyna stutters, fear flashing across her eyes.

"I declare this hold under siege. Greater Isle will be too if you do not surrender within 70 hours." Domhnall informs us all, declaring the fact to Light and to his army, with an eloquent flourish of his hand.

"We will fight you," Phyna growls, one shaking hand on the Moonbeam Bow, hanging from her belt, and another being brandished violently at Domhnall.

"With what? Your army of who, your handmaid, a foolish boy stupid enough to be in love with you, your ancient professor, a handful of Earls, the students, with as much experience as some hawks, and you, little sister, seventeen, in love, as much wit as our father, I'll give you that, but no battle skills, no charm and worst of all, leader of a dying House," Domhnall tests, bending Seraphyna in all directions to see if she'll break. Despite all the turning, twisting, pulling and pushing, she doesn't even crack.

"70 hours?" Seraphyna raises an eyebrow calmly. "I'll see you then."

"To surrender?" Domhnall quizzes.

"To see you die," she replies matter-of-factly, turning to walk away.

"I think that's where you're mistaken, little sister," Domhnall tells her. She stops dead in her tracks, stands up tall and whips back round to face him. She has cracked.

"I am never mistaken!" she yells. "I am Seraphyna Lux, Highest Lady of the House of Light, protector of the Eastern Isles and holder of the Sun Crown. I hold a power you have not cared to know, and that will be your downfall. You will have to drain the rivers and seas, watch the sky fall in and see the sun shine at night to watch me surrender. You will never wear the Sun Crown, you have enough shiny things already, you vulture." Seraphyna's quick wit and lightning remarks reduce Domhnall to be able to stay no more, he just stands there, small as Seraphyna's fear, silenced not by his sister's almighty magic, but simply her humble words.

Seraphyna walks back in on foot, her horse trotting back automatically behind her, back into the Palace. Seb and I turn back as well. Clancy and Conaire run in as Lorna lowers the portcullis and shuts against Domhnall and his army.

*

"Why? Why of *all* days is it today?" Seraphyna rants, pacing up and down her study.

"Phyna, dearest, calm down, please," Seb coaxes, kissing her forehead.

"How can I be calm when there are 3000 death soldiers outside my palace walls, threatening to murder my people?" She shrieks but still does not reject his gentle, supporting grip on her shoulders. "Today is either the day I die a failure or rise as a mistress of light, defying expectations that have been placed upon my house. You have to promise me something, both of you."

"Anything," I assure her, and I know I mean it.

"Anything for you," Seb promises, and I know he isn't lying either.

"If I die," she starts. Seb flinches again. "*If* I die, you have to take care of my people. Evanie, I declare you, my dear friend and Baroness of the Unknown Realms, my heir and you, Sebastian, my love, my dearest, as her heir after her. This is my will, not to be contradicted by anyone. I plan to live a long and happy life, but if anything happens to me, I dread to think, promise me you won't abandon my house and my people."

"Never," I say, the word making a smaller sound in the room we stand in but it takes significant effect in my mind. I have responsibilities now.

"Don't die," Seb asks of her simply, he takes her shoulders so vigorously it's almost like he's shaking her. "Please, Phye, darling, don't."

"I cannot promise anything, dearest," Phyna sighs sadly, hanging her head. "I love you, Seb, more than I thought I could ever love someone, but not light, not darkness, not even my love for you can prevent death or reverse its sting. Death is a most unhealable wound."

"Don't talk like that!" Seb insists, shaking his head angrily. "Please, I can't bear it." Quieter this time. I know that I can't bear these words either, though, and we're all tearing up.

"If... it's an if," Phye reminds us. "It's an 'if' not a 'when' just for now, I will be as careful as I can be, as long as you both are. I love you both, and you are worth infinitely more to me and the House of Light alive than dead."

"So are you," I tell her.

"And I know that," she confirms. "But enough talk of life and death, we must plan for it. We pledge our allegiance to each other today, each of us to one another. I promise that I am loyal to you both, if you both promise you are to me."

"I promise," I say.

"I promise," Seb repeats.

"I promise," Seraphyna finishes as we sit around the council table. The chairs are dusty, the map of the table printed on an ancient roll of silk, like a tapestry or a garment. During the strategy planning, we shoot concise looks at each other which carry clear messages. Loyalty. It's a simple thing, but we've promised and pledged it true. There are no empty promises here.

SUNRISE

"So, Evanie, you'll ride with Earl Luz and Count Ilene to here-" she points to a spot marked red on her map. "-You'll only have Ilene and Luz with you but they're good archers and swordsmen. You shouldn't be seen if you leave by one of the West Keep's passages and go straight to Hornblower Cave. Stay there for a few minutes, time enough to check for hoof marks, if they're there, head on to Old Oak, where hopefully Herminia and Dagan will be."

"Of course," I confirm, "and if not?"

"Wait where you are, Herminia will find you some way or another," Phyna assures me. Nodding, I glance back at Luz and Ilene who are standing silently in the corner of the study behind me, amongst rolled-up maps and cobwebs. They nod also.

"Conaire, Clancy, you will take my flagship, the *Vercinii*, to Greater Isle. Domhnall shouldn't have reached there by now. If you leave quickly, you can rally the men and women who want to fight. Those too young and those not willing to fight will be taken to a stronghold to the very north of the island by Ethelde. Do not force anyone to fight," she explains, straining the last sentence. "Understand?"

"Yes, your lightest," Conaire says.

"It will be a dangerous job, I hope you know," Seraphyna admits sadly, dipping her head slightly.

"Of course," Clancy nods. Conaire and Clancy look at each other nervously and start to walk out of the room. I grab Conaire's shoulder and gaze into his focused eyes.

"Don't do anything stupid," I murmur, my strong defiant grip on his armour holding him back.

"Conaire," Clancy calls from where he has paused in the doorway.

"I won't," Conaire says hesitantly, although I know he's lying. He's too much of a hero to be sensible.

I nod emptily, letting go of him. I don't need to say anything to Clancy, I know he won't do anything stupid. All I do is stare him straight in his brown eyes. And mouth:

"Good luck."

"You too," he replies silently, crossing his fingers. I watch him leave out of the door with Conaire and my heart sinks.

"Wait," I cry, reaching my hand out towards them both. I don't know which one I'm calling to.

"Yes?" They both answer, replying and turning in perfect and eerie synchronisation.

"Nothing." I shake my head, just happy to see their faces one last time. I purse my lips, watching them go. They're gone. I may never see either of them again.

"Are you scared they won't come back?" Seb asks me as the soft thud of the door shutting us in echoes throughout the study chamber.

"Of course I am," I tell him, pausing in reflection. "But I'm almost as worried only one will, for some reason."

"Why's that?" he questions.

"Because.... Well, I'm afraid I'll realise I love one more and then the one I don't is the one who comes back and bears the news of the other's death." I explain desperately, almost drumming the fact into myself, instead of telling it to Seb.

"Then the question is simple, which one do you love more?" Seb asks.

"That's the problem, Seb, I don't know!" I exclaim, louder than I was expecting. Each person who was looking down at work or plans looks up and towards me. I redden swiftly to the degree of an unpleasantly bright crimson.

"You need to ask yourself that question," Seb reminds me. "Which one do you love more?"

"Saints, I'm sure Oralee never had it this bloody hard!" I say agonisingly, placing my heavy head in my hands.

"Oralee the Great was killed by her brother, lost her son and stepdaughter to Star Fever and had to watch her sister be slaughtered by her sister's husband. Her husband died under *mysterious circumstances* so, I think we can quite easily say that even with your trials, Evanie, few people had it harder than Oralee the Great," Seraphyna intervenes calmly, not raising her voice or drastically changing her tone throughout her explanation of the suffering of Oralee.

"Well, I'm sure she never had to make a decision like this!" I conclude.

"You don't have to choose," Lorna reminds me, "be an old maid with thirteen cows who wields oak twigs at children for all we care, but we just need to focus on this now, alright?" She gestures to the strategy map she's working on, laid out on the table and dotted with various unknown marks. Shouldn't Conaire, as a student of wielding, be doing this?

"Sorry, Lorna," I sigh, taking my seat back at the table.

"Right, Evanie, when the clock strikes 10, you'll be leaving with Ilene and Luz. Remember, Hornblower Cave, 10 minutes, hoof tracks then Old Oak," Seraphyna reminds me.

I nod and put my hand tentatively on Seb's shoulder.

"Are you coming with me, Luz and Ilene?" I ask him quietly and privately.

"I'm staying here," he admits, almost ashamed of the fact. "I hope you understand."

"Of course I do," I smile, trying to tell him everything will be fine, although I hardly believe that myself. "Someone needs to stay here to take care of the palace... and Seraphyna."

"I'm just glad you understand. I don't want to be thought of as a coward," he replies.

"Just be safe," I ask of him.

"Only if you are," he promises. Just as I reach out to embrace him, the clock shifts and chimes 10 times, deep and echoing sounds.

"That's my cue," I grimace, reluctantly letting go of Seb. "I'll see you later."

Seb sighs worriedly and clings on to me.

"All I'm doing is going to get Herminia," I tell him. "And, hopefully Lorna will have Aella and Corentin by the time I get back, too."

"Alright, see you then, I suppose."

*

The weather is peculiar today, it's not that sunny but it's uncomfortably warm and I sweat continuously under my thick hooded cloak. However, a breeze flows through the woods every now and again, but it's rare and carries all sorts of dust through the gaps in the trees. The ride to Hornblower Cave is easy but nerve-racking, a clear and trodden path made by the horses guiding our way. We stop suddenly when we arrive in front of the cave, a large open stone structure with all sorts of flora sprouting from the top, sprawling out in all directions, some even covering the gaping entrance.

Luz and Ilene dismount their horses, their heavy tread making miniscule rustling sounds as they pass over the carpet of dead leaves lining the forest floor. I don't leave Melie's back, feeling as though something isn't quite right, as though someone is watching me. I can feel a thousand eyes burning into the back of my head, and the sensation is unsettling.

"No footprints or hoof marks here, Baroness," Luz tells me, creating a gap in the auburn blanket to check. Ilene moves to the edges of the glade, the parts free of leaves, where hoof marks could be clearly seen if there were any.

"General…" Ilene calls frightfully, brushing a single brown leaf away with his sword. "Look at this."

Cautiously, I dismount Melie and step over to where Ilene is standing. He's quite young and obviously frightened and chilled to the bone. Luz is much older, knocking on sixty, I suppose, and looks quite unfazed by the situation.

"What is it, Florean?" Luz asks.

"Look!" Ilene cries once more. A circle has been traced in the mud, filled in with a red ink that looks too much like blood not to be.

"Darkness is in these woods," Luz mumbles, frightened. I pull the hood of my cloak further over my head,

"Run," I order, "Forget the horses, if they have any sense, they'll follow. Run!"

We all shoot off at full speed, Ilene and I both have athletic builds so we move at a fast pace, but Luz's age hinders his speed. I feel terrible, but I daren't look back. As we continue to run for our lives, I hear a horn, low and fierce. Ilene, Florean I hear as his name, stops dead in his tracks suddenly. I pull his arm, trying to get him to move. I look down to his feet and drop Ilene's hand, shocked.

Slow, clanking chains of black metal wind up around his legs, over his riding boots and soft leather trousers. I'm extremely surprised Ilene's legs aren't ripped from his body. He is dragged down by the chains, not just to his knees of the ground but through the soil so all that is left on the surface of the dewy leaves is a pool of his claret blood in an odd, rigid shape so that it resembles a piece of burnt parchment. Miraculously, the red colour of the pool fades into the yellow of the autumn leaves and then into a cream parchment. Cautiously, so fearful that I may suffer the same fate as poor Ilene, I bend down. I don't need to pick up the note, I can see the writing easily, red, but too bright to be blood red. The words are chilling themselves, simple handwriting and simple words.

Look up – D

I probably shouldn't look up, but I do and by the Saints, the sight is awful!

I thought Ilene had been dragged through the ground to the boiling centre of the earth, but here he is, hanging by the same, black iron chains that dragged him under the ground, from a tree up above. The chains are thick and long, so that Ilene's lifeless, booted feet are handing just a few inches above Luz's head.

"By Oralee," Luz exclaims, trembling ever so slightly with the shock of the sight above him. "Just a boy."

"Stop," I hold my hand out as I notice Ilene's body is swinging violently.

The chains break in a great scream of iron and sparks. Ilene, a perfect 'O' of shock still painted on his face, falls to the ground like a falcon, landing on the leaves in a position like a man lies in his coffin.

I can barely cope with any more horrors and am so scared something else extraordinarily evil will happen, but the sight now before my eyes is a gentle one, surprisingly.

Vines, dainty green ones weave their way prettily around Florean's body. They make patterns in between his cold fingers like attractive spiderwebs lacing his hands.

I hear faint footsteps and the crunch of leaves. Swiftly, I draw my sword, again feeling comfortable with the sword in my hand. Probably because I've held it so much.

I've held it twice, what am I talking about?

More like a hundred.

"Show me your colours."

I am held by a powerful force, so strong I don't bother to resist it. A woman with floor-length hair like chocolate and chestnut, who I can barely make out from underneath her cloak, stands defensively in front of me and a man with a dark complexion and eyes like a night sky contently watches an arrow in his bow, ready to release at any moment.

"Colours?" I question. I cannot recognise the man or woman at the distance I am away from them and through the shadow of my cloak's hood.

"Your sword, General, uncloak yourself and show Lady Herminia your sword," Luz tells me urgently, staring alarmed at an arrow being aimed at his head. I am released from the force, letting my hood down and smiling at Herminia. She's changed much since I last saw her in the summer. It's like she changes with the seasons. To be honest, it wouldn't surprise me if she did.

As I draw my sword and lay it over my hands as though I was going to knight her, Herminia gasps and inspects the sword carefully.

"Is that…" Herminia asks, reaching out towards me apprehensively.

"Yes, this is the Sun Sword," I confirm, as Herminia traces her fingers over the jewelled hilt.

"You must be a special one, Lady Evanie of the Unknown Realms, my sister must know that if she gave you this sword. It only agrees to fight in the hand of certain people, and it looks like you are one of them," she tells me. Her voice is deeper and less excited than I'm used to. The autumn has changed her. That or she knows what a serious situation this is.

"We must move quickly, Lady Herminia, there are men of Darkness in this forest," I urge. Herminia nods, signalling for her archers and Dagan to follow her.

"I'm sorry," Herminia sighs, "This is all we have." She gestures to the small crowd of her archers and their two snow-white stallions. "We had another boat but it never left the harbour in Berr, Water's ships were on the horizon and I told them not to leave. I'm so sorry."

"It's not your fault, you were thinking of your people. Seraphyna will understand, I know she would do the same," I assure her. At this, Herminia seems to brighten a bit. She nods at me thankfully and mounts her horse.

"I'm so sorry about the boy," Dagan laments, stopping me before I mount Melie once again.

"Ilene? Yes, a cruel death," I agree, stroking Melie's chestnut mane. "Thank you for burying him," I can only assume that it was Herminia or Dagan who created Ilene's living coffin after his cruel death. I glance back the point where Ilene now lies. The small mound doesn't look out of place in the forest and is already covered in a variety of burning leaves.

"No man deserves to die like that," Dagan tells me. I nod in agreement. "It's the least we could do."

The ride back to the palace is much less nerve-racking than the one to Hornblower Cave. The trees and animals part to let us by, almost bowing to Herminia, which is understandable.

We have to sneak into the palace quietly, entering by a different tunnel concealed by a great pine tree, for the soldiers have almost completely surrounded the palace by now.

Seraphyna and Seb are standing on the balcony from the wall, watching nervously for our small parade. Little do they know, however, that our parade is one smaller than expected. As soon as we're in view, ready to enter the passage that enters the courtyard, Seraphyna flies down the stairs, Seb reluctantly following on her heels. We enter the passage, ducking and guiding our horses as we do so. Before long, we're in the courtyard, met with Seraphyna's worried, accusing face.

"Ilene, where's Ilene?" Seraphyna demands before we've even emerged into the daylight, counting heads and staring at me distraught, awaiting an answer.

"Seraphyna, calm down," Seb says, placing his large but trembling hands on Seraphyna's petite shoulders.

"What happened?" Seraphyna screeches, shaking my shoulder as I make an effort in trying to tie Melie to a wooden beam.

"He's gone, Phye," I tell her grimly. "It was awful-"

"Don't tell me, I've seen it all before, I know how terrible it is!" Phyna sobs, holding her hand up, white as sea mist, to stop me from elaborating. "No one is as cruel as Domhnall, now you know it as well as I do."

"We buried him properly," Herminia assures her.

"Oh, Hermie!" Seraphyna exclaims, embracing her sister and sobbing into her emerald-clad shoulder.

"It's alright, Phye," Herminia soothes, patting Phyna calmly on the back.

"A man has died at my hands!"

"Not yours," Herminia sighs, holding Phye's face and trying to drum the simple fact that she's not guilty into her.

"He has died because of my hatred for Domhnall," Phyna cries, slamming her face back into Herminia's shoulder again.

"Because of Domhnall's hatred for you," Seb interjects, "It is never your fault, Phye."

"If I hadn't sent Florean out he wouldn't have died," Seraphyna laments. "He was too young."

"Phyna, you're 17, you are more caught up in this war than anyone twice your age or otherwise. You have the wit and wisdom of a king who has ruled seven kingdoms his whole life, the beauty of a mermaid, a sea nymph and a Valkyrie put together, you have words in that heart of yours that couldn't be said by the oldest of pre-Omnian royal guards or warriors, you are something else," Herminia reminds her. "Age is but a number, Phyna, remember that well, mind you. You're seventeen, Phye, you have years to live."

"Ilene was young, too," Phyna mumbles, still fixated on the fact that he's dead.

"He was 23, a lot older than you, my lady," Luz corrects angrily.

"About the same, then," I point out, trying to lower the tension. "Please, everyone, come inside."

"Yes, it's getting dark," Dagan urges, going to push Herminia forward slightly.

"Don't say dark," Phyna warns, "I despise little else as much as darkness."

*

Even now with Hermina's warming presence in the palace, the night is still cold as every effort couldn't light the fireplaces. Seraphyna mumbles every time the flames fail to appear, damning Aidan and his control over fire. It gets to midnight. The moon is high and the sky is clear, the stars peeking through small wisps of clouds if they were the few who are concealed. Seraphyna paces the floor of the study impatiently as we wait for any sign of hoof sounds, whether they be from friends or foes.

"A parade approaching by the west keep," Seb tells us after conversing quietly with a messenger.

"West keep?" Seraphyna stares at him blankly but looks somewhat hopeful.

"Yes."

"Let me come and see this for myself," she concludes, seeming hopeful but she still slings a quiver of arrows over her shoulder and grabs the Moonbeam Bow from where it rests on the table.

I go with Phyna and Seb as they march solemnly to the balcony overlooking the west keep. Herminia is already at the west lookout tower, examining the landscape before her.

"Can you tell who it is?" Phyna asks Herminia, but she shakes her head and squints.

"I don't want to make assumptions," she explains, "that could be fatal."

"Down!" Seb yells and I duck accordingly.

"Oh, dear god," I exclaim, seeing a long, thin arrow wedged between the stones behind me.

"It's them!" Herminia exclaims. "Oh, thank the Saints, it's them!"

"Don't just stand there, then, go!" Seraphyna orders, yanking the arrow out of the wall forcefully.

"It can't be Aella, they just open fired at us!" I point out as Phyna fires an arrow of her own into the air with a faint ping. With the audible landing of the arrow, murmuring starts from down below.

"Exactly," Seraphyna smiles, turning abruptly to descend the crumbling steps of the west tower.

The west keep has a solid iron portcullis which has obviously hasn't been opened for months or even years as many vines and weeds have grown around the bottom spikes of the portcullis.

"It's me, sister!" A high, fluid and swaying voice calls through the night.

"Ssh," Seraphyna exclaims, pressing a bony finger to her lips, despite Aella not being able to see her through the night.

"God, Phye, just open the gate!" Lorna calls, even louder than Aella did and I see Phyna flinch with worry and slight annoyance. She flicks her hand apprehensively, cranking open the portcullis.

"Finally!"

There are only three people who emerge from the darkness, Lorna, Aella and a man sitting on a horse behind them. I remember his face well, a long, healed scar running over his left eye. The eye that is open is deep green and gazes purposefully at everything in the field of his view. All I can say is that Aella chose well when she chose Corentin as her husband, Lord and General. They look fantastic together, the feelings between them felt even by the surrounding air, which is notably sweeter when they are both together. Both sport silver armour, laced with intricate patterns which, on second inspection, turn out to be ancient script weaving lines of spells and scared prayers.

"Thank you for coming," Phyna says to Aella and Corentin.

"Our soldiers are stationed along the northern coast of Greater Isle, as you commanded," Corentin tells her and Phye nods thankfully.

"What took you so long?" Phye asks.

"We had a hold-up," Aella explains.

"Well, obviously," Phye sighs, "but what was it?"

"We had to avoid Water's ships on the horizon," Aella mumbles, turning her head away from Phye cautiously. I glance at Herminia nervously, and she gives me an expression that's similar to Aella's. Worry, apology, caution.

"What?" Phyna rages.

"Water's ships on the horizon," Aella repeats.

"I heard you the first time!" Seraphyna shouts, throwing her dark white hands up in the air. "So, he gets help too, of course he does that... ugh."

"You got help," Herminia points out.

"Look at me!" Seraphyna yells, distraught and fuming. "Look around you, Herminia, at the crumbling walls around me, at those few that are loyal to me! Dead men lie in shallow graves because they lay their honour and their lives at my feet! I'm 17 years old but I am here, ready to be murdered by my own brother, ready to lead my army to their possible deaths..." She sobs, choking, shrill sobs that paint a thousand words each in themselves. "And who stands with me?"

The pause is long and tense, the only sounds audible are heavy breathing and a gentle, welcome breeze.

Seraphyna takes a long, frustrated sigh. "That's right, no one!" she shrieks, wiping her sodden cheeks with the sleeve of her dress.

"Phyna, dearest, please look behind you," Seb urges, turning Phye's body towards the opening of the west keep. "Look and see who stands with you."

"Clancy!" I exclaim, running to the open portcullis. "Conaire!"

Clancy and Conaire have certainly done their job well, it's clear. They stand torches in front of an army of hundreds of men and women, loyally stationed behind them both. Each of the soldiers holds a weapon of some kind, whether it be a sword, spear or just the lightest magic concealed in their hands. Solemn and brooding looks are painted on everyone's faces but underneath shines blazing pride and bravery.

"Your Lightest, our Lady, we are your humble servants," Clancy announces, drawing his sword and kneeling to the ground. As he does, everyone, including Conaire, copies, those with weapons laying them upon the scraggly grass too.

I turn to Seraphyna and Seb who have joined hands spontaneously and subconsciously. Without thinking, I take Seraphyna's hand also.

Stepping towards the army, united, we watch them intently. Clancy and Conaire are the first warriors to rise.

"For the General, Lord and Highest Lady of our house!" One man decrees. The army erupts in an uproar of joy and pride.

*

Morning breaks abruptly with a beautiful sunrise and calm birdsong, a stark difference from the sea of black that is still swarming around the castle. We have not yet, thankfully, received a cannonball that manages to reach inside the walls, but our front battlements are damaged beyond repair and many arrows have broken our glass or penetrated our wood.

It has been 20 hours since the beginning of the siege but we're still doing comfortably. Herminia uses the bare soil of the courtyard to grow fruit trees in a matter of seconds and Aella brings a cool rain that muddies the battlefield and lowers Darkness's spirits but only brightens ours altogether.

I am sitting at the very top of the west lookout tower with Aella at the break of dawn.

"Is my brother up yet?" I ask her after the sun has peaked its crown up from behind the horizon. It's a terribly bright morning, and neither Seb nor Phye are anywhere to be found. "I checked his room, he's not there."

"Consider the circumstances, Baroness," Aella sighs, throwing a nut shell over the wall. She offers me one as she says it and I gladly accept it.

"Please call me Evanie," I insist.

"If your brother and sister are Lord and Lady of the house-" Aella continues, not acknowledging my request.

"They're not married," I tell her. Aella stares at me doubtfully and raises a doubtful eyebrow.

"Still, consider the circumstances. As much as she'll refuse the fact, my sister is a creature of passion, one who will always listen to what her heart says first. I think that there is a perfectly good reason that your brother and my sister have not emerged from her room. They're young and in love."

"Oh," I breathe, turning a deeper and deeper shade of red as I say it. "Thank you for helping me realise that."

"You strike me as a smart woman, Evanie," Aella tells me. I reply by smiling with gratitude. "But I do think you don't look around enough."

"Why should I look ahead when my path is a simple, straight one?" I ask.

"If your path is straight, General, then you're walking the wrong way," Aella reminds me. The words stop me in my tracks. Perhaps I am going the wrong way. "It is no crime to deviate from the path, Evanie, you should do well to remember that."

Quick, purposeful footsteps echo through the tower, getting more frequent and desperate as they gradually work their way up to being at our level.

"Ah, Lady Lorna," Aella smiles, budging over on her seat to make room. I sense that Aella and Lorna have become firm friends.

"No time for sitting around, princess, I'm afraid," Lorna shakes her head. It's an odd title that I don't think describes Aella in the right way, princess. In fact, Seraphyna, Aella and Herminia are all still, in fact, princesses and the fact frequently escapes my mind. They don't seem like they would carry out classic, stereotypical princess-like activities. They do not sit around, waiting for servants to bring them honeyed biscuits and fancy sweets, they certainly do not sit and wait for fate to happen to them. They are mistresses of their own fate, it's clear. Each one of them are queens, through and through, crowns are not necessary to show that.

"What's wrong?" Aella looks worriedly behind her over the grey and crumbling walls. She lets out a small, shocked and dainty gasp. I turn my gaze from Lorna's face to where Darkness's army is.

"Crazy bastard," Aella murmurs, turning briskly towards the door. I watch with horror as the innocent morning rays, golden and inviting, reveal the evil and sickening image of three colossal catapults standing proud and determined. Soldiers of darkness, arranged in a criminally neat production line of death load the catapults with all kinds of things surrounding the main, harsh grey boulders. Tiny stones, sand, dead horses, dead soldiers, beehives, wasps' nests, orbs of fire, arrows and weapons, you name it, it's in there. Somewhere.

"Oh, Saints," I exclaim.

"Could you fetch my sister?" Aella asks me, brandishing her staff at the tower door.

"Which one?"

"The one currently in bed with your brother," Aella says matter-of-factly. I shudder, taking my first reluctant step towards the door. "I'll get Herminia."

"No need," Herminia replies, throwing open the door of the tower. "I'm here, Dagan and Corentin are in the barracks alerting our soldiers."

"Thank you," Aella sighs with relief. "Now please, Evanie, go and fetch our Lady and her Lord."

Before I have time to protest the fact that my brother is Lord of Light, I am bundled down the stairs irritably in a daze.

There is no sound coming from inside Phyna's room, but I assume both her and Seb are in there thanks to Aella's awkward pointing out. I knock quietly on the door; a grand redwood and brass thing covered in scratches and etches like battle scars. My knock is not answered.

"Seb? Phye?" I call out as I open the door ajar slightly.

I've never been into Seraphyna's bedroom before due to lack of invitation, but it's clear that Seb has had plenty of invitations to visit. A lopsided stack of his things are piled into one corner, the clothes he wore yesterday scattered carelessly about the room. A boot is in one corner of the room whilst its partner is in the other. Seraphyna's garments are more neatly stored, it seems. A great wooden wardrobe is pressed up against one of the walls and a map of Omnia is pinned down on a desk next to it. A propped open glass door opens onto an expansive balcony, letting the morning air into the room. The view out of every window is different, whether it be the wide ocean, twinkling mischievously in the dawn sunlight or the ancient, rough walls of the castle that bear as many scars as the door to Phyna's room. On one of the latches of the windows, concealing the view from it, is a stark white dress and a lacy veil.

Wait a minute…. What?

"Oh, goodness, look at it!" I exclaim. "Look at the awful thing, what is it?"

"Your wedding dress, Oralee," Hestia explains tiresomely, taking a seat at my desk. She unrolls the map that resides on its wooden surface, a crisp new one crafted from Elspethian Cotton.

"It's a monstrosity!" I sigh. "I haven't worn white in three years!"

"And for a good reason, too. Maidens don't wear white apart from holy day and you know that," Hestia reminds me.

"I don't like white," I pout, snatching the dress off the hook.

"I didn't come all the way from Calia just to hear you moan about your wedding, Oralee," Hestia sighs, shaking her head desperately. I ignore her and continue to speak.

"Oh, and I suppose this man is already married as well, too? I bet he already has two wives he's grown bored of and locked up in some dark wing of his Greater Isle manor," I guess, which is only logical from what I've heard about him. Twenty-nine years old, Count of Ilene, has a daughter already, the exact type of man I hate.

"He's a widower," Hestia states. I scoff.

"So heartbroken, used and power-hungry?" I whine. "Honestly, you know, Hestia, if mama was here-"

"Well mama isn't!" Hestia rages. "Stop whining about every single little detail! This is supposed to be the happiest day of your life! Just try to be somewhat happy and not downright miserable, alright?"

I hear a knock at the door. I do not answer it, I can sense who it is. Luke.

I run to the doorway. Luke. He's here. I haven't seen Luke in a year and he finally turns up the day I need him most. I breathe a sigh of relief as he steps into my room.

"What are you doing here?" he asks, sitting on the bed.

"What?"

"What are you doing here?" he repeats. I furrow my brow in confusion and shut the door behind me with a mellow thump.

Seb rubs his eyes, around one of his wrists is a white ribbon but it appears that he wears nothing else.

"Evanie?" he questions. "What are you doing here?"

"Where were you last night?" I demand, noting the plain silver band on Seraphyna's hand, which grips Seb's muscular arm lovingly and tightly even in her slumber.

"We were... we..." Seb stutters. "Well..."

"Did you two get married or not?" I say, pointing first to the wedding dress on the window, then to the white ribbon on Seb's wrist and then finally to Seraphyna, all the while staring Seb down.

"Yes," Seb replies quietly, hanging his head. "At midnight, just us two, no one else was there. I'm... We're... I'm sorry," he decides finally.

"Don't apologise," I insist. "Put some clothes on and wake your wife up."

"What's happened?" Seb questions worriedly, shaking Phyna awake gently and tentatively.

"Evanie?" Seraphyna sighs, sluggishly sitting up, dragging the pressed white sheet with her to cover her bare chest. "Evanie, what's wrong?" she asks once she has fully awoken. "Evanie, tell me."

"I'd put some armour on, if I were you," I recommend. "And some clothes."

"Oh, that crazy bastard!" Seraphyna rages, running to the window that gives her a view of the meadow, covered in Domhnall's scattered army. She brings the sheet with her, leaving poor Seb just a fur coverlet to protect his dignity.

"Exactly what Aella said," I grimace, passing Phyna her silver gauntlets. "Meet me at the north keep in twenty minutes." I open the door to leave. "And no hesitating!"

The sun has fully risen by the time we're mounted and ready on our horses. The north keep is more widely used meaning the gates are easily opened, strong and sturdy.

Seraphyna nervously addresses her army, each holding or concealing menial weapons. She takes a deep inhale, lets out a sharp exhale, holds her head high and projects:

"Today, you stand here before me as my loyal soldiers. You willingly lay your lives down before your house. I say to each and every one of you that today you are all heroes-"

"Heroes indeed!" Lorna pipes up.

"Through and through-" Phyna continues, her words being met with a joyous roar from each man and woman, further proving their faithfulness and willingness. "Today, we face our greatest and most ancient foe. For this day, and all days, we are not counted by our number measured against theirs, or our number alone, we are counted as one. As one, faithful house!"

Each sword, bow or hand or spear is thrust into the air. I can almost see, hear, even taste, the pride radiating from Seraphyna and settling on all the soldiers, making the whole courtyard aglow with pride and faith.

I face Phye, who smiles strongly, taking Seb's hand. I can just see it when she looks at him, the obvious love. It's simple, like a book that stands alone and is read forever, one that has no sequels nor prequels, no chapters nor plot twists. It cannot be tarnished, broken or destroyed. Their love is nothing but an endless, stunning story, always returning the thing that matters to them the most. Each other.

Seb returns Phyna's besotted gaze except the look is more of a mask over worry than a genuine emotion. The moment becomes theirs, it becomes private as they lean in to embrace each other.

Aella is hand-in-hand with Corentin and Herminia with Dagan. I glance behind me, where Clancy and Conaire stand on the castle walls. I furrow my brow at them both, surprised they're not in front of or even part of our army. Clancy smiles knowingly in return to my confusion, Conaire merely sneers at it. Clancy jumps down from his position way up on the walls, Conaire hot on his heels to follow.

"I was waiting for you to notice," Clancy laughs as I tread heavily over to them.

"What are you doing?" I shake my head, having no time for comedy.

"What does it look like? We're the announcers!"

"Might I remind you that I'm not from around here? I don't know every obscure bit of unfamiliar vocabulary," I say, starting to become quite irritated.

"We announce that battle," Conaire snaps rudely. "It's quite self-explanatory, don't you think?"

"So it's a cheap and effortless way to save your necks and get out of fighting?" I scoff.

"We protect the castle and the battlements, fight off attacks. It's... it's quite an important job." Clancy says humbly.

I nod, understandingly and apologetically. I now understand, frighteningly, that Clancy and Conaire may be in more danger than I.

"Good Luck," I say to Conaire and he seemingly dismisses my comment, returning to his post as he climbs back up the wall.

"Please be careful, Evanie," Clancy pleads, taking my hand. "We... I couldn't bear to lose you."

"I couldn't bear to lose you..." I linger on my words and my thoughts suspend heavily above us both.

"Evanie, I have something to tell you-" Clancy starts but is cut off by a very loud shout of:

"Get down, General!"

I don't know who called out to me but they just saved my life. Rubble, debris and dust fly around the courtyard, threatening to hit me from all angles. I can only assume Darkness's catapults are working just fine.

"That's our cue," Seraphyna says calmly. "Evanie?"

"Ready," I confirm, Clancy turning purposefully away from me, hanging his head ever so slightly. I hesitate, knowing that last time I regretted not seeing Clancy's face one last time on the last occasion we thought we could both be dead.

"Clancy, wait," I call. He stops, turns around and grimaces.

"Yes?" he replies.

"What did you need to tell me?" I ask.

"Never mind," he replies deeply. "It doesn't matter now."

"Because I have something to tell you…" I debate in my mind what to do, but my feet decide for me. They decide that I'm done waiting, and I am. I rush over to Clancy, who is seemingly taken aback for a moment but then grabs my hand. Our faces are so close together that I can read every story his face tells me. I trace lines between a small scar on his upper lip, a cluster of freckles on his nose, a crack in his spectacles, his deep, rich brown eyes. He has ink on his cheek and I reach up hesitantly to wipe it away. The feel of his breath against my forehead makes me shudder, but in a euphoric way.

I go to say something but am silenced by Clancy's lips pressing against mine. I let out a long but sharp breath and smile weakly.

"At least you know it if I die," I breathe, letting go of his hand reluctantly. Nos is the moment that I realise everyone in the courtyard has stopped and is smiling over the moment Clancy and I just shared.

The gate opens with a slow, agonising crank as Conaire looks onto the courtyard scene sourly, taking most of his anger out on the gate crank, yanking it round and round and round…

"Inevitable," Seraphyna shakes her head but smiles all the same. "So inevitable. Mount your horse, General. We have Light's battles to fight now." I clamber onto Melie's back, holding Seb's hand as I do for support. When I am safely on, I don't let go. I take Phyna's hand also.

"I love you both," I say, clinging tighter to the both of them. "This is the test of all tests."

"The day of all days," Seb continues.

"The battle of all battles. This is history, this is war," Phyna finishes. "May light bless you both."

"And you," I smile, letting of her comforting and soft grip. Even after I let go, Seb doesn't of her hand. She nods understandingly and places the other of her hands over his.

"My dearest," he sighs, staring into Phye's eyes with more emotion that I could've felt in 50 lifetimes.

"My lord," She smiles back. She looks at him. He looks at her. He looks at her as though she is the reason love exists.

I glance up to where Clancy has retaken his post on the walls. He offers me a concise nod after catching my eye, before blowing into a long, thin horn. The sound is low and deep, bringing an unwelcome chill to my already frozen spine. The noise is almost identical to the one that warned us of Ilene's death.

Seraphyna is the first out of the gate.

Seb and I follow. Aella, Herminia, Corentin, Dagan and Lorna are next. The only cavalry of Light. Compared to Darkness's 300 mounted soldiers, we have eight.

We ride on and on into the warzone but our army doesn't follow, leading me to believe they're under strict orders not to. We still continue to ride towards Domhnall and his death soldiers, so close to them that we can see the white hooves of the black horses on the standards that the banner men grasp.

Domhnall still stands at the front of his army, talking to the tall dark-haired man I know as Darsey, General of Darkness.

I don't think Domhnall or Darsey notice us at first, only giving us their full attention when a soldier shouts and points with his bow at us.

Domhnall is as quick as the crack of a whip to turn as he shouts some inaudible and vague order at Darsey.

I expect Phyna to dismount her horse, but she doesn't. She makes no announcement, no order, no speech. All she does is steady herself on her horse, reach for the Moonbeam Bow and fire a single, silver arrow into the abyss of Domhnall's army. Whether it lands in a gap or wounds a soldier, I know not. I have little time to think properly as my mind is consumed by the roar and thud of our army's feet. I glance at Seb, who draws his sword and raises it in the air. He signals for me to do the same. I thrust the Sun Sword in the air defiantly, the iron and gold catching the sunlight, which is directed straight at Domhnall and his death soldiers.

Domhnall tries desperately to rally his army, but he has little precious time to. By the time he and Darsey are mounted, ready and fully aware of what is going on, it's too late.

We are upon them. The battle has begun.

*

I daren't look back at the palace once, even though I am dying to see how it and Clancy are. The thought of them both swills around in my mind like raging rapids, Clancy's soothing voice pushing me on another moment and when that moment is over, he tells me to keep going further. I am occupied on all sides at every second and minute, a soldier behind me, to my side, in front of me. A countess to help to the east or a soldier to help to the west; most of the time, I just carry on fighting as I can't escape the vortex that Domhnall's soldiers have created around me.

I stand out on the battlefield like a sore thumb. Sitting so high up has its advantages and its disadvantages. My position on Melie's back means that I can survey my surroundings if I just happen to have a split second to look up, but also means I'm an easy target to my foes.

I have no concept of time during the battle, weeks could have passed for all I know. I have no idea how long I've been fighting, but it gets to the point where the calamity is too much for Melie. She refuses to move forward, even when I grip the reins tighter and try to push on through the sea of black and yellow before me. Melie whinnies defiantly, yanking her head back towards the palace. I take a deep breath, jump down onto the bloodied grass and, finally, when I'm not occupied with fighting, unbridle her and stroke her mane scruffily. Melie bows her head at me thankfully, pushing through the soldiers as she runs back towards the palace, prancing among the dead.

I release my sword from my scabbard, just in time, too, for three separate men approach me from all angles. I have little time to react, so I swing my sword heavily, injuring all three of them and giving me the time to finish off two before more soldiers approach me menacingly.

I feel a pressure against my back. Alarmed, I turn to see who it is. Lorna is behind me, bow in hand, helping me to fight of the death-soldiers as well as she can with a slashed, claret arm. She's handy with a bow, pulling the arrows painfully from her quiver with her bloody arm, sending them off strategically in various directions. Once the bow string is cut by a rouge blade, however, she continues to pull arrows from her quiver, handfuls at a time, and uses them as disposable spears, plunging them in the chests of the soldiers can reach until there's a star of dead bodies around us.

"Lorna!" I exclaim.

"Thought you might need a helping hand," she chuckles, dropping her empty quiver on the muddy grass. "Speaking of which-" she continues. Pointing to a cleared area, she runs forward.

"Wait!" I call. "Stop!" My warning echoes and rings throughout the battlefield. As my vision focuses, I can catch sight of the danger better.

The battlefield is eerily quiet. Everyone has stopped fighting; some have even dropped their weapons. The soldiers that fight on both sides that are still alive watch intently, silently, as Seraphyna and Domhnall stand directly opposite each other, still as those around them.

Both are unarmed, and they stare into each other's identical eyes so furiously, I'm not surprised no one's moved yet.

I am so wrong about them being unarmed.

Domhnall takes the first swipe, knocking Seraphyna off her heels onto the ground. Her dress is muddied and splattered with crimson blood, hair matted and armour dented, but she still looks regal, passionate and fierce.

Phyna strikes back creating a slash in Domhnall's arm, which is unprotected as he never anticipated our emergence from the palace this early.

They fight continuously, one strike against the other. I catch Seb's eye from across the meadow, a restrained expression staining his face. Corentin is holding him back away from Phye but Seb knows. Only Seraphyna can fight this fight.

Domhnall knocks Seraphyna to the ground with every occasion she even raises her finger or tries to scramble to her feet. She looks defeated but, as I look beyond her face, I see something brilliant building up inside of her, ebbing and flowing, beating through every vein and bone in her body.

It may have been just me, but I am blinded and deafened by what comes next. I open my eyes and Seraphyna is the only one standing as she's diminished every single one of us with her magic. Seb stands, as do I, and without hesitation or acknowledgement or even agreement, run towards her.

She laughs and smiles, brushing the dust off her shoulders. She laughs again. Seb gazes adoringly at her, the love obviously mutual.

Her smile is a mile wide. It gleams and glows like the light within her. She coughs lightly and sighs confusedly a few times. Her smile diminishes until it is just a tight circle of pain. She falls to the ground so quickly, she's like a bolt of lightning, but Seb is at her side even quicker than that. I jolt forward too, seeing Seb cradling Phyna's face. A long, red gash runs through her abdomen and she gasps in pain and shock. A thick, black iron chain is wrapped around her hand which flops helplessly against its force. I pull the evil thing away from her crimson fingertips, which go to stop Seb who's making an effort to cease her bleeding with his trembling hand.

"Don't," she pleads, whispering feebly but passionately. "It's no use. There's little time for me now."

"Don't say that!" Seb insists, bitter, desperate tears forming in the corners of his eyes. I hesitate, thinking about what I could do to comfort him, but I can't as he's almost as faded as she is. She's broken, he's breaking.

"Listen, Seb, you are everything to me, everything," she pauses and grunts in pain. "You need to promise that you'll look after my people, you and Evanie."

I nod fervently and sob. "I promise, I promise."

For a moment, she smiles and looks up, then laughs, saying: "The Second Sun."

I tilt my head up, and next to Star Oralee, I can see another become brighter and stronger as Seraphyna become fainter and weaker.

"Hold on, hold on, my love," Seb asks of her. "Please." It's a simple plea, but one she cannot grant. She sighs tiresomely and shakes her head.

"The sun is rising, I should sleep now," she whispers. Seb shakes his head profusely and lets out a sob as she rests her frosted eyes and her hands go limp.

She's dead.

Gone.

Instead of sorrow, all I feel is anger. I find myself standing and staring right into the place where Domhnall stands, cackling like a vulture, ever so pleased with himself.

"Who's next?" he bellows, only to be followed by a huge eruption of laughter from his army.

Aella is holding onto Herminia, sobbing. Seb still clings onto Phye's lifeless corpse.

"Enough!" I shriek, throwing my arm across my body. To my surprise, the action unsteadies Domhnall's strong stance.

"You have killed her now, I hope you're pleased with yourself, you murderer," I growl. "Give us time to bury her."

Domhnall doesn't reply.

Sorrow

His expression is stone cold, showing no remorse. Slowly, I dare to take a step towards the man. The man whose eyes show no remorse, none at all.

None at all.

A girl. His sister. My brother's wife. My predecessor, for I'm Highest Lady of Light now that Seraphyna's dead. She's dead. The thought that Domhnall, a force of darkness and anger that stands before me in the evening sun as real as the blood streaming down my arm and onto the sodden crimson grass, has *murdered* Seraphyna makes my blood curdle. The thought sticks out at the front of my mind, jabbing furiously at my head from the inside.

"At least let us bury her, Domhnall, she may be your enemy, but she's still our sister," Herminia shouts tearfully from behind me, where she clings onto Dagan painfully.

"The fact that she is my sister concerns me not," Domhnall sneers nastily, chuckling as he says it. "Sister…" He spits the word as though it were a poison from his mouth. "But, as the *benevolent king* I am, I will give you until sunrise tomorrow to bury your *Lady Mother of Light.*"

I open my mouth to speak, to shout my anger and sorrows at the darkness, to whittle Domhnall down to nothing, but I know my words will do more damage than good. King. He uses the word so casually, a title he has picked for himself that no one would dare give to him.

I turn cautiously back to the palace, the first time I see the cream and grey walls, crying out from all of its wounds and gashes and breaks. I think momentarily of Clancy, whether one of the wounds the palace has endured is his absence, if he lies alone and dead in the courtyard.

From the palace I glance to the grass, Seb still clutching Seraphyna's robes and sobbing onto her etched armour. The small orbs of his liquid sorrow dwell upon the silver, gleaming in the evening sun momentarily until they fall onto the grass, simply to become part of the dew that scatters the meadow, never to be found again.

"Seb," I whisper. My brother doesn't look up, he just continues to hit the ground with his fist in pain and. "Seb." The second time I say it, more forceful and trying, he briefly looks up towards me, his red, pained eyes meeting mine.

"She's..." he mutters, quietly and solemnly, the sorrow once again flashing across his face.

"I know, Seb, I know," I nod, bitterly biting my lip to force the tears to stay in my eyes, to not fall and show my weakness.

"Sebastian, let go, please," Lorna coaxes, placing her own trembling hand on Seb's trembling shoulder. "It's alright, let go, we're here for you."

I nod, also crouching to Phye and Seb's side. "We are," I confirm.

"Oralee," he yells, the crisp, clear sound silencing all of us, even our breaths. I inhale in shock. "No!" He continues to open and close his eyes rapidly, throwing his head from side to side in a fervent disagreement of whatever is happening to Luke at the moment.

"Seb, what did you see?" I ask him cautiously, not sure of whether he's still stuck in Luke's mind or not. Very suddenly, his head snaps towards me, then back to where Seraphyna still lies dead.

"Everyone I've ever loved..." he whispers, pausing to let go of Seraphyna's hand, "gone."

"I'm here, Seb, *I'm* here for you," I breathe, "Seb?"

I'm desperate now, and I can see the army that stands behind me is growing reckless by the second. Tired, bereaved and afraid, I let out a muffled sob in defeat to my sorrow and grief. Before I know it, Seb's arms have been flung around me.

"Don't leave me, Evanie," he sobs.

"I won't, I won't. I promise. Come, it'll be fine," I tell him. "Come with me."

Domhnall looks upon our parade with a cruel eye. Seraphyna's body floats in mid-air as we surround her, each one sobbing, clinging to whoever is nearest, whoever will accept our desperate and comforting embraces. The portcullis of the north keep is closed. Lazily, I raise my hand for it to open as though it's natural. Nervously, I look up to here Clancy and Conaire should be standing. Are they? No.

Clancy, Clancy, Clancy. It's the first time I've properly thought about him since the battle started, but now he plagues my mind. If he's dead... oh, I hope he's not, but I'm sure he is.

The mud of the courtyard gives easily underfoot, and a collective squelch sounds as we all clamber inside the palace.

"What colour do you wear in mourning here?" I ask Aella as I don't even know, I had had no use for mourning clothes yet, no one had died.

"Well... black," she shrugs sadly.

"Black," the word lingers in my mouth sourly. "Darkness." I remember what Seraphyna said, just less than a day ago. *Don't say dark, I despise little else as much as it.*

I pause on the thought for a while, my mind flitting back and forth on what to do.

"Then we shall wear white," I conclude to them.

"Well chosen, General," Dagan pipes up, before realising my new status. "My lady."

They all, apart from Aella and Herminia, drop to their knees. Even Seb, in his blinding grief, bows to me as Highest Lady. It breaks my heart, I pull Seb up by his trembling arms.

"Please, do not bow. No one should bow to me," I plead, shaking my head. "I say that you all have leave to go about your business until sunrise tomorrow."

The crowd murmurs, slowly disbanding alongside friends and brothers. Seb saunters silently back to Seraphyna's body, following it inside as it floats gracefully. I go to follow him, but step back as Lorna is the one who takes her turn to embrace me.

"Let him be," she whispers to me. "You go and mourn her yourself; I'll make sure he's alright."

"Thank you, Lorna," I sob, hugging her tighter. I spin towards the entrance to leave the courtyard, looking up towards the walls, trying just to spot a glimpse of Clancy.

If he's alive.

I expect the corridors to be a picture of chaos, except they are quite the opposite. In fact, few people wander along the south wing corridor, but those who do dip their heads at me silently, in respect. I reach my chamber, which is at the end of the corridor, and the door and walls show no signs of distress. Slowly, I open the door even though I know I'm safe.

My room is sparsely furnished, but I have a chair at a desk to sit on. Lying the Sun Sword down on the trunk at the foot of my bed, I slump into the chair in exhaustion.

It takes me a while to look around, gather myself together and extinguish the thoughts of Clancy still attacking my mind before I start to cry. I don't even know when my sobs switch from sorrowful ones to angry ones and back to sorrowful again, I just scream and sob so loudly I can't hear my heart pounding inside my chest anymore. I don't know if anyone can hear me, but I don't really care, I just need the time and space to let all of my emotions out. Sorrow, anger and confusion mix their way into my tears equally as I sob into my sweaty palms.

It reaches midnight, and I sit on the end of my bed, polishing the Sun Sword angrily and maniacally and ridding it of all the blood and muck that coats the silver. I reach the point where I have polished it so thoroughly and vigorously that I start to bleed onto my rag from the many cuts on my hands.

Just as I go to set the Sun Sword aside, a low, mellow knock sounds at the door. It makes me jump, but then my heart races from fear but also hope. I pace over to the door, trembling hand on its brass handle.

"Who is it?" I whisper, nervously opening the door slightly. I catch a glimpse of brown shoes, muddied and worn. My heart beats faster, to the point I have to clutch my chest.

"Open the door, Evanie."

I don't need to be told twice, to hesitate or question who the caller is. Clancy.

My Clancy.

"You're alive," I sob, throwing my exhausted arms around him. "Oh, Clancy, Clancy."

"So are you," he holds me at arm's length, examining my now scarred face. I embrace him again as he kisses my forehead tenderly.

"I thought you were dead," I sigh, closing the door behind me.

"I was caught downstairs in the professor's library. I locked Conaire and myself in with the Sun Crown and some of the important scriptures," Clancy explains. "I thought you were dead!"

"Better I than anyone else," I grimace, biting my lip.

"Don't say that!" he asks of me, guiding me to sit on the bed. We grab onto each other, holding on in sheer terror of losing each other.

"Is Sebastian with Seraphyna?" Clancy asks me after a while.

"They're embalming her now, so I wouldn't expect so," I sigh, resting my hand on his chainmail clad shoulder. Suddenly, he raises my chin and perks up to full height.

"What?" he trembles, lip quivering. He doesn't know.

"You don't know?" I question, placing my hands over his shaking, folded ones.

"She's dead?" he breathes. I nod silently.

"I'm sorry, I thought you knew; I really thought you knew," I explain. Clancy pulls rapidly and coldly away from me. He sinks off of the side of the bed onto the cold stone floor, on one knee.

"My lady, Highest Lady of Light," he mumbles, directing the address at me. Me.

I plunge down to his level, grabbing him by the shoulders, for whose sanity, mine, his or both, I don't know. Sorrowful tears stream down my cheeks as I fervently shake my head at him.

"Do not bow," I sob, pleading and holding his hands as I raise him to his feet. "Please."

I watch the emotions shift behind his eyes, back and forth between sadness, grief, anger and passion. I watch him intently like the sunrise in winter. He's cool, calming, but ever-changing.

"This doesn't change anything," I promise him.

"No," he agrees, "It doesn't."

"Just for now, just for the night, can we just live in the moment and not care about what tomorrow might have to say about it?" I question desperately, slowly closing the gap between us.

"I love you, Lady Evanie," he whispers. I smirk, pulling on the corner of his shirt.

"And I love you, just Clancy," I smile back.

"Just Clancy?" he questions, raising an eyebrow.

"My Clancy," I confirm, his lips meeting mine. As we hold hands, I can't help but notice the tiny sparks that erupt from the ends of our fingers.

*

The morning's mood doesn't match the situation. The horizon sits flat where it's supposed to be, the sun begins its daily dance as normal, and the usual birdsong is no more sorrowful that usual but is still shrill and beautiful to wake me in the morning. As I sluggishly open my eyes, the sky is still somewhere between darkness and sunrise, but it's approaching dawn quickly. Prying Clancy's embracing arm from around my shoulders, I slam my feet onto the cold stone floor, reaching for a hanger that holds my robes. After pulling them on and fixing the cape around my shoulders, I walk to the trunk that the Sun Sword rests on. I pick it up gingerly but tenderly, watching it catch the light as I turn it around in my hand. The stones on the hilt are especially reflective, the opals that the fireworks are weaving their way around. I stare at the stones, arranged in an odd pattern, I suppose they've moved around with age. It's not until I notice a sparkling, new opal just under the central stone that I realise what the pattern is. The Temple of the Eastern Sun, now with Phye's star, the Second Sun. The perfect star pattern. I remember Clancy showing me the stars and the names of each of them, Oralee and Phye in the middle, Ledan, Caspian and Luke to their left and Xanthe, Erich and Hestia to their right.

I look over to where Clancy is still asleep, peacefully and undisturbed, his face not even letting any of his sorrows away. I smile at his handsome and calm resting face, just the slight hint of a beard coming through on his pale face.

A sporadic, sharp tapping jams my mind out of thought whilst I look down at Clancy. Sighing, I open the window where, perched on its sill, a magnificent, proud, black raven stands. Its eyes gleam mysteriously

Anger boils violently inside of me, working its way up my throat until the fury is moving my mouth for me.

I wave my hand again, knocking Domhnall completely onto the mud and off his feet.

"Will you not at least grant us that grace?"

as I approach it with caution. It squawks once at my approach, a low and ominous sound.

For some reason, I reach my hand out towards it, wanting nothing more than to stroke its ebony feathers. It goes ballistic, flapping its great, wide wings all over the place. As it flies away, I see that attached to one of its legs is a thick black chain. Vaguely, I see a dash of yellowing parchment, the chain wrapped around it. As the raven flies away, it's met by a partner. Panicking, I command the parchment towards me and it flies into my hand, fitting in my closed fist comfortably. I watch the two magnificent birds as they frolic in the in the very early light, as the black of their chains fades into the feathers of the servants of their Lord.

I debate for a few moments whether to open the parchment, afraid of what the black seal marked with Domhnall's crest conceals. Eventually, curiosity bets the better of me and I rip the parchment open, tearing the black wax seal as I read the blood-red cursive.

One for Sorrow, two for Mirth,
We're coming for your people, only you can stop it.
-D.

I stare down at the letter in horror, reading the words over and over. The writing is as red as the scars all over my fingertips, but the cursive loops around the page like magic.

I ponder what to do for a while, trying to interpret the letter, although I practically know what Domhnall's asking of me. Sacrifice myself at his hands for my people. For Light's freedom, for what Phyna died fighting for. Eventually, I decide there's no question about it. I stare out of the window, knowing it'll be the last time I look over the ocean. I don't even feel scared or nervous about my upcoming demise, as a voice at the back of my head, I swear it's Seraphyna's, carries on repeating the same, soothing words. *Thank you, you are light's saviour.*

At least I'll die a hero's death.

Gingerly, I reach for my quill and parchment and drag it across the page, explaining to Seb what I am doing and why I must do it. I try not to cry as I sign my name after *Your dearest loving sister,* but I do, and one of my tears tumbles onto the page, smudging the ink slightly.

I'm all ready to charge down to the courtyard and onto the meadow until I hear Clancy stir. The noise, which despite being so quiet leaves a strong impression as it cuts through my pensive silence, makes me question myself. I observe his charming face, his opening eyes, his widening smile as he sees my face.

"Good morning," he grins, stretching his arms above his head. He's removed his spectacles for sleeping so he looks different to how I'm used to seeing him. My heart swells as I continue to gaze longingly into his eyes. For a shred of a second, I decide that I should just screw freedom and just live and be happy, live out my days with Clancy as he needs me. He's not even the only person who needs me. Seb needs me.

But Light needs me more.

"Morning," I reply, trying to mask my secrets with a smile.

"I see you're all dressed," he points out, observing my white ensemble.

"Yes, yes," I nod, trying not to glance at the window or the door or even the note in my hand.

"Where are you going?" he questions as my eyes move themselves to stare at the brass handle of my door.

"I'm just going down to the courtyard early to attend to some..." I pause, before deciding on the right word, "...business."

"Alright then," Clancy smiles, standing from the bed and making his way over to the mirror that rests on my desk in one corner. He observes his chin and hair in it before shaking his head comically and sighing.

"Saints, I need a shave," he laughs.

"I love you," I sigh, making my way over to him and kissing him tenderly. I place the note on the windowsill face down before making my way over to the other side of the room where the door is.

"And I love you," he smiles.

"Oh, Clancy," I mutter as I close the door behind me so he doesn't see my tears.

*

I'm happy to see that everyone has gathered in the courtyard even before the sun has fully risen. Several friendly faces greet me as I float along the muddy ground. My white robes shimmer in the rising sunlight as they trail along the ground behind me. I wear no armour, I don't even carry the sword on my belt, I don't even wear a belt at all. The only thing I do wear apart from my robes is the gold circlet Seraphyna gifted me on choice day. The Sun Crown lies untouched in the Professor's library, where it stays in its locked cabinet. I never even saw Phye wear it, as it was so precious. All around me is white, whether it be on the bodies of everyone around me or hung over the sides of the walls.

"Evanie?" Herminia asks as I part the crowd, just trying to reach the gate of the north keep. "You look troubled."

"It's fine," I assure her, sending her a concise, polite smile before heading back towards the north keep.

"Evanie, are you alright?" A supportive hand rests on my shoulder and Conaire's concerned expression looks down on me. In any other circumstance, I would be irritated at his presence, but I don't have enough time left to be angry or let the darkness in.

"I'm fine," I sigh, "I don't see Seb, is he alright?"

"Lorna and I tried to visit him in his room last night but his door was locked, he's set some kind of spell on it," Conaire explains.

"Spell?"

"Yes, I couldn't unlock it," he confirms.

"Leave him be, but can you give him this?" I ask, snapping my fingers to summon the sealed letter into Conaire's hand. He looks at me with bewilderment and I chuckle.

"It's a long story," I tell him. "One I barely know myself."

"You've changed so much from that girl I knew who arrived at the dock all that time ago," he sighs, shaking his head as though it's a bad thing.

"I am different, I changed then, I changed on choice day, I changed just now, I'm ever changing, like the light. I am changing, Oralee's changed me."

My dreams are usually funny, dreams about men called Conaire and Clancy, how Conaire pushes me around and doesn't let me breathe. Conaire places a hand on my chest.

"Conaire, what are you doing?" I ask, trying to pull his hand away from me.

"No, no!" he yells, our parting pushing me over. I wake up in a cold sweat in my own bed to a rhythmic knocking on my door. I groan.

"Oralee?" Caspian calls through the wood.

"Oh, Caspian," I smile, peeling the covers from my legs and opening the door to his smiling face.

"May I?" He asks before stepping over the threshold.

"Of course, come in," I smile, gesturing for him to sit on my bed. "Wait," I sigh as he sits next to me. I run a finger over a fresh scar on his cheek.

"What?" he asks, oblivious.

"Oh, Caspian, not again," I shake my head in disapproval.

"He's my son, I have to keep him occupied somehow," He explains, removing my concerned hand from his face.

"Not when he does this to you, he's too powerful to just play games with," I chastise, opening the chest next to my bed. I thrust a vial of ointment at him. "Here."

"I don't need that," he says, walking to the window. "He may be powerful and he may be able to scar me with his magic, but I suppose that's what happens to children born under the Morning Moon. He just needs some fresh-" he stops mid-sentence, turning back around and staring at me in horror.

"Cat got your tongue? Don't you mean air?" I laugh, standing to join him by the window.

"Darkness," he gasps.

"What do you-" I start to ask before seeing what's outside the window. Donovan leads the army that heads towards my palace. "Oh, Saints."

"Again?" Caspian asks in a true state of disbelief, *blinking and shaking as he stares at me with wide eyes.*

I hold my hand out to command the Sun Sword into my hand, and when it's secured on my belt, I go to send myself onto the meadow. I'm about to snap my fingers before Caspian grabs a hold of my wrist and stops me.

"No," he tells me sternly. *"The crazy idiots have already taken too much from me. First my mother, I'm not going to let them take you from me as well."*

"If I lose the battle, I'll die with our defeat," I tell him sadly. *"Tell Xanthe and Erich I love them,"* I sob, *welling up. I wipe my tears from my eyes so I can see his face. I snap my fingers. And I'm gone.*

I lift my hands despite their heaviness. I blink uncontrollably and Conaire places his hand on my shoulders in concern to steady me.

"Oralee, come back!" Caspian yells. Stop!

"Stop!" I shout. "Stop, stop, please."

"Stop what?" Conaire asks quickly.

"Stop all of this!" I wail, collapsing into Conaire. I pause to close my eyes for a second and flit back and forth, deciding what to do.

What would Seraphyna want you to do?

"Listen, Conaire, I'm going to do something you won't like, but tell-" I start before I'm interrupted by two people tearing through the crowd.

"Evanie! Evanie, I won't let you do it," Seb yells, running up to me, Clancy following closely on his heels.

"Evanie, please," Clancy pleads, clawing at my robes. "I found Domhnall's note, I know what he wants you to do and I won't let you do it!"

"Don't try and stop me," I warn them both. "Otherwise you'll end up dead."

"You're worth infinitely more to me and the House of Light alive than dead," Seb whispers, quoting Seraphyna's wise words.

"It's losing me in exchange for the freedom of thousands," I sigh. "It's a small price to pay."

I stare at them both hopefully but they refuse to budge.

"Listen," I tell them quietly, "I let Seraphyna die, I refuse to let anyone else be killed by Darkness. Let me go, and you'll all be free."

"I won't lose you too, not now!" Seb begs, bitter and sorrowful tears running down his face.

"You'll never have to lose anyone else," I sigh, embracing him warmly. "Seb, you know what I have to do."

He closes his red, sorrowful eyes. Silence. "I do," he whispers, nodding understandingly. I turn defiantly towards Clancy who grabs my arm.

"I won't let you do it, Evanie," Clancy growls at me fiercely. I frown so I don't sob from his hostility. I place a trembling, powerful hand on his cheek and sigh, closing my eyes.

"I love you," I breathe,. "I can only pray that you love me."

"I do-" he insists angrily, moving my hand away in his vigorous fury.

"Enough to let me go," I finish, hanging my head. Clancy glares at me, his deep eyes darting about my face. Our fixed gaze looks more like a standoff of foes than anything else, which breaks my heart.

"So, you're asking for me to fall in love with a beautiful, smart, inspiring, amazing woman, discover feelings I thought I was incapable of feeling, to know

I've met the woman I want to see at the end of an aisle, the woman I would die for-" Clancy pauses. The silence is a painful thorn in my side, but his words are a dagger through my heart. "I love that woman with all my heart, but you're asking me to let her go, watch her be slaughtered?" He spits the words poisonously, aggressively. All out of his love for me.

"I want to say no," I promise him, wrapping my unsteady arms around his wide torso. "But I have to say yes." The words destroy me and I willingly accept the tears that roll down my cheeks like a hot river from my cavernous eyes. Those eyes dart around the courtyard, the last time they ever will.

No more goodbyes. I can't stand the pain they cause me.

I don't address my people, though perhaps I should. I open the portcullis with my command and stare out at the meadow where Domhnall is waiting for me. The battlefield where I will die. Again. The place where Seraphyna died in darkness and fury.

By the time I have stood in front of the north keep's portcullis, pondering my entire life with my hand on my heart, my people, I gather, have realised what's happening.

"Our lady, our hero!" someone shouts from the back of the crowd. Lindera holds a young girl back, smiling at her support of me. I send her a sad smile. She's now a widow, but she'll at least be free after my death. The girl is young, innocent and sweet. They're the reason I'm doing this, laying down my life for light. It's a small price to pay. I smile at my people one last time as Seb walks up to me.

"If you're going to-" I start, but I'm cut off as he throws his great, strong arms around me. I accept his embrace gladly. We break apart and when he turns to re-join my people, *his* people now, I reach out and place my fingertips on his shoulder.

"Take care of them, do what she would've done," I ask of him, there's no need to explain who *she* is. He nods concisely and leaves.

It takes all of my courage, building up inside of me, before it's clawing at my throat, to take my first step.

With it comes chaos.

Every single one of the archers in the front row of Domhnall's army fire their uniform arrows on his command, all of them focused on me. I take a deep breath before taking my second step, then my third. Fourth, then my fifth. When the arrows reach me, I'm not fazed. They bounce off my skin in all directions, leaving no scars or marks at all. A few get caught in my robes and do not deflect away from me, but their weight does nothing to drag me down.

I'm almost entranced as I continue to take step after step after step. I catch sight of Domhnall in the front and our eyes fix. He smiles evilly and laughs I can only assume maniacally as I can't hear him over the relentless and frantic shouts of:

"Evanie! Evanie! Stop!" I daren't look back in case my mind, in its adrenaline-fuelled frenzy, is making it up. It's not until Clancy's foolish, daring hand grabs onto my shoulder that I deviate from my path.

"Evanie," he gasps, staring at me, a madness behind his eyes. "Evanie, I won't let you do-"

This. He never finishes his sentence, his words cut off by an arrow plunging straight through his abdomen, crimson already seeping through his shirt. His mouth forms a wide grimace of shock as he falls to the ground.

No. Not again.

Not again, no, but there's no saving him now, no loving him anymore. Clancy struggles, fixing his gaze with mine the whole time. His message is clear. *I love you.* I nod in amongst all the confusion and the tears.

"I love you too," I sob, placing my hand on his heart. His gaze shifts when he places his own hand on mine. His eyes gloss over, his breathing becomes more and more ragged until those breaths are his last.

I gather myself, my sorrow radiating out from my red, tired eyes in the form of bitter brine. I take Clancy's hand in mine, kissing it tenderly.

"Goodbye, my love," I whisper.

I have to use every ounce of courage, might and determination that resides in my trembling body to part myself from Clancy. I rise shakily to my feet, staring at Domhnall's amusement painfully.

Momentarily, I see a shred, a mere slither of shadowed remorse, or is it doubt, cunning perhaps?

No, that's ridiculous.

I take menacingly slow steps towards Domhnall. His eyes glisten in the morning sun. When I reach the area that is close enough to Domhnall, he gives me a chilling, toothy smile.

Meekly and humbly, I kneel down, the thick mud of the meadow dirtying my white robes. Domhnall nods in approval of me bowing to him. Angrily, I turn my back to him and face the palace and the meadow where Clancy lies dead.

I refuse to bow to Darkness.

Domhnall raises an eyebrow in surprise and moves in front of me, beckoning for Darsey to do the same. Domhnall, preparing for my murder, slips a great leather gauntlet over his wrist and snatches a broad sword from Darsey's serving hands. The hilt of the sword is decorated with deeply coloured stones, tiger's eyes and black diamonds.

"My lady," he sneers, looking down on me, black cape flapping in the breeze. "*Highest Lady* of the *Faithful* House of Light, formerly Baroness of the Unknown Realms and General of the House of Light, I applaud you, I really do, for managing to evade me for so long!"

Domhnall pauses, laughing happily on reflection. He rolls the sleeves of his cotton shirt so that the inky black material gathers in rigid bunches over his strong biceps.

"This girl claims to be Oralee of the Eastern Sun!" Domhnall announces, shooting me with another degrading, mocking sneer. A loud chuckle erupts and waves through the army, but I can tell each laugh is forced out of their fear of Domhnall.

"Oralee the Great, Highest Lady of the House of Light and Mistress of the Eastern Sun," I correct him quietly, subconsciously hoping he wouldn't hear me.

"The girl has the nerve to question me!" Domhnall cackles again and that same, dull and familiar chuckle bounces around in the crowd. I hate how he calls me 'the girl'. I am not just a girl. I am a Lady. I am Evanie. I am Oralee.

"Your crimes are extensive," Domhnall tells me, signalling for Darsey to drop the bottom part of an ornate scroll. The parchment reaches beyond Darsey's knees as his eyes examine the words I cannot see.

"Conspiring with Seraphyna Lux, Herminia Arbour and Aella Caeli to take down the monarchy and strip the Noble Lords of their titles; wielding the Sun Sword in the face of its rightful holder, the highest Lord of

Darkness; murdering the Count of Ilene-" Domhnall lists.

"I did nothing of the sort!" I insist.

"Murdering the Count of Ilene," Domhnall continues, "falsely claiming your loyalty to the realm."

Domhnall pauses, snapping his fingers for Darsey to re-furl the scroll.

"The list, as you can see, goes on," Domhnall explains. "Do you plead guilty to your crimes?"

"I plead guilty to being faithful and devoted to the House of Light and rejecting the forces of Darkness, Water and Fire. I plead guilty to conspiring to abolish the evil of the established monarchy. I plead guilty to those crimes and I plead guilty to nothing else," I declare, wincing slightly as Domhnall's lowered sword digs into my shoulder, making the white of my robe blood red.

"Then you shall die for your sins," Domhnall declares, raising his sword in the air. The silence of everyone around deafens me.

In the moments before my death, my world stops moving. I take time to dwell on what to say to Seraphyna when I see her again. Will she be disappointed in me? Will she understand? Will she be thankful?

The light in my veins rushes through me, spreading to every corner of my body. Whether it be behind my eyes, the end of each fingertips or the very soles of my feet, the light's there. I'm ready.

I wait for the pain.

It doesn't come.

TRUST

My eyes swing open, fighting against the weight of my heavy lids. I take desperate breaths as though I haven't tasted air in centuries. I'll be fair, it certainly feels that way as the moist, bitter breath swills around in my mouth. I move my hand to my soaked forehead, mopping up the crowds of beaded sweat with my fingertips. It is only at this point my vision clears and I manage to make out a little of the room they've decided to dump me in.

The first thing I notice is the depressing lack of light. No lanterns hang from the wall, no chandelier or even candles are suspended from the ceiling. The only light I have to see the room by is a miniscule slither of silver moonlight that is peeking just slightly through drapes hung over a tiny, closed window. The moonlight hits the very few items of furniture in my sparsely furnished cell of a chamber. A black wood dressing table strewn with black glass bottles holding black liquids is pressed up against the far wall next to a black wood wardrobe with black iron handles that open black doors to black, rigid robes. That is all apart from the bed that sit up in. The covers are dark and grimy, dotted with worryingly red patches and small moth-eaten holes. I throw them off my legs in disgust. I swing my feet over the side of the dark wood frame, but quickly undo the action when I hear purposeful and menacing footsteps.

The steps pause, a rusty lock creaks and the shrill sound of the door inching closer open cuts into the room like a sword. The door opening lets no more light into the room. I pretend to be asleep, returning to the position I found myself waking up in.

"Do you really believe that she's Oralee the Great?"

The voice is low, masculine and solemn, but also pitying. I feel the voice's shadow loom over my supposedly sleeping figure like a thick, suffocating veil.

"Seraphyna believed so," another voice whispers. I feel a pressure on the end of the bed, making me believe that someone's seated by my freezing feet. The voice, exhausted and feminine, speaks again.

"I do believe she is, Darsey, but even if she isn't, I want her to live. I owe it to my Seraphyna."

My Seraphyna.

My muscles tense at the mention of Darsey's name, but I'm surprised when I'm not as alarmed as I expected I would be. Come to think of it, Darsey's never raised a bow or sword to any of my people. But, even worse, he just stood by and watched it happen.

"You really loved her, didn't you?" Darsey sighs. There's no answer but the woman sniffs, standing from the bed.

"Melaina?" Darsey continues, confirming my suspicions. The woman is Melaina. The woman who raised and loved Seraphyna like a mother, who saved her from living in Darkness for eternity, the one who has lived as the worst sufferer of Domhnall's cruelty.

I stir, turning to the side of the bed Darsey and Melaina are now standing. I peel my eyes open slightly.

"Darsey," Melaina reaches out to stop Darsey from placing his huge, paw-like hand on the brass handle of the door to leave. "The child, she's stirring."

I sit up, my undone braid flying around my head as I do so. Melaina places a soothingly cool hand on my shoulder.

"Peace, my child, don't worry," Melaina soothes, gently pushing my body back down to lie on the filthy sheets. "You're safe."

"What is your name, child?" Darsey asks cautiously.

I try to speak but my throat prickles when I go to form my name. I make an effort to mouth the word.

"I'll get you a quill and parchment, child," Melaina offers, opening the door kindly. She smiles at me genuinely before taking a peek into the corridor and firmly shutting the door, frightened to the degree that she's shaking.

"Domhnall," she whispers, bounding across the room, nestling among the dark robes in the spacious wardrobe and slamming the door.

Hastily, Darsey sits back on the bed, signalling for me to sit back against the splintered headboard. The door swings open grandly, purposeful footsteps pounding against grubby tiles as Domhnall enters the room. I crinkle up my nose in disgust, his foul stench suppressing even my roaring appetite.

"Ah," Domhnall sneers, squinting at me curled up in one corner of the bed. "So, here she is."

Domhnall cackles, pulling Darsey from the edge of the bed to his feet. Darsey laughs along evilly with Domhnall's cruel mirth, all the while sporadically glancing nervously and discreetly towards the wardrobe that conceals so many secrets.

"Stand, girl," Domhnall commands. I throw my legs onto the floor, bare feet hitting the filth. My white robes are so dirtied by soot, ashes, dry blood, fresh blood, mud and general filth that they're no longer white. They're halfway to being black and I hate the fact so much that I pull uncomfortably at the fabric.

"Isn't she lovely, Darsey?" Domhnall questions, although it's more of an order to Darsey. The look in his eyes is telling Darsey to join him in his entertainment. *Say she's lovely, Darsey, say it.*

"We'll have to clean those wounds, won't we?" Darsey sighs, trying to please Domhnall by sounding like he doesn't care, but still trying to tell me he's my ally. "But apart from that, my lord, yes, she's a picture."

"Good," Domhnall concludes proudly. "Girl, you will go with Lord Darsey to clean yourself up. I shall leave you some clothes more suited to the... *situation.*"

Domhnall says nothing else, leaving the room with a flourish. I stare at the door in hatred, my eyes stabbing a thousand daggers into his back. Darsey and I watch through the open door as Domhnall turns a dark corner into another dark room. We wait for his sluggish pace to fade into silence before Darsey darts to the wardrobe, opening the door. I expect Melaina to jump out, but Darsey rifles through the clothing, gesturing for me to move over. Confused, I reluctantly follow.

"You're fine," Darsey assures me, clambering inside the wardrobe. The wood has been sawn into a small door, leading into a stone passage the size of a large barrel.

"You'll have to crawl, I'm afraid," he apologises. I shake my head in a way to tell him that it doesn't matter.

Darsey, who's muscular and well-built, has to shimmy through the passage in its narrowest areas, whereas I seem to have lost a considerable amount of weight in however long I've spent unconscious, so I fit though all the narrow gaps comfortably.

Eventually, Darsey and I tumble out onto a carpeted floor where Melaina is towering over us bundled up on the floor.

"Oh, my love," Melaina gasps, pulling Darsey up to her level so their lips can meet. I gawk at them, staring up helplessly.

Melaina chuckles, offering me her hand so I can pull myself to my feet.

"You'll learn many new things here, my dear, and one of them will be how to avoid the attention of Domhnall," Melaina explains, clinging onto Darsey.

"And you never managed to tell us your name," Darsey asks.

"Evanie," I rasp.

"A pretty name," Melaina smiles, guiding me over to a velvet chair in the corner of her room.

"We want to help you," Darsey assures me, "but you have to be open and honest with us, you have to tell us everything."

"From the start," Melaina continues.

I open my mouth to speak before quickly closing it to glance nervously at the ajar door and then to the wardrobe we just emerged from.

Calmly, Melaina saunters to the door, pulling a glinting silver key from her pocket to lock it from the inside.

"You know where my loyalties lie," Melaina assures me, "and Darsey's are with me. We know you're scared, but you'll be safer if you trust me."

I pause momentarily, my eyes following the patterns on the intricately carved oak panels that line the walls.

"I was born in the Darker Realm," I start quietly. Melaina and Darsey's eyes widen from bewilderment in synchronisation. "I had an older brother named Henry and an older sister called Penelope and I have a twin brother, Sebastian."

I hesitate as I recover from the stab that my vocal chords took saying Seb's name. My head throbs from how much I'm worried about him.

"My brothers were forced into the army to fight in some goddamn pointless war and my sister dragged me off to a war hospital to work as a war nurse, shortly after Sebastian and I turned eighteen and he was forced into the army. One day I was waiting by the postbox for a letter from Seb, and a girl who seemed to me, at the time, madder than a march hare. She told me my brother was in danger and she accurately guessed my name. Next thing I knew, I was on the frontline surrounded by soldiers. One of the soldiers was pressing my brother up against a wall; he was about to be shot for cowardice because he tried to run away. I begged the girl, I didn't even know who she was, to help us and she said there was only one way," I explain, astonished at how much of my old life I could recall.

"I arrived in the Lighter Realm at the beginning of summer. Sebastian and the girl, who by now I'm sure you've guessed is Phyna, had an instant connection. They loved each other until... until the day she was murdered. Even now he still loves her more than anything in the whole realm. We became members of the house, the Palace of Light became my home and I forged friendships like I never knew I could form. I travelled to Olympia with Seraphyna, Sebastian, Herminia and the students. I became a baroness and Seb became a baron," I tell them. I wonder whether to tell them about Penn, I decide not to. "I caught Star Fever when I returned, everyone had doubts about my survival, except Seraphyna, who believed I would recover. That's how I got the star."

"I think star marks are beautiful things," Darsey interjects, rolling up his right trouser leg and exposing a tiny black star on his calf.

"Clancy, one of the students, he-" I start before trailing off.

Oh, Clancy.

"Only my Clancy and his sister Avie, as well as Seraphyna and one of the students, Leora, sat with me over that week and a half, but eventually, I recovered ten times as strong. It was only shortly after that Domhnall arrived in the Eastern Isles and I think you know the rest..."

"Oh, you poor child," Melaina sighs.

"Domhnall killed not only the wife my brother loved with every inch of his being but also the man I had only started to love wholly," I explain desperately. "I loved Clancy with my heart and soul for that one night. And now... I still love him, but he's not alive to love me."

"Oh, don't weep!" Melaina pleads.

"I have lost so much to get here," I sigh, wiping my eyes with the torn edge of my muddied sleeve. "And now, I could die here. My people need me. I thought I was going to die when I stepped out to plead guilty to my crimes, but now Domhnall has foolishly given me a chance to live a while longer, I'm going to grab at it with both hands."

"Which is why we're going to help you escape as best we can, my dear," Darsey promises. "You can trust us."

"Oh, oh, thank you!" I smile, the first time I have really done so since I arrived here.

"Now, my child, I have no power over Domhnall, but you have the power of being Darkness's only foe and only you can defeat him," Melaina explains solemnly.

"But Seraphyna couldn't..." I start.

"They say that you're Oralee the Great," Darsey says quietly from his shadowed spot in the corner.

"To some extent, I am," I shrug. "Sometimes I don't believe the fact myself, but other days I am more Oralee than Evanie."

"Seraphyna had only trained her magic for four and half years. Oralee trained almost her whole life, you have that experience behind you," Darsey explains. "Domhnall is a man weak in power, though he'd kill anyone who would dare say it."

"He married me when I graduated from the Imperial Academy as I was incredibly powerful when I was young, I was the professor's prodigy. Only problem, I was a woman, so I wasn't entirely accepted by the other students at the time. I trained Domhnall with the little power he possessed but he could barely create a chain of seven links," Melaina grimaces.

"What's that about?" I question.

"To show their prowess in their magic, men of Darkness see who can create the longest chain using their power. It used to be a way to decide who would be the Duke when a Highest Lord or Lady was absent. The record for the most links was 900, made by Blake XVI around a century ago, but there has been someone who had produced more links since then," Darsey tells me.

"Who?" I ask.

"Me," Melaina smiles meekly. "But women aren't allowed to partake in the competition. I was so angry one day, I just sat in my room and made a chain of a thousand links. It's used to hang the chandelier in the great hall. Domhnall was proud of me, but also jealous. The only time he excels in his fighting is when he's so infuriated the anger fights for him. Ever since we married, he's managed to control me more and more, as I'm sure you saw on choice day."

"He treats you terribly," I nod sadly.

"I can't argue with that sentiment," she sighs.

Apprehensively, Darsey glances at the clock on the wall, watching the second hand drag itself around the face.

"You should head to your room," he tells me quietly. "Domhnall will start looking for you." He opens the door, scanning the corridor before beckoning for me to follow him. I glance back at the wardrobe in confusion.

"Can't we just-" I start. Darsey holds his hand up to stop me, waving goodbye to Melaina as he ushers me out into the corridor.

"No, you will be staying in a different room, closer to Domhnall's," Darsey explains quietly, guessing my question accurately. He grimaces in apology as I stare at him with alarm. "I'm sorry."

He leads me to a splintering, bolted door off an unlit corridor in the west wing of the castle.

"I'm under strict instructions to lock you in until Domhnall asks to see you, I'm sorry," he apologises as he presents a tiny key to open the rusty lock on the door.

"It's fine," I assure him as he gestures for me to enter the room. As I gaze around at the tiny area and its furnishings, I wonder if they've just cleared out a broom cupboard and given me that to sleep in instead. There are no windows and a dying candle hangs in a lantern from a collapsing peg on one wall. A bed is pushed against the other wall with a dust-caked shelf hanging above it. A roughly cut shard of mirror is resting against the bedframe, just about snagging on the burlap covers that encase a thin duvet that lies under a papery cotton blanket. The final thing I notice is a huge set of heavy black robes hanging from the shelf above my bed like a shadow.

Darsey grimaces as he exits silently, the bolting of the door squeaky and sharp. I plunge myself down against the wall, knees pulled up to my face. I stare at the robes, a long, black dress with an uncomfortably suggestive slit up the slinky skirt and a trailing cape with a train that must be at least a few feet long. The patterns that lace the bodice are in a green so dark, it's basically black. I hit my head against the wall several times to hold the tears back, watching the candle above me become progressively dimmer as time goes on. I pull my arms around myself, shivering from the cold. Even though Shee is very far south, it's colder than the Eastern Isles, so much so that I remember seeing ice around the window. I wonder for a moment whether that's just Domhnall's presence. I fall asleep with my head resting against the wall, tears streaming down my face and Melaina's kind words running through my mind.

An angry knock wakes me up after a few hours of sleep. My eyes fight against my desire to open them as they ache furiously.

"I'm changing," I lie rapidly, standing and walking around the miniscule space to make it sound like I'm actually doing something.

"His Majesty has requested your presence in the dining hall for dinner, Lady Evanie," someone calls through the wood.

"How long do I have?" I ask hastily.

"His Majesty asks that you bathe first and then Lady Melaina's maids will take care of you from there," he tells me, unlocking the door. I open it, clutching the robes that hung from my shelf.

"Fine, then," I reply, gesturing for the boy to lead me to where I need to go. He stares at his twiddling thumbs the whole time he walks down the dim corridors, pausing at Melaina's door before darting away silently into the darkness before I even have time to give him my thanks. Melaina answers the door almost immediately, smiling.

"Ah, you must be Evanie," she nods, acting as though she's never even met me before. She opens the door wider, gesturing for me to enter. She grabs my arm before I have the opportunity to advance much further.

"My maids are loyal to Domhnall, they're slaves but he still favours them, I'm sure I don't need to tell you why," Melaina whispers into my ear discreetly. "Act as though we've never met before and you'll be fine."

I nod concisely at her and take a seat at her dressing table as one of her maids leads me to a small room off the bedroom that has an over-spilling bath in the middle. The maids fuss over me for a few minutes before Melaina instructs them to leave me alone. I don't bathe for long, just long enough for the dirt that cakes my skin to be cleaned off and for my hair to be washed and cleaned of all the blood and muck that tangled its way among my dark locks.

After I get out, one of the maids irritably hands me a hairbrush and gruffly tells me to start brushing as one of her friends starts to brush on the other side of my hair. They style it with ease, using too many different vials to count, whose contents they brush into my hair and spray on it. A very young girl, she couldn't even be older than Avie, wanders over holding a tray of perfume bottles, asking me sweetly to choose which scent I liked best. I look over to Melaina for guidance, and she smiles knowingly, selecting one from the front row and spraying it on my neck. Then the girls start to apply my makeup, dark kohl eyeliner and deep, wine-red lipstick. I grimace at the deepness of the colour. I try to dip my head around Melaina's maids to catch a glimpse of how I look in the mirror before me.

Finally, they force me into the incredibly tight corset and massive skirt of the robes that were left for me. Surprisingly, they fit perfectly on my narrow hips and thin waist. It takes me back to when Avie and Lorna effortlessly created a dress for me out of one from Aella's wardrobe. This is different. I'm skinnier, I'm sicklier, the dress makes me look like a shell of a person.

Exactly what I am.

I eye myself up and down in the mirror, my eyes adorned with thick black liner and painted with dark shadow, although that may just be my agonising exhaustion despite the few hours of sleep I had earlier. My lips are covered with a paint of the darkest red, so deep and pigmented it's practically black.

The familiar nervous knocking sounds at the door again and Melaina answers it kindly, beckoning for me to follow her into the corridor. As I drag my aching, high-heel encased feet along the black and red patterned carpets a few steps behind Melaina, the horrible feeling that I'm on show encroaches on me like a swift-flying arrow. I observe Melaina's simple ankle-length, rather conservative gown and minimal makeup, compared to the huge mountain of material that hugs my body tightly, paired with a plunging neckline and opera gloves. Most of my face is adorned with some kind of powder or liquid, and under it all I'm uncomfortably hot, even in the harsh cold. Melaina shoots me smiles with varying ranges of pity as I hurry along to her side. The Palace of Darkness is of titanic size, but all of the corridors are narrower and darker than any of those in the Palace of Light, which is barely a cottage compared to the extent that the walls around me reach. The great hall lies at the centre of the complex maze of rooms and passages that Melaina and the escort lead me down and the doors tower over me in an intimidating sheet of dark wood and gold gilding.

Domhnall sits in his golden throne on the opposite end of the hall from the doors, observing a document that rests in Darsey's hands. Darsey doesn't look up when we enter, Melaina escorting me down the aisle of the great hall. Domhnall's face curves into a cruel smile as he sees us approach, nodding in approval.

"This was the girl I was telling you about, gentlemen," Domhnall tells the crowd behind him, all just slightly less gaunt and greasy as Domhnall, who is enjoying himself far too much.

"My dear," Domhnall looks over at Melaina, "I have some good news for you, my angel."

"What might that be, my lord?" Melaina replies obediently and meekly, bowing her head, which makes the circlet that rests among her golden hair fall lopsided on her head.

"You have leave to go and see our son in Arx," Domhnall tells her as Melaina and Darsey's eyes meet momentarily.

"How long for?" Melaina asks hopefully, her thin lips curling into a hidden smile.

"A week or two, he'll be glad to see you," he replies. "You shall leave immediately, the General will escort you."

Darsey nods quietly, bowing as he escorts Melaina out of the room, not hiding his happiness well. They glance back at me with contrasting solid faces. I read Melaina's look, she's apologising profusely through the stone mask she's putting on. I nod curtly and smile. Once they have disappeared from sight down the narrow corridor completely, Domhnall leans towards me, beckoning wickedly for me to approach the dais. Gingerly, I pace towards him, my shoes clicking against the harshly cold tiles as I do.

"I trust you're feeling well, Lady Evanie," Domhnall asks in a surprisingly kind and genuine tone.

"Very much so, my lord," I tell him through gritted teeth, tightening my already white-knuckled fists. I watch Domhnall intently as he rises from his throne slowly, his cape trailing behind him along the ground. Extending his hand as he stomps down the shallow steps, I take it, glad that both of our hands are gloved so that we may never have to touch.

Despite us not touching, Domhnall makes a flourish with his hand that isn't laid upon mine and locks my arms in place, outstretched in front of me. Gasping, I try to run, but my legs won't move either. Looking down at my skirt and bodice, I see that my body has been limited by a thin chain that extends all the way down to my ankles, around my neck and hanging off my wrists. My hands still lie flat as Domhnall takes the other one. Snapping his fingers, he commands one of his men to move his throne to the side, another to stand in the middle of the platform holding a silk cushion and an ancient, ruined book.

"What's going on?" I question desperately, my words coming out as a mere whisper rather than a shout as I intended them to.

"Lady Evanie," Domhnall looks me in the eye, his pupils dilating as he smirks roguishly. "Today is the happiest day of your life, my pearl, today is the day when we can finally marry."

"No!" I yell, the words echoing around the eaves and walls melodically. *Marry Domhnall?* I'd rather die.

"No, I will never marry you," I shake my head profusely, my eyes producing bitter tears as I break the uncomfortable gaze that Domhnall is holding. "You already have a wife."

"That hasn't stopped a thousand years of my forefathers, so it won't stop me," Domhnall laughs proudly.

"I refuse," I insist.

"Very well, then," Domhnall concludes, gesturing for another of his noble courtiers to step over. "We're going back to the Eastern Isles, I want the heads of every single person loyal to the faithful houses, and I want them displayed on the walls of the castle for Lady Evanie to see."

"No!" I gasp, trying to move my hands in protest, but Domhnall only grips them tighter.

"Then say it!" Domhnall spits. "Say that you will marry me."

I hyperventilate for a good few minutes, debating what to do. Is it even a debate? I won't have any people to save or come back to if they're all dead.

"Say it!" Domhnall insists, holding his hand in the air, ready to give the signal for his men to move at any moment. "Say it now!"

"I... I... I will... I will marry you," I sob, the words tasting like blood or poison in my mouth.

"Good," Domhnall's face softens as he lowers his hand carefully. He returns his gaze to me as he pulls me forward to face him. I have no choice but to look into his vulture eyes.

I repeat the words that I am told to say with hate, masked just enough by my panic and sadness.

"I, Evanie, promise to take you, Domhnall, *King of our Noble country of Omnia,* as my... husband, I promise to love you, serve you, trust you and obey you, *'til death do us part,'* I sob as Domhnall's harsh grip becomes tighter and tighter with every word I say. I bit my lip from the pain to save myself from crying out.

"And do you promise to allege yourself to the House of Darkness?"

"I..." I pause, not sure if I can say it. Domhnall raises a brow as he watches my hesitation as though this is just a juvenile game to him. The tears that were running down my cheeks reach my chin and he tenderly wipes them away. I keep my mouth shut in protest. Suddenly, my mouth is opening, I'm unable to control myself, it's as though an invisible hand is moving my mouth and tugging on my vocal cords for me. I inhale as I say it.

"I do."

*

Melaina and Darsey eventually come back from visiting her son (who I'm almost certain is Darsey's son, not Domhnall's). She greets me with open arms upon her return, with Darsey following closely behind her in a dizzy haze of happiness. I was overjoyed to finally see people who were my allies. Melaina talks relentlessly as we walk to her room about how Deene, her son, was able to hit a bullseye on an archery target even though he's only ten, how he's grown up so fast. I smile and nod as she continues to talk. Darsey chimes in every now and again with a small anecdote or compliment on Deene, but he makes sure not to seem too happy about everything that the boy is up to as people are always listening.

When we reach Melaina's room, she takes my hand gladly and smiles. I sigh with relief that I'm safe. I haven't seen Domhnall since the wedding, nothing even happened afterwards. He just sent me back to my room alone after slipping a huge black diamond on my ring finger. Melaina glances down at the ring, furrowing her brow at the sight of it. Eyes wide, she raises her head and stares at me in disbelief. The words pass across her lips like a breeze.

"No," she whispers as Darsey wanders over also. He gasps as I take off the ring and slide it into my pocket.

"He threatened to kill my people," I explain desperately. "I'm so sorry."

"Oh, no, my child, *I'm* the one who should apologise," Melaina insists, forcing me to sit down as she wraps her lean arms around my shoulder. "I shouldn't have left you there alone with him, I should've known, my dear, *I'm* so sorry, I just hadn't seen Deene in almost a month, and I was so excited when Domhnall said Darsey could come with me, he could finally meet his son."

"It's no one's fault but Domhnall's," Darsey interjects bitterly, crossing his arms and leaning against the wall by the corner of Melaina's room as he usually does.

"Evanie, it is more important than anything that we seek to help you to escape before Domhnall decides that it's finally time for you to die," Melaina tells me hastily, grabbing a tiny, pocket-sized book from the small shelf of books that hang above her roaring, warming fireplace.

"What's that?" I ask.

"A queen's map of the palace," Melaina tells me. "It has all of the secret passages marked on, we're going to find one that will help you escape."

"We can't do it now, though," Darsey stops her quickly, glancing nervously to the door. "He'll most likely host a wedding ball in the next few weeks to announce his marriage to Evanie. That's when we'll have the best chance of distracting him and helping you escape, Evanie."

"But won't I be centre of attention?" I ask. "Won't Domhnall want to show off his 'pearl' to his courtiers?" I gag as I say it. Domhnall, every time he sees me, calls me 'my pearl' so as to make a mockery of me. He calls me the name with that wicked smile he's always wearing across his face and it only becomes wider when he sees me. Not a smile of love or affection, but a smile a hunter makes when he sees his prey.

"You really think Domhnall cares about you?" Darsey asks, scoffing. I shake my head fervently. I *hope* he doesn't care about me. No one wants the love of a monster, I most certainly don't.

"Domhnall will only want to show off the fact that he's now a man who has it all, an heir, two wives, a 'thriving kingdom', not that it is, and hundreds of rich and powerful men at his feet. He'll only use your marriage as an excuse to spend more of his people's money on his friends and allies," Melaina sighs, opening the tiny book and scanning the pages closely.

"We'll have to find someone to distract him," Darsey concludes, placing his large hand to his face in thought, staring out of the window.

"I'll do it," Melaina offers, closing the book. "As much as I hate him, I'm still his weakness. Under all that twisted evil, he still loves me, somewhere."

"You don't have to put yourself in that position," I tell her, "Please, Melaina, don't, you could get hurt."

"For the sake of the realm, I'll risk anything," Melaina insists stubbornly. "There's a passage by the minstrel gallery that leads to the south tower, which isn't guarded at night."

"No, it is," Darsey admits., "But I can dismiss those guards, tell them they need to be in the hall on the lookout for dangers to guests, they'll listen to me."

"You are their general," I shrug.

"Yes, and I'm going to use that to my advantage," Darsey nods. "I'm just not sure how we're going to get you up to the minstrel gallery."

"The harp player," Melaina says quickly. "The harp player takes requests. Evanie will go up there, request a song and leave through the passage in the broom cupboard, which you will see if you're up there."

"What if Domhnall doesn't throw a ball at all?" I ask nervously.

"He's an Omnian, my child," Melaina laughs. "Trust me, he will."

*

Melaina was right, Domhnall did throw a ball. A raven landed on Melaina's windowsill when we were discussing forthcoming plans, holding two small pieces of parchment in its beak. Both of the notes said exactly the same thing, except they were to different people. Not our names, no, that would be far too humane of Domhnall. No, Melaina's was addressed to 'my angel', mine to 'my pearl'. I think I never want to see or wear another pearl again in my entire life, even if I live forever. The notes were written in the same, blood-red cursive that all Domhnall's notes were written in.

This evening, midnight, Great Hall, make sure to look lovely.

I'll be waiting.

-D

"I'll be waiting?" I scoff in disgust. "Is there no end to his games?"

"I've been playing chess for years," Melaina tells me sadly. "Now you've joined, I'm going to do everything in my power to put him in checkmate."

I return to my room whilst it's still light. My door is locked but I have no key. I try to budge the stupid thing open with all my might, but I have no success. Suddenly, out of the darkness, a hand rests on my shoulder. I jump, yelping slightly.

"Good evening, my pearl," Domhnall cackles, turning me around to face him as he grins.

"And to you, my lord," I smile at him through gritted teeth.

"I trust you received my invite," he whispers, hissing like a snake as he says it. Slowly, he starts to push me backwards, cornering me as my back is against the wall. "Will you attend?"

"It… it would be… my honour, my lord," I nod, crinkling up my nose, facing away from him to avoid the reek of ale he emits.

"I look forward to seeing you then, my pearl," he laughs under his breath, hissing and slurring from his drunkenness. Despite turning his head away from me, he doesn't leave, his hands still linger on my shoulders. My mind starts racing as fast as my heart is pounding inside my chest as I prepare myself for the worst.

"Don't worry," he whispers wickedly, throwing his hands up beside his head and stepping away from me. "I would never hurt you, Evanie, not yet, at least," he chuckles as I turn to try and force the locked door open.

"It's no use, Evanie," Domhnall tells me, shaking his head at me like I'm a toddler.

"Why didn't you just kill me?" I growl, the tears in my eyes dangerously close to exposing themselves by running down my cheeks.

"Oh, Evanie," Domhnall breathes, approaching me once more with a menacingly slow pace. He places his arms around my neck. I don't know whether he's embracing me or strangling me. "Oh, Evanie, Evanie, Evanie."

I hate the way he says my name. The way he lingers on the syllables, the way his lips twitch as he forms the vowels. I hate it. I hate it more than anything.

"Get away from me," I threaten, struggling against his grip.

"Oh, my pearl," he smiles. "I'm going to make you *suffer* until you *beg* for death."

*

After I am finally ready at 11 o'clock, I head to Melaina's room alone. I've just about figured out the way on my own now, and I know when to turn from one dark corridor into another.

"Good evening, your *lightest*," someone calls to me through the darkness. A hand rests on my shoulder, making my blood run cold as winter. I turn hastily towards the figure. She smiles at me gently, her deep brown eyes gazing at me sincerely.

"I'm sorry, do I know you?" I ask, my brow knitted as I observe her. She starts to laugh, retracting her hand away from me.

"Oh, you've definitely heard of me, Lady Evanie," she chuckles. Her dress is of the deepest blue, so dark it's hard to tell whether it really is black or not in the darkness. Her incredibly platinum hair shimmers in the moonlight that radiates from the windows, the only light in the corridors.

"I assume you're Isoletta," I raise a brow.

"And you have assumed correctly, Evanie," Isoletta nods.

"How did you know it was me?"

"You have the mark on your hand," she smiles as I lift my star-marked hand up to the moonlight.

"So it seems," I chuckle. Isoletta, upon reflection, is unlike Melaina or Eithne in so many ways. Whilst

Melaina and Eithne have incredibly kind and caring personalities underneath the submission they display in front of their respective husbands, Isoletta obviously displays her confidence every waking moment of her day, a fact I can tell even when Daileass isn't anywhere near her.

"Well, I suppose I'll see you at the ball, Lady Evanie," Isoletta says kindly. "And my condolences."

"On what?" I question.

"My condolences on your marriage and on the loss of your freedom," Isoletta frowns, sinking back into the darkness.

I knock on Melaina's door when I finally find it and Darsey answers with a smile.

"Good evening," he grins.

"And to you," I reply, stepping onto Melaina's plush carpets.

"How are you feeling?" Melaina asks me as I enter, standing to embrace me. I'm happy and relieved to see that she is just as dressed up as I am, her makeup extremely dark and brooding, sadly an ugly contrast to her pale brown eyes that sit under the darkness. Her dress has a train that sweeps around the room as she walks, throwing up the dust and ashes that sit around the fireplace. It's only when that happens that I realise her dress is on fire.

"Melaina!" I exclaim, running over to her train, patting the fire out with a rug beater that was hanging from the wall. Try as I might, the flames refuse to extinguish.

"I know," she sighs sadly, turning to face me. Despite her train being on fire, the flames do not spread to the rug or anywhere else in the room but are still moving at a snail's pace up the fabric of her dress.

"Why?" I ask in bewilderment.

"To keep me at bay," Melaina grimaces, flapping her train to remove the dust from it. "If I say one thing wrong then I can burn up."

"Wait..." I stop them. "Does that mean Aidan is here?"

"Yes," Darsey replies suspiciously, raising an eyebrow at my alarm.

"Aidan has met me before, he knows what I look like, except he thought I was a Myriean brothel runaway. That's when I found out I had Star Fever. If he finds out that I know things that the faithful houses were never supposed to know, he could try and kill me. I know of his cowardice and his cruelty and Aidan won't like that," I panic, placing my gloved hand to my chest to slow my breathing.

"Oh, Saints be damned!" Melaina exclaims sighing in frustration. "You're right, Evanie."

"If I fake an illness, could I get out of going to the ball?" I question awkwardly, removing my gloves from my hands, which are sweaty and clammy with anxiousness and nervousness.

"I don't think that Eithne and Aidan are arriving until the early morning. There was a delay as the babies were tired and unwell so they had to stop a few miles down the coast of Calia," Darsey explains, his eyes darting around the room as he calculates my new escape plan.

"How long is the ball going to go on for?" I question in disbelief. It was already a shock that the ball started at midnight, but now I find out that it goes on until at least the early morning? I'm already exhausted.

"Until midday usually," Melaina laments, yawning as she says it. I throw my head back against the velvet chair in exhaustion.

"Domhnall's a proud man, he wants as long as possible to show off his fine life," Darsey sulks, crossing his arms. I turn to Melaina.

"How *in the realm* did you end up marrying that man?" I exclaim, throwing my hands above my head in disbelief.

"Do you really want to know?" she asks.

"I don't know," I say slowly, observing her expression.

"It's a long story, it will pass the time," Melaina offers. "It may help you to understand the man more. Understand me more, even."

"Alright," I conclude, sitting back in my chair.

"I was born in a far-off land, which they call Calanda. My father was the warden of an island nearby that was owned by the Omnian royal family. They used the island, Staré, as a prison, and my father would travel there once a week and check on the prisoners and send a letter back to Domhnall's father on the state of the prison. Anyway, my family was quite rich from my father's position. I was the eldest daughter, I had an elder brother and three younger siblings, a brother and two sisters. When I was about eleven, my father developed a horrible gambling habit, and by the time I was 13, he had gambled all of our money away," Melaina starts.

"That's awful!" I exclaim, pressing my hand to my mouth.

"Yes, it was awful," Melaina confirms. "My mother made the decision that my siblings and I would be safer away from Calanda, as there were many men on our island that my father owed money to and my mother feared they may try and force him to pay by threatening us. My little brother, my sisters, my mother and I all left Calanda, leaving my elder brother and my father behind. I haven't seen either of them since, that was almost eighteen years ago now."

"No letters? Nothing?" I question in disbelief.

"Nothing," she sighs in lamentation. "We arrived in a terrifying, dark land a few weeks later. Surprisingly, the land's king was kind and welcomed us with quite open arms. He referred me to the care of his son."

"Domhnall?" I guess. Melaina nods, lips pursed.

"The boy was incredibly charming, he asked me about any power I might have or whether I wanted to try for a choice day. Of course, I didn't know what a choice day was, and my mother was sceptical, but Domhnall liked me so much and had so much faith in me that he persuaded his father to let me be a candidate on the same choice day that Domhnall's brother Daileass chose. I was right at the end, which scared the life out of me, as so many of the candidates before breezed through the process so easily like they'd practised in their sleep. I was unsure of what I was doing, whether I was going to be chosen for a house at all, or whether one in a million possible things would go wrong. I think you can guess the rest, I was chosen for Darkness. I practically knocked the whole crowd over with my power, at least, that's what Daileass said, and I was chosen to be student of wielding, which caused some murmuring in the library as I was a woman and they'd never had a woman in the library before. Slowly, over the four years I completed my studies, my family settled into the village near the palace quite well, and my siblings found jobs at the palace. None of them were ever put in for choice day, but I don't think they wanted to take the risk of possibly having to leave my mother," Melaina grimaces, pausing to sigh deeply.

"And that's when things started to go wrong," she laments. "Domhnall eventually fell in love with me, and there was some part of my mind that fell in love with him, the part that wasn't ringing with alarm bells, that was. He became fed up with just being Baron of Darkness as he wanted to marry me and his father said no. So, he killed his father. I was there. And just for fun, he killed his mother and his father's other wife, Arista."

"Seraphyna's mother?" I ask.

"Yes, he killed them on the floor of the royal palace's ballroom and fled the scene. The king and his wives, as well as his daughter, a little girl I grew to love because of her sweet charms and smiles, I'm sure you can figure out who that was, were eating when Domhnall stormed in with his guards and murdered them all. Domhnall was going to kill Seraphyna too. I begged him not to. I physically got on my knees before him and begged him to spare her. Reluctantly, he agreed."

"And if he hadn't..." I start.

"Oh, I dread to think, my child," she presses her hand against her forehead lightly, closing her eyes in thought. "I'm so glad he spared her. So glad. We married the next day. There was still a part of me that loved him. Even though I'd seen him murder in cold blood. I still stared at him the way newlyweds were supposed to stare at each other, I still overlooked all his incredibly imperfect imperfections. He became bitter and furious as his claim to the throne was challenged, he was no longer my

Domhnall. He was a force of Darkness to be reckoned with and woe betide you if you questioned him on anything. He started to see other women behind my back, this was less than six months after we married. I occupied myself with Seraphyna's care to distract myself from the fact that I was stuck with him for the rest of my life. He started to limit my power. I didn't realise until it was almost too late. He was doing it with the help of the professor, who I thought was my friend. That really hurt me, almost as much as the fact my husband felt I needed controlling like an animal in a cage."

I look over at Darsey, whose fists are clenched. His lazy smile has twisted into a furious, agonisingly pained grimace as he hears of Melaina's torture. You can tell he loves her more than anything.

"The last thing I could do with the power I had left when I realised what Domhnall was doing was cast one single spell," Melaina tells me in a hushed tone.

"And that was?"

"He can't have children," she raises her eyebrows. "He will never have a true heir and his blood will never pass on. I know it sounds cruel, but he had his chance to be happy, and it died with my respect for him. Even after all that, I still felt guilty, I nearly lifted the spell, because I'm sure somewhere inside me, at the deepest and dustiest point of my heart's cellar, there was some love for him shut up in a box," she pauses to scoff.

"It sounds stupid, after the way he treated me and the things he did to me. I can assure you though, that box was smashed with a sledgehammer and thrown into an ocean of tears. I went away to visit some friends a town away from the palace. I was gone for a few days. Whilst I was gone, my little sister, who worked as a maid to one of Domhnall's mistresses, was approached by him and asked to go to bed with him. She refused as, bless her soul, she didn't understand that just because he was married to me that he would stay with me and me only. He became so angry at her refusal that her head wound up on a pyre on the palace walls, displayed in full glory for me to see in the moonlight as I returned."

I never even knew Melaina's sister, but my eyes water in memory of her, in memory of her cruel death and how she didn't deserve to die at Domhnall's cruel hands. I reach out to slide my trembling palm over Melaina's paling hand.

"But then I met Darsey," Melaina smiles, glancing over at him shyly. "And then Deene was born, and of course he wasn't Domhnall's, but he didn't know that. But Deene was sent away to a few towns along for his 'safety'. He was sent away because Domhnall couldn't be bothered with fatherhood, in short."

The clock chimes in a low and mellow tone, just once, as the cross-breeze in the room shifts.

"It's quarter to midnight," I state, heaving myself up from the armchair as Melaina does the same and Darsey pulls himself away from the corner in the shadows. "It'll take us a while to reach the ballroom, anyway."

When we finally knock on the doors of the ballroom at five to midnight, Darsey marches ahead into the ballroom to avoid suspicion. Melaina and I are told to stay back to be properly announced as we descend the stairs. Isoletta is held back as well, including some other rather scandalously dressed ladies from the court of Water... and the court of Fire.

Oh, no.

Eithne approaches from behind me, luckily no Aidan by her side, but accompanied by a few of her ladies-in-waiting, one of which carries a small baby in her arms.

"Eithne!" I exclaim, trying to be hushed. "I thought you weren't arriving until the morning?"

"Evanie?" Eithne questions, furrowing her brow in confusion about my presence. "No, we managed to make up time, Aidan was anxious we'd miss the first dance and he wanted to be there for it."

"Right," I mutter. Shouting a hundred curses in my head.

"Are the rumours true? Domhnall forced you to marry him or else he'd kill your people?" she widens her eyes.

I hold my hand up to show her my horrible ring. "I'm afraid so."

Discreetly, she places her hand on mine in solidarity, which brightens my spirits.

"I'm so sorry," she sighs.

"Don't be sorry," I reply sadly. "It's no one's fault but mine."

Hestia looks upon me with pity and sympathy. Her frown says it all.

Eithne's frown says it all, the doors open with a creak as Melaina pushes for me to get into position behind Eithne.

"I just can't believe Caspian's gone!" I wail, "First I lost my son and now my husband. Luke's still away and Xanthe won't talk to me, it pains me more than anything, Hestia."

"It will get better," she promises, rubbing my back supportively.

"Did he even think before he did it?" I question.

"Grief does terrible things to people, Oralee," Hestia *frowns.*

"We could've got through it together," I sob, *failing to dry my eyes with my sleeve because of the sheer depth of the waterfall that flows from my eyes.*

"You had Star Fever, he probably thought he would lose you too, Oralee," she offers, *but I hold my hand up to stop her.*

"Please," I beg, *"just go. Please. Go."*

"Go!" Eithne exclaims, pushing me forwards into the sight of the entire ballroom. "Evanie, go!"

"Alright, I'll leave you alone," Hestia *concludes.* *"But promise me that you'll think twice about everything you do."*

Melaina smiles gracefully at me as I stumble up next to her.

"The wives of his majesty, the king. The queen consort, Melaina, and her highness, Lady Evanie," the announcer declares to the crowd as my head cartwheels violently like a spinning top. I descend the steps only with the help of the bannister, which I cling onto so tightly my knuckles are white.

Domhnall takes my hand to kiss it first and, again, I am grateful for my gloves, which I wish I could burn. He takes Melaina's hand next, and she makes intense eye contact with Darsey as Domhnall takes her hand to his lips. After Eithne and Isoletta as well as their ladies have descended the steps, I frantically start looking around the hall for Aidan, trying to spot if he has caught sight of me. Nervously, I glance back at Eithne, who shakes her head comfortingly at me, turning her head back towards the door herself. Just in that moment, Aidan enters the hall, descending the steps before the announcer has even started to announce him. Eithne signals for me to turn around, and I keep my fingers crossed that my dark makeup and intensive slimming over the past month or so is enough for him to not recognise me enough to alert Domhnall and just shrug it off as a passing coincidence.

"May I have this dance, my pearl?" Domhnall asks me, extending his hand in expectation for me to take it. Melaina barely glances at me, but just enough that I know she's going to intervene.

"Wouldn't you prefer to dance with me, my lord?" Melaina giggles, lowering the shoulder of her gown to expose her bruised skin. Domhnall purses his lips in approval.

"I'm sorry, my pearl, but my angel always comes first," Domhnall apologises, gesturing for the minstrels to start playing. He places his huge hands around Melaina's waist and I can tell she's trying not to keep staring at Darsey, who's dancing with a lady of the court. He nods to me discreetly. I nod back.

"Thank you," I mouth, which is followed by another nod. Melaina catches my eye as I start to ascend the steps to the minstrel gallery. I don't need to tell her thank you. I know it's not the last time I will see her again. As for Domhnall, it may be the last time I ever see my husband alive.

I smile at the thought.

I have a brief chat with the harp player, an extremely shy woman who hides in the corner of the minstrel gallery by the broom cupboard. *Perfect.* I press a finger to my lips as I fiddle with the handle of the broom cupboard and the harpist is too frightened to question me. As I go to turn to step into the cupboard, a hand is placed on my shoulder. My blood runs cold.

"Looking for something, my lady?" Aidan asks me as he spins me around forcibly to face him. "An escape, perhaps? In a broom cupboard?"

"Uh... no, my lord, I'm just looking for a broom," I lie. "One of the servants spilt something and I..."

"Don't play games with me, girl, I know who you are. Little did I know that I'd met you before," Aidan chuckles as he pulls me out of the corner, the eyes of the harpist gradually becoming wider and wider.

"I don't think so, my lord," I stutter.

"Don't lie, I'd recognise that cursed mark on your hand anywhere, in such plain sight, such a valiant battle scar, don't you think?" He mocks me tilting his head in false concern.

"Please don't tell Domhnall..." I plead, joining my hands together, begging him.

"I think it would be more fun to tell him, don't you think?" Aidan smiles, his wicked grin the same as Domhnall's, the same bone-chilling, evil expression painted on their faces. "Oh, Domhnall!" He exclaims as he pulls me down the gallery steps by my dress sleeve.

"What do you want, little brother?" Domhnall asks tiresomely as Aidan leads me up to him. "And get your hands off my wife, get yourself another wife if you're so desperate for mine."

"Guess where I found your little pearl?" Aidan quizzes, making Domhnall sigh. "I found her in the minstrel gallery broom cupboard, where there is a passage to the south tower."

Anger briefly passes across Domhnall's face, his eyes pure fury as he gazes upon me.

"Thank you, Aidan," he says through gritted teeth, before exhaling and addressing me. "You, girl, go back to your chamber. Now. We will discuss this later. Go!"

He shouts at me so loudly that the whole ballroom hears him say it and goes quiet. He smiles calmly at his subjects and raises a glass, which signals the room to start mumbling again. Tears in my eyes and fearing for my neck, I stumble back up the stairs and hurry out of the doors into the darkness. I reach my room in almost total darkness and I have to fumble around in the pitch blackness to unlock the door. One I am inside, I light the room with my command, and the light spreads from one corner to the other. I play with the light as I sit on my bed and jump at every sound that I hear. Even if it's the breeze that blows under my door or the mice in the corner, I jump. The light gradually becomes darkness as my sorrow and fear takes control of what I am doing. Consumed by the darkness and my feelings, I pull my knees up to my chest and sit with my back against the wall, staring through the darkness at the damp wall opposite me.

Just as I give up and decide to get up again, a knock sounds at my door. I don't even know what time it is, so it might not even be Domhnall, but my heart starts racing faster than an eagle. I light up the room again, staring at the shadow of the knocker's feet under the door. I don't ask who it is, I just open the door.

"Message for you, my lady," the knocker tells me.

"Avie?" I question, not daring to believe my eyes. I must be dreaming.

"Come on, Evanie, let me in," she whispers. I oblige, shutting the door behind her.

"Avie what are you doing here?" I ask her, sitting her down on the bed.

"What does it look like? We're freeing you," she tells me.

"We?"

"Herminia and Aella are waiting in the next town down the coast," she says, opening the door and checking if anyone is there.

"How did you get in?" I ask her as she leads me down the corridor, holding her hand out to silence our footsteps.

"Turns out anyone can just walk into a ball if the doors are open and you have a well-faked invitation," she laughs. "Domhnall's not the smartest man in the world, and I was really the only one who could come as I'm the most unrecognisable of us, you know?"

"Mm," I reply, although I'm distracted by the sight of a guard in the next corridor.

"Avie," I whisper, pointing discreetly towards the guard.

"Oh, don't worry, they can't see us," she chuckles. "Or hear us," she waves at the guard frantically, shouting things after him as he patrols the corridor. I smile fondly. She leads me to the South Tower which, luckily, Darsey still has assured is absent of soldiers, not that it would matter so much.

"Here we are," she says. "A Valkyrie should be along to fly you to the port where Herminia and Aella are waiting for you."

"You're not coming?"

"I'm staying here to take your place," she frowns, placing her hand on my shoulder and turning to leave.

"Avie, no," I tell her forcibly. "I won't let you do that, you're too young, you don't know what Domhnall might do to you."

"If you die or get hurt, my brother dies for nothing, and that scares me more than anything else," she insists, tears in her eyes.

"Clancy wouldn't have wanted you to do this, Avie," I assure her.

"He would've done if it meant you living," she shakes her head.

"Avie," I plead. "Clancy would have wanted us both to live."

"It'll be risky," she whispers quietly. "But you're right."

I smile widely, extending my hand for Avie to take it. Just in that moment, a huge Valkyrie appears in the sky next to the tower.

"I can't get any closer," the Valkyrie shouts over the roar of the breeze that her wings emit. "You're going to have to jump, Avie."

I nod at the Valkyrie and then at Avie, and we run up to the wall of the tower and leap over the stony barrier, hands still clasped together tightly. I close my eyes as I jump, and when they're opened, we're floating away from the Palace of Darkness through the night sky.

Freedom.

I can taste it on the tip of my tongue, hear it roaring through my ears, surging through my body as I throw my hands behind me, emitting a trail of light behind us as we soar away amongst the stars.

It doesn't take long for us to reach the port that Herminia and Aella are stationed at. The Valkyrie lands gracefully on the roof of a small castle that faces the sea, glinting in the slithers of moonlight that touch the waves.

"Thank you," I smile at the Valkyrie as she takes off and heads back towards Berr, over the ocean. Avie and I stand on the roof, looking around for a way to get into the castle. Behind us, I hear an excited scream.

"Evanie!" Aella exclaims, running over to me to embrace me in her fur-laden arms.

"Aella! Herminia!" I grin, embracing them both. "Oh, I'm free, I really am!"

"Did he hurt you?" Herminia asks worriedly, looking me over as she holds me at arm's length.

"Not terribly," I assure her. "But he underestimated me, and now I'm away from his clutches."

Six Queens

Herminia and Aella escort me and Avie back across the sea to Berr, where we should be safe. We keep glancing worriedly behind us as we sail over the rough waves to see if any of Domhnall's fleet are following us, but, surprisingly, they're not. Either he hasn't noticed I'm gone, or he's waiting for me.

Luckily, he's not. We reach Berr by sunrise. The small port by the capital and Herminia's palace is as bustling as the markets of Olympia. I see a small crowd of people waiting right at the end of the pier, at the furthest point you can stand without falling into the glistening ocean. As our small boat pulls into the dock, they all attack us with relived embraces and smiles.

Lorna, Conaire and the professor are the first ones to greet me, and my heart pangs as I notice a Clancy-sized gap in their crowd. He should be here to greet me, say he's glad that I'm alive, tell me he loves me. But he's not, he's looking down on me, unable to tell me any of those things.

"Evanie!" Seb calls from the back of the gathering. I push through the others to get to him, clinging on to his shirt as I embrace him like I never have before. *I understand your pain.* I try to tell him, but my tears prevent me from opening my mouth to do anything else but sob. *I understand what it's like to lose someone you love with your whole heart. I know what it's like.*

"I thought you were dead," he whispers to me.

"Alive as ever," I tell him. "How are you coping?"

"Am I even?" He sighs, breaking our embrace, trying not to cry out. "Now that she's gone, it's like I'm screaming and no one can hear me."

"I can hear you," I reassure him, frowning at the wooden ground of the dock. "You really miss her?"

"Every day. Everything I see, I hear and touch brings her memory back to me accompanied with an agony I can't extinguish. I'm destroyed, Evanie, I have no heart anymore since it died with her. God, I can't even bring myself to say her name. It's not right."

"Nothing is anymore," I assure him. "But you'll heal, somehow." Even though I say the words with hope, I'm still apprehensive to believe there is any, because I really do think what he says is true. His heart died with Seraphyna.

"If I asked every person in all the realms what pain was, they couldn't describe this," he laments, shaking his head, the light catching on his curls.

"Sebastian? Evanie?" Herminia asks, ushering us towards the palace.

"Coming," I call back, smiling sadly at Seb. We join hands, sauntering towards the palace together.

The Palace of Earth is nothing like the palaces of Light, Air and Darkness. Whilst all the other palaces I've been in have been great turreted castles, the Palace of Earth is a row of huge, amazingly gigantic oak trees, joined together by fraying rope bridges. It looks like something from a fairytale, with squirrels and birds scuttling around the branches and eating the leaves of the trees, those same leaves growing back immediately. The windows of the palace are carved into the trees, and the great hall sits in the very middle of it all, inside a tree that is as large as the Palace of Light in its own right, with huge stained-glass windows adorned with charmingly overgrown ivy and wreaths of roses. The doors of the palace lead straight into the great hall, and the west and east wings branch off from there. The minstrel gallery is reached by climbing a bough of ivy at the rear of the hall, and the instruments that stand alone in the gallery are spindly and charming.

I turn to Lorna and Conaire, who are gazing around at the great hall in wonder, at the vines that hang from the ceiling, at the carved eaves that have limbs of trees with blossoming flowers.

"Just a tad more impressive than the Palace of Light?" I ask them, and they nod in unison.

"More than a tad, this is the most amazing place I've ever been in my life," Conaire sighs.

"How long was I gone for?" I question.

"About a month and a half. It took them a while to travel back to Shee from the Eastern Isles, and they kept you asleep the whole time, and then you are in the palace for a month or so, yes?" Lorna says.

"Correct," I nod, watching as Aella and Herminia beckon us to step towards the east wing.

"Evanie, we need to discuss strategy, but if you're tired, I understand," Aella tells me kindly.

"No, I'll be fine," I lie, trying to stop my eyes drooping.

"Here," Herminia offers, handing me a small vial suspended from her belt on a vine. "It'll liven you up a bit."

"Thank you," I smile as I accept it gracefully, taking a small sip of the golden liquid from the vial. Instantly, I feel better, my shoulders even out and I stop slouching. My eyes open wider and a warm glow spreads around my body. Aella leads us into the library, seating us around a long table with a map pinned in the centre. Dagan, Corentin and Rosaleen, the professor of Earth, are already sitting around it. I stare at Rosaleen for a moment. Apart from Phye or perhaps Eithne and Melaina, I have never seen a more beautiful woman in my life. Even though she is a professor, she is as young as me, even. From what I've heard of her she's the youngest professor for five hundred years and can grow a 10-foot-tall oak tree from just one flourish of her hand. I have also heard some less savoury things about her, like how she was the mistress of the Count of Ilene, and even has a child by him. I have seen her once before on choice day, and her eyes are more drooped and saddened than they were then, so perhaps she did have some relationship with him. I smile at the three of them as Seb, Lorna, Conaire, Aella, Herminia, Avie and I all sit down at the table. In some ways, Avie's presence is bittersweet. With Clancy's absence comes Avie's presence, and she has almost replaced him as the incredibly intelligent, knowledgeable, shy but curious member of our group. Somehow, she has almost replaced her brother, but not quite. Clancy is irreplaceable.

"As most of you have probably figured out by now, Domhnall is going to start looking for Evanie," Aella starts, fiddling with the small wooden boats that were laid out on the pinned down map on the table. "We have to make sure that she's protected."

"I'm not hiding away like a crown to be kept safe," I insist. "If we're going to fight him, I want Domhnall to know who he crossed. I want to be there to fight for all of the people who couldn't be there."

Silently, we agree to stop talking for a moment and bow our heads in memory of those we have lost. The battle moved so quickly on from fighting to me being taken away from the Eastern Isles, we haven't had much time to stop and mourn, to just be quiet. We hang our heads and imagine the faces of the fallen passing through our minds. We're silent for them. For Ilene. For Clancy. For Seraphyna. Herminia is the first to look up at us, signalling for me to stand as she walks over to the cabinet next to the bookshelves suspended from the ceiling. She unlocks the top cupboard, pulling out a velvet cushion with a dainty, golden crown resting amongst the fabric. I gasp.

The Sun Crown.

It's beautiful. The way that the gold manages to weave its way around itself, sprouting out in places that reflect the light so well. The jewels are clear but change colour as the light shifts when Herminia presents it to me.

"May I?" I ask quietly, not daring to drag my fingers across the smooth gold for fear the power may knock me over.

"Only the worthy can touch the crown, only the true leader can wear it," Herminia tells me with a raised eyebrow. I exhale in panic. *What if I'm not worthy?* "I'm absolutely certain that it will look perfect on you."

Slowly, Herminia passes the crown to Seb, who holds it by the sides in his hands. He raises it above my head and places it among my hair. I suddenly become very conscious of the fact that I am still wearing my ballgown from the Palace of Darkness, and it feels wrong that I am being crowned in such attire.

"It suits you so well, Evanie," Herminia smiles as every one of the people around the table stare at me with mouths agape.

"Are you sure?" I ask uncertainly.

"Really, Evanie, you look perfect," Someone says. I look around at the gathering in front of me, but none of them opened their mouths. It's only when I realise that, I notice that the voice sounded exactly like Seraphyna's kind, reassuring, smooth tone. I smile, staring up at the sky. *Thank you,* I mouth.

"Now, we need to discuss what the plan is after we defeat Domhnall," I conclude, sitting back down at the table and rubbing the thick eyeliner from my eyes.

"Well, Seraphyna had an idea she told me about," Aella pipes up, almost shyly.

"Proceed," I urge her.

"She said that the only way to achieve peace is to abolish the royal family altogether and separate the ruling party of Omnia into six, one for each house. The king or queen of the house would name an heir who is a member of the house, which doesn't necessarily have to be his or her child. The kings and queens of the houses would rule the entire country together and meet together regularly, but ultimately has claim over their territory," Aella explains.

"Well," Rosaleen starts, "Seraphyna was a very wise woman."

"She's obviously read the right scriptures and researched what would work and what wouldn't," Avie tells us quietly.

"Do we all agree that?" Herminia asks. "That's half of the leaders of the houses."

"We'll never get Daileass and Aidan to agree though, Hermie," Aella points out nervously. "And who will take over after Domhnall? His son? He's ten!"

"Deene isn't Domhnall's son," I disclose. "He's Darsey's son. Melaina cast a final spell on Domhnall which meant he would never have an heir. I think that Deene's too young, but I know someone who deserves a crown after all she's been through,"

"Melaina?" Seb guesses. I nod.

"You have no idea what she told me Domhnall has done to her, I was lucky he didn't have enough time to start with me," I sigh in relief but also worry. What's Domhnall planning now? Is Melaina taking the brunt of his anger?

"And then for Water and Fire? We can't have Daileass lead water, he's a half-decent man, but a terrible ruler and a selfish creature above all else," Lorna adds.

"Isoletta does all his diplomacy, and she's the best general Water's ever had," Aella holds up a finger. "The people love her, they'd *worship* her as a queen."

"It's the same with Eithne for Fire," Lorna sighs. "They've already tried to overthrow Aidan and put Eithne on the throne. She's so incredibly talented in her power the Calians don't even care that she's a woman."

"So, it's agreed," I nod. "Instead of one king, Omnia will, for the first time, have six queens."

*

We wait for days. Domhnall doesn't even make a move. No ships even leave Shee. In the end, I snap from the worry. I barge into the library at exactly midday.

"We're leaving for Shee," I order. "Now."

"That's exactly what he wants us to do, Evanie," Aella sighs, reshuffling the deck of cards laid out in front of her and Herminia.

"No, I'm worried about Melaina," I tell them. "You haven't had a proper conversation with your brother for years, he's become cruel as a northern winter."

"His palace is unbreakable," Aella points out. Seb enters the library casually, slumping down in a chair by the fireplace. I smile. It's the first action I've seen him do that makes him look like himself since Seraphyna's death. Although, I know he'll never go back to being his true self. Seraphyna wasn't just a part of him. She was half of everything he did.

"Unbreakable? Impossibility? Nothing's impossible," Seb shakes his head.

"Titanic!" I exclaim. Aella and Herminia furrow their brows, Seb raises a finger.

"Ah, yes!" He nods. Aella and Herminia become more and more confused by the second. I chuckle.

"The Titanic was a great, huge ship built a few years before our war started, back in the Darker Realm," I tell them. "It was said to be unsinkable. Lo and behold, in the middle of its first voyage, it hit an iceberg and it's now lying on the ocean floor."

"And?" Herminia says, still not catching on.

"My point is, if unsinkable ships can be sunk, why can't unbreakable fortresses be broken in to?" I start to pace the floor of the library, waiting for a reaction from Aella or Herminia. Seb still looks at me encouragingly.

"Well, Evanie," Herminia concludes. "You certainly are the Queen of Light Seraphyna would be proud of."

*

Our boats sail from Berr that afternoon. Men from all the Faithful Houses sit in the boats and wait as we cross the waters. The Palace of Darkness sits overlooking the ocean before her, the shadow creating an ominously dark patch on the waves and beach as the breeze blows the sea foam and the sand along. The turrets of the palace aren't guarded and no one sees us coming. The grounds are incredibly quiet. Too quiet. Dangerously quiet. Carefully, our boats land on the seashore and we stand at the base of the black walls that ascend so high they almost touch the ground. It feels so strange to view my prison from the outside for once, it almost feels wrong. I beckon for my army to clamber up the banks of the beach to where the path starts to the palace. As we stumble up the hill, clinging on to the reeds and kicking the sand behind us, the sight of a small crowd comes into view. A woman heads the gathering, a few soldiers behind her. Her back is turned to us but the soldiers, bearing arms I have not seen before, a deep green lion on a black background, can see us if we move even an inch closer to them.

"Is that Melaina?" Seb asks me quietly, pointing to the woman in the front of the crowd. It's hard to tell as I'm not paying my full attention to her, but my doubt kicks in when the soldiers bow to the woman. The soldiers never bow to Melaina. It was Domhnall's way of demeaning her further.

"No, it's not he-" I start, but the woman turns around, alarmed at the whispering from behind her. "Yes, it *is* Melaina!" I signal for the soldiers to back down, but I stand and greet her, worried that Domhnall might be with her, posing this trap.

"Evanie!" she exclaims. "Oh, Avie found you, thank goodness!" She steps forward to embrace me.

"Are you here alone?" she asks in disappointment.

"Are you?" I question.

"Domhnall isn't here, if that's what you're asking, Evanie," Melaina smiles.

"What do you mean?"

"I mean that he's in the west tower, locked up, and he's no longer the Highest Lord of Darkness," Melaina tells me triumphantly.

"What?" Aella exclaims, appearing from behind the reeds. "Melaina, you did it! How?"

"I don't know the full story myself. After Evanie escaped, he took his anger out on me, and then Darsey defended me, and Domhnall, well, naturally, he became suspicious, and he tried to hurt him, and that's just when it all came out of me, all the magic that Domhnall had held back from me all those years ago and I just... I don't know, honestly."

Herminia springs up at this moment. "He deserves to die for all he has done," she points out, presenting a scroll from her pocket. "This is a list of all grievances made against him from the Faithful Houses,"

"I, too, made a list," Melaina nods. "A list for myself, a list for the House of Darkness and a list against Domhnall, Aidan and Daileass along with their houses."

"Domhnall's lists are enough to testify for his death," I say. "But Daileass and Aidan deserve to live. Aidan, though, doesn't deserve to walk free, he's a worse man than Daileass. Eithne has been wronged by Aidan more than Isoletta has by Daileass, so she should decide his fate."

"Agreed," Melaina grimaces. "So, Evanie, Domhnall's fate is up to us."

I pause for a moment. Domhnall is the exact opposite of a good man. He's a terrible man. He's a tyrant first and foremost. If he was a father, I would consider letting him live for the sake of his child, if he had a wife who loved him, I would let him live for the sake of that poor woman. But no sane, living creature could ever love a man so dark and brooding.

"I say we send him to hell," I conclude. "Where he belongs."

*

Domhnall sits in the corner of his dark cell, staring at the door as we enter. He has plenty of room, but he's confined himself to the smallest place he could find in the tower. He simply looks departed, the evil and wicked glow in his eyes replaced with shame. If I didn't know his true monstrous nature, I would feel sympathy for the man. Instead, I just stare at his bemusement.

"And here they are," Domhnall whispers as we enter, his eyes not rising to meet ours. He carries on staring in the same spot, his eyes still fixed to the same brick on the same damp wall.

"We have decided your fate," Melaina announces to him. He glances up at us, that evil shimmer finally returning to his eyes.

"So it seems," he chuckles, gesturing to the Sun Sword, resting on my belt.

"There have been several lists of grievances made against you and your brothers. Naturally, your list is the longest, would you like to hear them?" Melaina continues.

"Do I have a choice?" he asks tiresomely.

"I think you know them already," I snarl, pointing a finger at him threateningly.

"I do," he sighs. "But do you care to elaborate?"

"Even in your final minutes, you play games with us, Domhnall!" Melaina yells, turning back towards the door in anger. She takes a few deep breaths and faces him again. I beckon for Aella, Herminia, Avie, Lorna, Conaire and the other soldiers to enter the cell.

"Those you have wronged should see you die," I declare. "But the whole realm can't fit in this cell."

"Oh, you are a smart one, my pearl," he laughs.

"I am *not* your pearl," I growl.

"Well, not anymore, but I'll always be your husband, even in death," Domhnall smirks. "Let that be my parting gift to you."

"Let's get this over and done with," Melaina concludes. She takes a few steps towards Domhnall, who, despite maintaining his confident, wicked smirk, backs further into the dim corner of his cell.

"You said once that you would love me, 'til death do us part," Melaina starts, encroaching on him even further. "How dare you lie to me!" she yells, the sound ringing throughout the chamber. Melaina takes a moment to breathe, cooling off her blinding anger as she paces around the circle we've formed around Domhnall.

"Would you mind just getting it over and done with, I'm incredibly tired?" Domhnall sighs. Melaina's head snaps around so that her furious gaze meets his.

"No!" she yells. "You do not know tired! You do not know tired until you've been travelling across the ocean because your father's gambled all of your money away, your mother is dying, your little siblings are crying, you've been awake for almost three days and if you even close your eyes just once, you fall asleep. You do not know tired until you've been married to the same man for ten years and you're tired of his words that tear you apart, his stares that break you down, his actions that destroy you. You have wronged me in so many ways, Domhnall Omnia, and it is the greatest regret of my life meeting and marrying you, I hope you know that. I hope that's your dying thought. I would stab you a thousand times if it was my right, but you have wronged the people of Light more than anything, therefore it is Evanie's right to see the little light you have ever had in you leave your evil eyes," Melaina, slowly, turns to me, gesturing for me to draw my sword. Wide-eyed, I reluctantly draw the Sun Sword from its ornate scabbard and pause. Gingerly, I lay the sword and across my hands and present it to Melaina.

"It has always been your right," I insist. "My lady," Melaina stares at me for a few moments, before nodding and placing her fingers around the hilt of the sword. I remember Herminia saying that only special people can hold the sword. I panic for a moment, wondering whether the sword will reject her grasp. I had no reason to be worried. It fits perfectly in her hand, and she turns it about in her palm before facing Domhnall. She points the end of it towards him, nicking his already torn shirt. Closing her eyes to exhale, she swings the sword aggressively across his arm, leaving a deep red mark. It surprises me how much the wound bleeds. Domhnall catches the blood with his other hand.

"That was for my sister," she hisses, before swinging again and slashing his other arm.

"That was for Seraphyna," she continues, snarling at him. My heart sinks. Seraphyna. She cuts him on his shoulder as his face twists into a grimace of agony. Still, he shows no remorse.

None at all.

"And that was for all the other people who have died on your order or at your hands," she shouts. She raises the sword above his head, ready to slay him once and for all.

"You don't have it in you to kill me," he laughs weakly, but still, even half-dead, his cackle still chills my bones.

"You underestimate me," Melaina spits. "That will be your final, fatal, mistake."

There's no time between her finishing her sentence and lowering her sword.

"And that," she finishes, as Domhnall's heads lulls over to the side and his arms turn limp and cold. "That is for the realm you tore apart with your wrath."

Domhnall's deep red blood scatters the hay that litters the floor and the wood planks under it, the walls behind his corpse and Melaina's white skirt. She wears white, I notice only in that moment, just like I do. A mark of respect to Seraphyna.

I look up as Melaina turns back around to face us, dropping the Sun Sword, stained with blood, on the planked floor. I sigh, examining Domhnall's lifeless shell.

"The tyrant," I declare, "is dead."

*

"Evanie," Melaina taps me on the shoulder, her black dress shimmering in the morning light. Eithne and Isoletta fuss over their hair behind her, and Aella and Herminia are shooing Dagan and Corentin to their seats in front of the temples. Ethelde embraces Eithne gladly as she goes to take her place in front of the temple of light.

"Yes?" I reply.

"You look nervous," she states, placing her hand on my back in support. My pale yellow and white robes flap behind me in the breeze as I twist my belt around so that the Sun Sword is at my side.

"I am nervous," I admit. "I don't even know what to do."

"None of us do, Evanie, there's never been a coronation of six monarchs before, let alone six queens," Melaina laughs, beckoning for Eithne and Isoletta to come over. Isoletta waves away the nanny holding her daughters, Nadiya and Julianna, and Eithne waves away hers, holding only one child, the boy, Kit.

"Where's your daughter?" I ask her nervously.

"Laelynn?" Eithne questions. I nod. She sighs worriedly, ushering me over to the side so that we may talk in private.

"You know they were born under the Morning Moon," Eithne tells me quietly. "Well, Kit has already started summoning the flames to the candle."

"That's wonderful!" I exclaim, but Eithne waves my hand down.

"And Laelynn, well," Eithne starts nervously. "She... I thought she was doing the same with the flames but she was just lighting the room, Evanie, I think she has the power of Light."

"Well, that's even more wonderful!"

"Maybe for you, but I was so excited and I was foolish enough to tell Aidan, and he went mad, told the whole court and now, well, some of those still loyal to Aidan tried to kill her, and I had to lock her in the west wing of the palace to protect her, but I'm more scared than anything that she'll get hurt because of who she is," Eithne explains sadly.

"I have an idea," I tell her hopefully. "What if she comes and lives with me in the Eastern Isles, I raise her as an... aunt say, she still visits you and her brother but she'll have me and Seb and her grandmother, and we can train her in her power, she'll be safe."

"Oh, I don't know," Eithne sighs.

"Just think about it, Eithne," I suggest. "I'm not trying to take her away from you, but Laelynn would thrive in the Eastern Isles, I know it."

"Thank you, Evanie," Eithne smiles.

"Evanie, Eithne, it's time," Aella calls, gesturing for us to walk over to the centre of the aisle. The temples on Holynest now have altars outside them, and the professors of each house are waiting for us. Along with the Sun Crown, crowns from each house have been forged for each of the new queens. The Flame Crown for Fire. The Wave Crown for Water. The Wind Crown for Air. The Rose Crown for Earth. The Night Crown for Darkness. And, of course, the Sun Crown is the same and waits for me.

"Good luck, Evanie," I hear from the back of my mind, and I have no doubt that it's Seraphyna wishing me the best. I close my eyes and nod, thanking her a thousand times in my head, before lining up behind the others.

Melaina walks down the aisle, her train brushing the dusty ground behind her. It's been two months since she slayed Domhnall in the Palace of Darkness. She carries the burden well, but her shoulders droop slightly as she passes the empty seat in the front row. Seraphyna's seat. She was meant to be here. The Sun Crown was meant to rest on her head. Except it's not. She's gone.

Isoletta follows next, then Herminia. They all pause in front of their temples, staring at the beautifully forged crowns that rest on the altars. The professors of each of the houses stand facing them, ready to coronate their queens. Aella and Eithne follow next, floating down the aisles in their beautiful robes. I take a deep breath and start walking. I pass Lorna and Conaire, a rather pregnant Leora, Ulric and Avie, sitting next to an empty chair.

"I wish you were here, Clancy," I mutter under my breath. I half expect to hear an answer, but the only sounds around me are the breeze rustling the trees and the birds singing. I finally reach the temple of light, kneeling down in front of Ethelde. She smiles widely at me.

"My lady," she whispers meekly. She nods at the professor of Darkness, who, regally, picks up the crown and holds it above Melaina's head. The other professors do the same, stopping just a foot above each queen's head.

We are all crowned in succession, Melaina first, then the canon works its way down to me. The audience stands and turns to Melaina.

They all bow to her. "Long live the Queen!"

They turn and bow to Isoletta. "Long live the Queen!"

They bow to Herminia. "Long live the Queen!"

They bow to Aella. "Long live the Queen!"

They bow to Eithne. "Long live the Queen!"

I smile. The smile stays. Peace. It's here. Finally.

Finally, they turn to me.

"Long live the Queen!"

Sunset

Laelynn stares down at me, a grimace of pain painted across her face. I reach up and stroke her cheek.

"My time has come, my child," I tell her weakly as my eyes droop further.

"Aunt Oralee," she begs, clinging on to her fingers.

"One day, you will know me better, Laelynn," I promise. "You will know who I am and who I am not. Who I was and who I became."

"Stay," she pleads, her face a waterfall of sadness and sorrow.

"It has been the greatest joy of my life raising you, Laelynn," I whisper as her face becomes further and further away.

"Aunt Oralee!" she yells, for that is how she knows me. She never knew who I really was. "Aunt Oralee! Stay with me! Don't go! I'm not ready."

"The sun is setting, I should sleep now," I smile, clutching her hand tighter. "What a beautiful woman you've become, Laelynn."

"I am who I am because of you," she sobs. "I can't be that girl without you!"

"Care for them, Lady Light, I'm going to join my brother and my love and the queens before me," I sigh. "When the light calls, follow it."

Laelynn continues to scream for me to come back, but I can't hear her. I lose control of my hand and it falls against hers. She cradles my face with her hands. I smile at her for one last time.

Darkness.

Then Light.

Light everywhere. Above me, below me, next to me, within me, walking alongside me, it's there. It's everywhere. It's inescapable.

I raise my head, looking ahead. In front of me is a postbox. I'm waiting for a letter. From who though? I don't know.

"Welcome, Evanie," a voice calls. I turn my head. I see nothing. The voice speaks again. "We've been waiting for you." I don't know the voice. I've never heard it before in my life. Even so, I start to walk towards the voice.

"Stop," I hear. I do. I stop dead in my tracks. I gasp, not daring to turn around. I know that voice better than I know my own. Seraphyna

"Waiting for a letter?" she asks me, placing her hand on my shoulder. I turn, finally. Her face remains unchanged. She still wears her battle armour. The blood still stains her robes. Her eyes are still as bright as day. I throw my arms around her.

"Yes," I whisper.

"You can go that way if you want," she sighs, pointing behind me. "But, you could come this way, it's much brighter. After all, when the light calls, follow it."

I look behind me, at the endless, cold, dark void. Suddenly, in front of me, not only Seraphyna stands, but so many faces I haven't seen in years.

"Seb," I gasp, his eyes kind and welcoming.

"Come this way, it's much brighter," he smiles. I nod, stepping forward.

"Come this way, it's much brighter," another voice says quietly.

"Melaina," I sigh.

"Come this way, it's much brighter."

"Clancy," I sob, running to him. I feel his hair between my fingers, his skin against mine, his heart beating in his chest. I turn once more back to Seraphyna. She opens her arms to me. So does the light.

"Come with me," she says.

I do.

ACKNOWLEDGEMENTS

When I set out to write *This Lighter Realm* last year, I never expected to be here when I wrote the first words about Evanie and Seraphyna and the journey they took me on. That journey was the wildest, most wonderful and diverse journey I've ever been on.

First of all, I should thank all readers who have got this far. To anyone who has loved my characters and world and magic as much as I do, thank you. I am frequently told no one reads the acknowledgements anyway, so to any reader who is taking the time to read this, thank you as well!

I obviously need to thank my wonderful parents and grandma. To my mum, for absolutely everything you have done for me and for my book. For everything you have ever done to encourage me in my writing, for making me restart when I lost ten thousand words that one time and for being as invested in *This Lighter Realm* as I am. To my dad, even though you probably didn't understand what I was actually writing, thank you for understanding when I say I have writing to do. Thank you for making me as much tea as I wanted and thank you for taking me to castles and houses during the holidays, without those days my book would be very different. It may not even exist. To my grandma, for your endless generosity and support. Thank you.

To those who aren't here to see the publication of my book, I hope you're proud of me. This book is dedicated to both of my grandfathers who, despite me only knowing them as a small child, have made huge impacts on my life that come in the form of this book and everything I do.

Of course, I have an abundance of the most wonderful friends a teenage author could ask for. In any other situation, I wouldn't have this much acceptance, but you've all blown me away by how amazing you all are. To all the girls in my class at school, you are amazing (as always, thank you for being my cheerleaders!). To everyone at my fencing class, everyone in my musical theatre group, everyone at space school and to anyone who has ever asked me about my book or said, 'that's so cool!' when I tell them I write. Every single one of my friends has made some impact on this book. Every single piece of support, small or huge, means the world to me.

I especially need to say thank you to my closest friends as they have put up with so much. To Jananee, Isabella and Beth, thank you for putting up with me when I told you, 'I have another book idea!' or 'I've started another book!'. (Thank you for at least trying to hide the groans of disappointment!) Thank you for listening to every problem or plot hole I had trouble with and being generally lovely and tolerant and wonderful and just the best.

To all the teachers who have influenced me in my life. Not just my English teachers, but my history teachers, maths teachers, science teachers and all my teachers, really. Thank you as well to my school, who encouraged me in my writing and have supported me through writing and publishing *This Lighter Realm*.

I have been writing and reading since before I can remember, so to the writers who wrote the books that became a part of me, thank you. Shakespeare, J.K. Rowling, C.S. Lewis, Jane Austen, Charlotte Brontë, Rebecca Ross and Keira Cass, you have all made me who I am and what this book is. Thank you.

I know this sounds really narcissistic, but I'd like to say thank you to myself because I'm allowed to be proud of myself! I still can't believe some days that I actually sat down and wrote eighty thousand odd words, and it was no small feat.

Finally, I would just like to thank everyone again who was mentioned here. Your support, praise and enthusiasm is the most wonderful gift I have and will ever receive.